CU00497471

TIME STANDS STILL

JAY NADAL

Published by 282publishing.com

PROLOGUE

Two years ago

The bare concrete floor chilled her bones as she stared into the abyss. Each tug on the wrist bindings sent stinging bolts of pain up her arms. At some point, the lines of time had blurred. What was probably only a few hours, felt more like days. Her jeans were soaked. She stared at the bucket in the corner. Even though he'd left her with enough slack on the chain to reach it, she hadn't been quick enough.

A plastic cup of water and a ham sandwich sat untouched beside her. Though her stomach growled, she was in no mood to eat or drink anything.

He had left her alone, promising to return soon. She had begged him to keep the lights on, but her pleas fell on deaf ears as the door slammed behind him, the key rattling in its lock while blackness enveloped her.

Drifting in and out of consciousness and desperate to stay awake, she let her head drop down towards her chest. But only long enough for the primitive and subconscious part of her brain to jerk her awake, her breath ragged and her heart thumping in her chest from the sensory shock.

A while later, her eyes searched the darkness for what she thought was a noise. Slow footsteps from the corridor. Her eyes widened in fear as the sound grew. Was someone coming to rescue her? Had someone heard her cries for help? Over to her right, the first signs of light crept around the edges of the door and frame, illuminating it like a weird halo. The key turned in the lock and the door slowly opened. She scurried back across the floor like a terrified mouse, pulling her knees up to her chest, her hands balled tight to her throat.

His outline appeared in the doorway, one hand holding a portable lantern, the other carrying a white plastic bag. He stepped into her space, forcing her even further back into the wall. With the cold, hard cement firmly against her back, terror gripped her entire being. Her skin was cold and clammy, her eyes small as they fought to adjust to the light.

Through cracked and dry lips, she pleaded. "Please. Please don't hurt me. Just let me go. You can have it all. I promise I won't tell anybody."

The man closed the distance between them and towered above her. He exhaled deeply and tutted. "You know I can't do that. You've already seen my face. There's a very strong likelihood the first thing you will do is tell the police everything about me. Admittedly, you won't be able to tell them about this place since you were unconscious when I brought you here. However, I know you will certainly tell them about me and how I treated you. It would only be a matter of time until they found me, and I can't have that, can I?" he said, bending down to study her more closely.

Shaking her head wildly through fear and the need to get away from him, she cried. "I won't. I won't. I promise."

He laid the lantern down beside them, and in the soft glow studied her closely. Her soft, pure skin was now grubby, sweaty, and dirty. Her hair, once glowing with a sheen, clung matted to the sides of her face. She reminded him of civilisations buried deep within the Amazonian rainforests. With no connection to the outside world, they knew nothing about personal hygiene, appearance, or even the modern English language.

He ran his finger along her cheek and admired her. "You've been courageous while here. You've put up a fight, hoping to talk me round. Then a wonderful phenomenon kicks in. Learned helplessness. This has been such a stressful experience and you've come to believe you cannot control or change the situation, so you've given up trying." He glanced over his shoulder towards the open door and smiled as he looked back at her. "Even if I left the door open with the opportunity to escape, I really don't believe you would have it in you. Or... Maybe you still do. Go! I won't stop you. Why don't you try to leave? You don't know where you are, but maybe you'll take your chances."

The woman narrowed her eyes in suspicion, glancing at the man before looking over his shoulder. *Is he being serious? Is this another one of the games he plays? Will he come after me?*

His shoulders shook as he laughed. "See... I told you so. Learned helplessness. You just haven't got it in you any more." He stroked her hair before wrapping a curl around his finger. "'Tis a thing of beauty. Your time with me has come to an end. The police are clueless. They are in the dark as much as you are. And your poor, poor family. Your husband and parents must be beside themselves. Though they'll see you soon," he muttered, as he emptied the plastic bag, the contents falling out. Stanley knife, rope, and a bar of Dairy Milk.

He pushed all those things aside and inched closer to her, gripping the plastic bag in both hands. "It's time for you to leave."

"Please. Please don't hurt me." Tears tumbled from her eyes as she gasped for air, her chest rising and falling at speed. "I don't want to die. Please!" came her plea as she dug her heels into the floor to slide away from him.

"It comes to all of us. There's nothing to fear. You'll be at peace soon," he replied as he thrust the carrier bag over her head and wrapped it tightly around the base of her throat.

The woman thrashed as she fought for air. Her hands clawed at the bag, but the harder she resisted, the tighter the bag clung to her face. Each gasp felt like it tore at her chest. And then to her surprise, he whipped the bag off. Confusion and panic muddied her thoughts.

"That was no good. I think we need to try again," he said, grabbing her legs and pulling her away from the wall before positioning himself behind her.

Her moment of reprieve was short-lived as he thrust the bag over her head again, but this time placing his arm around her neck and squeezing tight.

The woman screamed as she thrashed around on the floor. With his arm in the way, her hands couldn't reach the bag as it starved her of oxygen. Muffled screams bounced around the space as her heels scraped across the floor searching for traction.

A few moments passed before she fell silent, her body limp in his hands. He let out a deep breath as he fought to control the hammering in his chest. Rising to his feet, he let her body slump to the floor. Checking his watch, he made a mental note of the time. He nodded approvingly before he set about disposing of her body.

1

"I see you have an eye for the abstract?" he asked, moving beside the woman.

The woman smiled softly and nodded, not taking her eyes off the artwork as she tilted her head from one side to another, appreciating it from different angles. "It certainly challenges perspectives on how we think about things."

"Indeed, it does. Howard Rutland-Pym, organiser of this fine exhibition," he said, extending his hand.

"Nice to meet you. I'm Ruth. You've gathered a fine collection here. I've travelled to many places to explore my fascination with abstract art, and…" she pursed her lips, narrowed her eyes deep in thought and nodded again, "I would say these pieces are as good as any I have seen."

Howard smiled and nodded appreciatively as he stepped in closer to Ruth. "It's very kind of you to say. Are you here to admire or are you looking to buy?"

"A bit of both, I guess. I have a tiny collection at home. And I mean *tiny*," she said, bringing her thumb and forefinger within a centimetre of each other.

Howard laughed. "We all have to start somewhere. It doesn't matter whether a collection is large or small. What it means to you is far more important. And I guess what it means to many of the artists who have their works on show here today. I've spoken to many of them and asked them about their thoughts on abstract art."

"And what do they say?" Ruth asked, taking a sip from her champagne flute.

Howard Rutland-Pym turned towards the piece of art Ruth was admiring. "Many of them say painting abstract art gives them the freedom to throw out the rules. It allows them to tap into their feelings, intuition and inventiveness, and work in a more spontaneous manner. They enjoy the creative process in which nothing is *wrong*," he glanced towards Ruth, "and the joy that comes from playing with materials, colours, and shapes. There's no narrative and no symbolism. Abstract art always has to remain on one level because it conveys only aesthetics."

"That's deep." Ruth smiled as she moved along to study other pieces in a quieter part of the exhibition.

Howard nodded and followed, placing a hand on Ruth's arm a short while later as he admired her beauty. Ruth's dark lips glistened beneath the lights. He was sure her smouldering dark eyes stared back at him, asking for more than simple conversation. "How deep is deep? It's so subjective. I'm drawn to relationships and the interconnectedness we all share. Colours and shapes are universal and form a kind of unspoken language which can be interpreted on a unique and energetic level." Howard let out a satisfying sigh as he loosened his grip on her arm but didn't let go. "You know, it's here where I find an evolution of expression. A growing and moving onwards, a shift I hasten to add, which affects the tapestry of relationships around me."

"You're very knowledgeable, Howard, and you have some very insightful opinions," Ruth replied, shifting her position to free herself from his grip and the invasion of her personal space.

Howard raised his hands to his sides. "It's what I live for. I have two exhibitions running at the moment. There's another in an adjoining room, though its theme is more about the cries for help. It's far more abstract and sinister and appeals to a very different market. That one doesn't start until ten p.m. each night just to add an air of mystery and danger which only heightens the experience of those who visit." He examined Ruth for a moment, assessing her reaction before continuing. "It's certainly not for the fainthearted and it's unique. I have repeat customers who travel from around the country to visit the exhibition. Those who come have a very special desire which needs fulfilling."

"Wow. It certainly sounds scary."

"You should take a look." Howard checked the time on his phone. "It's not long until we open. Why don't you hang around and view the other pieces in the meantime? I could walk you around a few of the finer pieces from *that* exhibition and we could discuss the meaning behind them a little later?"

"Thank you, Howard, I'm not sure it appeals to me. And besides, it's getting late, and I need to head home." Ruth placed her empty flute glass on a table close to them before extending her hand. "Howard, thank you for your time and well done on such a fascinating exhibition."

"The pleasure is all mine. It's on for a few more days, so you are more than welcome to come along again. It would be nice to see you and perhaps I might even tempt you to purchase one of these fine pieces."

Ruth tilted her head to the side. "Perhaps. I'm sorry it's been rushed for me this evening. I haven't had the time to enjoy these pieces as much as I would like to, so yes, another visit might be on the cards."

Howard watched Ruth leave as she slipped through the crowd and headed towards the exit. He narrowed his eyes as he admired her figure. She had brains and beauty, qualities he cherished in women. He placed his hand on her glass and stroked his thumb up and down the stem, affording himself a small smile. Lifting her glass to his lips, he placed his on the exact spot she'd left her lipstick impression. The connection was there. He could feel it as a surge of raw sexual energy charged through him like a herd of wild horses charging across a field.

2

"HOME SWEET HOME," Zac said, as he slid his key into the front door and stumbled through while manhandling two suitcases. Summer breezed in behind him with Karen following a few moments later.

"Summer, can you do me a favour and open the downstairs windows? We need a bit of fresh air," Zac asked, sniffing the air and noticing the lingering stale odour.

"Sure, Dad," she replied, disappearing into the lounge singing to herself.

Karen puffed out her cheeks and ran a hand through her hair as she followed Zac into the kitchen. "Cuppa?"

"Yes, please. I'm gasping."

Karen flicked on the kettle and grabbed a couple of mugs before dropping teabags in each. "Summer! Do you want a cuppa?" Karen shouted.

"No, thanks. I'm going to have a Coke," she replied before thundering up the stairs to her bedroom.

Zac came around behind Karen and wrapped his arms around her waist, pulling her body into his. "You okay?"

Karen let out a happy sigh and closed her eyes as she wrapped her hands over his. She had never been happier. Though initially nervous about going away on a family holiday, it was probably the best thing she had ever agreed to. Cala Bona in Majorca had been everything Karen could have imagined and more.

The hotel had been fantastic with great food and amazing entertainment. The resort itself was positioned in a stunning location alongside the harbour and marina, and as Zac held her tightly, her mind drifted back to when they had walked hand in hand past the jetties and the rows of small boats tethered to the platforms. With the roasting sun of the day and the sultry heat of the evening, it couldn't have been more perfect.

"I'm more than okay," she replied, thinking of how her life had changed since coming to York. A family holiday, a gorgeous, loving boyfriend, and now a holiday where they had spent hours by the pool soaking up the rays, before splashing around trying to dunk each other. She laughed as the memory tickled her.

"What's so funny?" Zac asked.

Karen shook her head. "Nothing. I was just thinking about our holiday. So many memories I'll always cherish. And I'm glad Summer enjoyed herself so much." Karen had noticed a change in her. She was happier, forever smiling, and jumping in and out of the pool more times than Karen could remember. It had proved the perfect opportunity for Summer and Zac to bond. During the brief moments where Karen had pulled herself away from reading a book, she'd watched with affection as Summer and Zac had larked about in the water. Summer had been constantly hanging on to Zac's back trying to pull him under. Screams had echoed around the pool and at times, she'd wondered if it was Summer or Zac.

"I don't think I'll ever forget it either," Zac remarked as he squeezed her tighter. "Thank you."

With the kettle boiled, Karen poured the boiling water into both mugs and let the teabags stew before she turned and faced Zac still wrapped in his arms. "For what?" she asked, furrowing her brow.

"For being the amazing person you are and for loving me and Summer. She's really taken to you. I swear I'm going to have to watch the pair of you. I feel outnumbered and vulnerable when you two are together!" He laughed.

"Well, someone needs to keep you in check," Karen said, playfully punching him in the chest. "I'm glad Summer didn't feel left out. It was her holiday as much as ours."

Summer had met a few other girls her age at the complex and had soon formed a friendship with them. When Zac and Karen had needed a breather, Summer would join her friends in the pool or head to the games room to play on the arcades. They had even sat around chatting while drinking non-alcoholic cocktails and pretending to be older than they really were, which had attracted the attention of a few boys. Though Zac had played the concerned father, Karen's steadying hand and voice of reason had kept his protective streak in check.

"I know, and it's why I wanted to say thank you. You've changed our lives. And I'm not sure what I would do without you…" he whispered before kissing her softly.

Their moment was interrupted as Summer's heavy footsteps thundered down the stairs appearing in the kitchen moments later.

"Ew, get a room," Summer teased as she opened the fridge door and pulled out a can of Coke, flipping the ring pull and taking down a large gulp in one swift movement.

Zac turned to face his daughter. "Did you say thank you to Karen for joining us on holiday?"

Karen elbowed Zac in the ribs.

Summer rolled her eyes. "Dad, get with the programme. While you were in departures grabbing a coffee, I said thank you to Karen."

Karen elbowed Zac again. "Yeah, Zac. Get with the programme. You can be such a grandad sometimes."

Zac stood open-mouthed and wide-eyed as Karen and Summer burst into a chorus of laughter. He jabbed an accusatory finger in their direction. "See, outnumbered."

The doorbell rung, and Summer raced down the hallway. "I'll get it!" she shouted. A few seconds later, she hollered down the hallway to let Karen know Jade, Karen's Detective Sergeant, had arrived.

"Right, my cue to go to Sainsbury's and get the food in." Zac kissed Karen on the cheek and headed for the kitchen door, bumping into Jade as she appeared in the hallway. "Hi, Jade. I'm popping out for a bit. I'll leave you ladies to it. Three on one is too much for me to handle."

Jade smiled, looking perplexed. "It looks like you've caught the sun well," she said, admiring his deep golden tan.

Karen greeted Jade with a hug. "I've made a cuppa. Do you want one?"

Jade nodded. "Blimey, I'm well jealous of your tan. I need a holiday now I've seen you. I feel pasty and white in comparison."

"Funny, I was about to say that you…" Karen cut off her sentence and winked.

"Cheeky cow," Jade said, dropping into a chair at the dining table. "So, go on, let's hear all the juicy gossip? Was he always whipping off your skimpy bikini?"

Karen rolled her eyes as she sat opposite Jade and pushed a mug towards her. "Get your mind out of the gutter."

Jade's eyes widened. "Pot and kettle. If it was the other way round, you'd be giving me a Gestapo interrogation about what I got up to and how much sex I'd had. So don't give me all that bollocks."

Karen took a sip of her now lukewarm tea and wished she had made herself a fresh cup. "It was good. In fact, it was fantastic."

Jade heavy-handedly slammed down her mug on the table as she choked on her tea. "What the sex?"

"Oh, for crying out loud, Jade. The bloody holiday, you perv. The holiday was fantastic. And, well yes, the sex was wonderful as well. It always is. Mind you, we didn't get much time alone apart from when Summer was with her friends playing pool or watching a movie." Karen blushed.

They both burst into a cackle of laughter.

"You're terrible, Karen."

Karen shrugged. "Well, I blame it on the heat, the good food, and plenty of wine."

"Now I'm really jealous. It sounds like you had an amazing time. So, no regrets about going on a family holiday?" Jade asked.

"Nope. Not one bit. I must admit I was nervous at the idea, though once I was out there it felt right," Karen said as she looked beyond Jade and stared into the emptiness. "I think for the first time in my life I can honestly say I'm really happy, but I'm sure tomorrow when I return to work I'll come back down to earth with a heavy thump."

Jade agreed as they spent the next half an hour chatting and catching up. Though Karen was desperate to find out what was happening back at the station, Jade masterfully steered the conversation away from the topic every time Karen dropped a hint.

Her time with Jade flashed by and it wasn't long before Zac returned laden with shopping bags. It was getting late, and Jade said her goodbyes before heading home, leaving Zac to take Karen back to her apartment.

3

"YOU HAVE ARRIVED AT YOUR DESTINATION," the scratchy male satnav voice announced.

Getting the unwelcome early morning call from the station wasn't how Karen had hoped to start her first day back at the office. Post-holiday blues were in full swing as she set off. The directions given to her by her team meant she needed to travel north from the city centre and head towards a location near Pilmoor. The further she travelled, the more remote became her surroundings as roadside hedges were replaced by thick woodland which offered Karen little opportunity to see beyond.

"No, I bloody haven't," Karen shouted at the satnav. "There's nothing here."

"You have arrived at your destination," came the voice again from her dashboard.

Karen shook her head in annoyance. "I might have arrived, but you're way off the mark, buddy!"

Karen pulled over and switched on her hazard lights before calling Jade. "Jade, the satnav says I'm here, but I can't find anything. Where are you?"

"You can't be far, Karen. There isn't much around here. Did you see the kennels?"

"I don't think so, unless there was a big red arrow the size of a double-decker bus hanging above the road pointing it out to me." Karen looked around, glancing over her shoulder in case she had missed it. "Nope. It's trees. Trees. And more trees."

"Hang on a sec, Karen. Press your horn."

Karen pressed on her steering wheel. She heard the feedback through her phone.

"You're close, Karen. If you go over the bridge crossing the rail line, then you've gone too far. I think you need to continue for perhaps another hundred yards or so, and you'll see us. Well, you'll see me, because I'm standing in the middle of the road."

Karen hung up and set off again, soon spotting Jade waving like a lunatic in the middle of the road. Beyond Jade, a line of police vehicles and unmarked cars confirmed her worst fears.

Karen pulled up behind the last vehicle and stepped out into the early morning sun. The fresh smell of nature wafted around her. Glancing around, she surveyed her surroundings. It was becoming a familiar story. A body dumped in a remote location.

"Welcome back, boss," Jade said, offering Karen her broadest smile.

"There was me hoping I would gently slide back into my role today, catch up with my team, have a spot of lunch with you and have a day with no dramas. What have I done to deserve this?" Karen said, looking up towards the sky.

"Well, whoever dumped the body knew York's finest detective chief inspector would be back at work today."

Karen and Jade signed in at the outer cordon and stepped over a large tree trunk lying on its side blocking access to the grassy field beyond. Karen cursed as she pushed past overgrown bushes which blocked her way. The ground beneath Karen's feet was dry, grainy and crisp, starved of rain from the hot summer, and the surrounding patches of grass and tree leaves were scorched mottled green.

"What have we got?" Karen followed Jade through an area of grass which had been taped off and checked by SOCO as being clear to walk through.

Jade updated Karen as they neared the crime scene and the inner cordon. "We believe the victim is Ruth Tate, aged thirty-two. No signs of robbery or sexual assault. We found her handbag beside her, which contained her purse, keys, lipstick, and other personal effects. No sign of a mobile, though."

"She known to us?" Karen asked.

"Nope. She's not in the system. Her husband logged a misper report in the early hours of this morning when she didn't come home after visiting an art exhibition."

"Who found her?"

"A local who was out for his early morning walk. Gerald Wiggins. Uniform have taken a statement already. I said we would follow up with him later today."

"Does anyone else come through here?" Karen asked, surveying the scene.

Jade shrugged.

Karen paused and looked around. Farm buildings in the distance, at least half a mile away and partially hidden behind a copse of trees. From where she stood, there was nothing close enough for anyone to see what was happening here. As she neared the tent, officers were conducting a sweep of the immediate area while a small team of forensic officers kitted in white Tyvek suits, blue booties, and gloves dipped in and out of the white tent.

"Morning, Izzy," Karen said as she spotted the flame-haired pathologist perched on her silver case, busily adding notes to her book.

"Ah, morning, Karen. Glad to have you back. Nothing like being thrown in at the deep end!" Izzy laughed.

"So everyone keeps reminding me. What have we got?"

Izzy pointed her pen in the tent's direction. "Caucasian female, no signs of sexual assault, but I'll confirm once she's on the table. The only visible injuries I can find are bruising around her neck, wrists, and right cheekbone, and lacerations to her wrists. We've completed the preliminaries and done the photos."

"Her wrists?" Karen probed.

Izzy placed both of her wrists together. "I would say her hands were bound like this and she struggled to free herself. There is bruising and open wounds to the outside of her wrists but nothing on the insides."

"And her neck?"

"There is evidence of compression to suggest strangulation, with bruising beneath her jawline and around the front of her neck."

"Time of death?" Karen asked.

"I'd say within the last eight to twelve hours. The body is still warm and stiff. No sign of flaccidity. Rigor may have slowed because of the warmth in the air."

Karen and Jade exchanged a glance as they formed their own theories before they headed towards the tent. Several clear evidence bags were left on a small table. One bag contained the victim's handbag, another contained a purse, and several others contained small items like her keys, driving licence, and make-up bag. Karen picked up the one which had the driving licence and studied the photo before taking it with her.

Pulling the flap to one side, Karen saw the victim lying on her back, her eyes fixed wide staring into emptiness. After stepping on the inspection plates, Karen came around to the side of the body and crouched down, while Jade joined her on the other side. Karen looked away from her face and focused on the rest of the body. She preferred to get a general sweep, a snapshot of the victim, before focusing her attention on the face. Ruth's long brown hair had been swept out to form a decorative fan behind her head. Sinister, dark blue bruising stained her right cheekbone and jawline. From where she was positioned, Karen observed the purple bruising around Ruth's slender neck. Lips shining with cherry morello lipstick pouted out from the centre of the violation.

Karen held up the evidence bag containing the driving licence and positioned it alongside the victim's head. "It certainly looks like her," Karen commented.

"She looks odd in the way she's lying here," Jade said, scrunching up her nose, glancing up and down the victim.

Karen had considered that same thing the moment she'd stepped into the tent. "Her legs seem at odds with her arms."

Ruth's legs were laid out straight and together, her ankles touching. Her arms were positioned at odd angles, with her left arm placed out to the side and her right arm extended above her head.

"What do you make of that?" Jade asked.

Karen pursed her lips. "I haven't got a scooby doo. Some kind of symbolism?"

"Not sexually assaulted, not stabbed, not set on fire, and not robbed. So what was the motive?" Karen pondered.

"Opportunist? She was in the wrong place at the wrong time?" Jade suggested. "Or a jealous lover?"

Karen sighed as she lifted Ruth's left hand, which was protected by a plastic bag to preserve any evidence and examined it for signs of any trauma. Fresh bloodied wounds to the wrist and dirt beneath her fingernails. "I hope not. Dealing with stranger killings is our worst nightmare. It makes it practically impossible to work out motive let alone get inside the mind of the killer. And we're hardly expecting to catch him on CCTV," Karen remarked, getting back to her feet and wincing as her knees cracked.

"Seen enough?" Izzy asked as Karen joined her, slipping her notepad into her case and tugging on the zip of her Tyvek suit.

"For now," Karen replied, doing the same with her suit as she watched Jade head over towards the nearest SOCO for a quick chat.

Izzy tapped out a fresh mint and rattled the container in Karen's direction, who shook her head. Izzy opened her mouth and flicked in the mint. "I think the PM should be straightforward, however, I doubt it will give you much in terms of clues to a motive."

Karen tipped her head back and blew out her cheeks. "I fucking hate cases like this. There's so little to go on. I'll send officers to her home. They can take her personal effects for identification by the husband, and I'll visit him after the briefing."

Jade joined her a few moments later. "SOCO has taken DNA samples and a few shoe print impressions. Although to be honest, the walker contaminated the area as he walked around the body while calling it in."

4

KAREN STOOD at the front of the room and waited for the final few stragglers to leave their desks and join her. With the news of a body being discovered, her team had gone into full murder case mode by clearing their desks, adding extra whiteboards at the front of the room, one of which had a large map of York and the surrounding area pinned to it.

Case officers, extra support staff, an exhibits and disclosure officer, a digital media investigator and family liaison officer had all been allocated to Karen's team in the interim period between Karen being at the scene and arriving back at the office. It was a smooth and well-oiled operation, something all of her officers had been through many times.

As Karen looked around the sea of faces jostling for positions and exchanging a few pleasantries, and the odd not so pleasant, tongue-in-cheek comment, she had to admire their dedication and professionalism. The first twenty-four hours after the discovery of a body were crucial to any investigation. The forensics team had already undertaken a preliminary search of the area. With SOCO still on site, there was much for them to still do, so Karen would have to wait until Bart Lynch, the CSI manager, and his team had completed their investigation. Until that point, many questions remained unanswered.

Karen checked the time on her phone before placing it on her notepad beside her. "Okay, team. Can I have your attention? Earlier this morning we were called to the discovery of a body, a white female, early thirties, who we believe to be Ruth Tate." Karen picked up a white A4 envelope and retrieved its contents before turning to the whiteboard and attaching images of the victim taken from the crime scene. She turned back towards her team and gave them a minute to study the images. "Her husband, Mark Tate, called the police at eleven thirty-two p.m. when his wife hadn't returned home. His attempts to call her went to voicemail. At one forty-seven a.m. we received another call from him. On this occasion, the distress in his voice was enough for a patrol car to pay him a visit. He had already contacted the hospital in case she had been in an accident."

"What did the officers do after their visit?" one of her team asked.

"They undertook a risk assessment and deemed her low to medium. She wasn't a child nor a vulnerable person. Yes, it was out of character for her, so officers began making local enquiries before escalating the case to us when she had disappeared without a trace."

Karen took a moment to replay the 999 calls Mark Tate had made.

"An initial examination of the victim appears to suggest she was strangled. With her personal possessions beside her,"

Karen said, attaching several other close-up images of a handbag and its contents, "we are ruling out robbery at this stage."

"Was there a sexual nature to the crime?" one of her officers asked.

Karen shook her head. "Izzy doesn't believe so. Ruth Tate was still fully dressed. There didn't appear to be any disturbance to her clothing. Cause of death was strangulation as you'll see from the close-up images," Karen said, tapping a picture closest to her which highlighted the purple bruising around Ruth's neck.

"Motive?" Preet asked, her large dark brown eyes fixed firmly on the image.

Karen shrugged. "At the moment we haven't got one. It could be a random stranger attack. Ruth may have been known to her attacker?"

"Colleague or a lover?" Preet suggested.

"It's an avenue," Karen replied, nodding in Preet's direction. "Though she was married, going by the images on her Facebook page, many of which were in mixed groups, she could have been involved with someone else and the affair turned sour." Karen reached for another envelope and pulled out several other images of Ruth Tate taken from her online profile. Karen examined Ruth's face. She possessed a natural beauty with dark brown, straight hair, plump lips, a clear complexion, and earthy brown eyes which carried a warm softness. She gave off an air of elegance and sophistication.

Turning to her team, Karen continued, "Maybe she had tried to call it off, and her lover, not willing to let her go, attacked her before dumping her body. Forensics will look for the usual things like hair and fabric fibres not matching hers, semen traces, and saliva spots."

A few nodding faces agreed with Karen's suggestion as the team took a few moments to digest the photos and form their initial opinions.

"There doesn't appear to be any defensive marks?" Ed pointed out. "Either she was taken by surprise and subdued quickly, or the attacker was known to her."

Karen turned towards Ed and chewed on her bottom lip as her mind traced back to the crime scene. "There were certainly no defensive scratch marks on her face. She had some disturbance around her wrists, but we believe her hands were tied together, and the cuts and bruising around them were from where she struggled to free herself."

"That means someone could have held Ruth somewhere before she was killed?" Ty offered.

"Exactly. For how long, we don't know at the moment. We could be talking of only a few hours. What we need to find out is whether she was killed somewhere else and then dumped where the killer hoped she wouldn't be found for a while, or if she was taken there and murdered at the scene. A detailed forensic analysis of her clothes and shoes will help us determine where she was murdered."

A few officers broke out into a general discussion about the positioning of Ruth's body, which they found odd. Someone had neatly positioned her lower half compared to the chaotic top half, with her arms left at odd angles. No one in the team offered anything of substance as theories were thrown about.

Jade sighed as she rubbed her temples. "Okay, where do we start?"

"Right, considering you were the first to ask," Karen said, jabbing a finger in Jade's direction, "you can get the ball rolling. Shoot."

Jade repositioned herself in the chair and cleared her throat. She offered Karen a tight-lipped grin as if to say, "thanks." Jade turned to a clean page in her notebook. "Ty, can you build up a full victimology on Ruth Tate? Second, we need to visit her husband, Mark Tate. I suggest you and I visit him," Jade said, looking in Karen's direction, who nodded her approval. "We still need to formally ID the body and we'll need him for that. The FLO can be on hand to help."

Karen always felt proud when Jade took the lead in an investigation. This was all part of Jade's training to give her the best chance of becoming a DI in the future and something Karen wished for her more than anything else. It was the main reason she had pushed back when Detective Superintendent Laura Kelly had made noises about appointing an existing DI to Karen's newly formed team. Karen needed Jade to show authority and leadership in order to cement her case as DI material.

Jade looked over her shoulder and spotted Claire, one of the junior members of the team. "Claire, can you and a few other officers search her socials? Look at her friendship circle, anything related to the work she did. LinkedIn seems to suggest she was a freelance graphic designer, so let's find out who her recent clients have been and who she's been talking to regularly."

Claire nodded enthusiastically as she jotted down her instructions.

"Any ex-boyfriends still on the scene?" Jade asked, throwing it out to the audience. "And then let's cross-reference that with her mobile phone records. Find out who she was with and speak to the phone provider. We want access to texts and call records under RIPA." RIPA, the controversial Regulation of Investigatory Powers Act, had made access to phone records an automated process with no warrant, and speeded up many investigations where Karen had been the SIO. A simple online request was all that was required without the involvement of any phone company staff and cut out days, weeks, or months of bureaucracy and red tape.

Claire answered, "Will do," even though the question wasn't aimed directly at her.

"Okay. Thanks, Jade. Can someone organise cell site analysis for her number please? Let's figure out her last known location. That's all for now. Officers are with Mark Tate at the moment, so we will see him there. Let's catch up later," Karen said, closing the briefing.

5

"I NEVER LOOK FORWARD to this bit," Jade said, finding a convenient place to park up.

Karen sighed as she unbuckled her belt and stepped from the car. "Me neither, but it's part of the deal."

It always surprised Karen how a visit from the police would always stir up curiosity in the street. It was clear to her today when she spotted a neighbour across the road washing his car. Several strokes with his soapy sponge were intermingled with long pauses as he stopped to stare at the police car parked outside the Tate house.

A police officer at the front door stepped to one side and gave them a quick update. The female officer shook her head and pulled a face as she whispered to make sure her words weren't overheard. "Ma'am, he's not in a good place. His legs gave way when we broke the news."

Karen grimaced. A death notification was the most devastating news any police officer could deliver when they turned up on a doorstep unannounced. It would turn lives upside down. The devastating news tore families apart and shattered dreams. Reactions by loved ones were so unpredictable which meant officers never knew what to expect. Some family members would sit in silence, while others would cry or scream hysterically.

"Where is he?" Karen asked.

The officer pointed towards the first room on the right. Karen thanked her and headed down the hallway. Turning into the first doorway, she stepped into a through-lounge. It was a well-proportioned room with large comfy cream sofas, light grey walls, a big flat-screen TV hanging above the fireplace, and a few vases of flowers dotted around the room to add an air of lightness and fragrance. Contemporary was a word which sprung to mind.

"Mark, I'm Detective Chief Inspector Karen Heath from York police. This is my colleague, Detective Sergeant Jade Whiting. I know this is difficult, but as you know we discovered a body this morning which we believe may be your wife."

Mark Tate sat quietly in an armchair wearing a white crumpled T-shirt, black Adidas shorts, and black flip-flops. His face was thin and hollow. Overnight stubble and teary eyes only added to his weathered look. He glanced up at Karen through watery eyes and nodded once. "Can you be sure it's her?"

"We believe so. We have to identify the body. I know it's not an easy thing to do, but we need someone who knows her. Of course, if that's too difficult for you, we can contact another member of your family on your behalf."

Mark sat, his eyes dropping to the floor as he retreated within himself. His shoulders curled towards his chest as he clutched his mobile phone in his hand as if it was the most treasured possession on earth.

"Can you tell me what she was wearing when she went out yesterday?" Karen asked, taking a seat opposite him on a large comfy sofa that swallowed her up as she fell backwards. Seeing Karen's ungraceful collapse, Jade opted to stand to one side.

Mark cleared his throat and scratched his stubbly chin as he struggled to maintain his grasp on reality. His breath came heavy and ragged. "She was wearing a white blouse, which had blue stitching on it. Dark blue Balmain jeans, black ankle boots and a brown, short leather jacket."

Karen glanced across at Jade and gave her a slight nod. The description Mark had given them matched what the victim was wearing, and with Mark already confirming the personal effects showed to him earlier were Ruth's, Karen was confident they had found Mark's wife.

"We are really sorry for your loss. Based on your description we believe it's your wife."

"What happened to her?" Mark asked, searching the faces of Karen and Jade. "No one has told me yet. I was told a body was found matching Ruth's description."

"We believe she was attacked and murdered before her body was taken and placed in a field beside Jobbing Cross, north of Pilmoor." Karen couldn't think of another way to put it without causing Mark any further distress.

Mark swallowed hard as the tears tumbled. He cried silently as his shoulders shook. "Why?" he asked as his voice cracked.

Karen didn't have the answers. Whenever faced with this situation, the next of kin always wanted answers, many of which she could not provide. At least not yet. "We don't know at the moment. I know it will not be easy, but do you mind if we ask you a few questions?"

Mark sniffed hard before nodding.

"When did you last speak to her?" Karen asked as Jade got out her notepad.

Mark cleared his throat again. His eyes scanned the room as he looked for answers. "Um... seven thirty last night. She had finished work and was heading off to an art exhibition. It's not my thing. She loves that stuff and wanted to pop in and have a look and said she wouldn't be long."

"And where was this exhibition?" Karen asked.

Mark slowly rose from the chair and shuffled to a side table where he retrieved a flyer and came back to hand it to Karen before taking his seat again.

Karen took a few moments to scan the details. "Thank you," Karen said, handing the leaflet to Jade.

"Did she meet anyone there?"

Mark shook his head. "No. She normally goes to these things alone."

"And how did she sound on the phone when you spoke to her?" Karen continued.

A shrug was all Mark could offer to begin with. "Fine. She was looking forward to going. It was one of her passions."

"Ruth had finished work and was heading there?" Karen asked for clarity. "We understand she was a freelance graphic designer? Who was she working with yesterday?"

"She mainly works online. Occasional face-to-face meetings when she's taking a brief and then when she's presenting her final pieces of work to her clients. Yesterday, she was doing research at a few places in the city and then on to a business café to work remotely."

"We would need the client details, as well as where she was working yesterday afternoon. Would you have those?" Karen asked.

Mark nodded, before swiping the screen on his phone and searching for the details. He read out all the information he had, while Jade made notes.

Though Mark was struggling, Karen noticed moments of focus and a determination to cooperate with the police as best as possible. That meant little in Karen's eyes. In any murder investigation, those nearest and dearest to the victim would be the first people to fall under the police spotlight. Family feuds, relationship issues and money problems were motives for murder. "Mark, do you know of any fallouts or disagreements Ruth has had in recent days, or even the past few weeks?"

Mark sat back wide-eyed shaking his head. "No. She had mentioned nothing like that. Why? Do you think she had a falling out with someone? Is it someone I don't know about?"

Karen shrugged. "We are trying to build a picture of Ruth's last known movements. It would be helpful to know the people she came in contact with socially or professionally."

"I can't think of anyone. She's not that kind of person. Ruth is very honest, sweet…" His voice trailed off as he sniffed loudly as a small cry broke from his throat. "She wouldn't hurt anyone. Ruth hates confrontation. It's not her."

"I have to ask this, Mark. Where were you last night?"

Mark's jaw fell open as he stared at Karen. Disbelief written all over his face. "No. No. Are you insinuating I had something to do with this?"

"Not at all. It's standard procedure. We always have to ask the next of kin about their movements."

Mark threw his phone on to the sofa beside him as he gritted his teeth. "Why the bloody hell would I want to hurt my wife? It was me who phoned when she didn't come home." Mark jabbed a finger into his chest. "Me."

"I appreciate that. Like I said, it's procedure. It doesn't necessarily mean anything. I need to account for your movements."

Mark tossed his head back and let out a sigh of frustration. "I was here. I was here all night. Check my phone. You'll see a string of calls I made to friends and family throughout the night asking if they had heard or seen her. We've got a Ring doorbell. You can check the history on my phone. It will show you if I was in or out. But I was here all night. I didn't go out."

"Thank you. We'll need access to your phone just to confirm that."

Mark picked up the phone and held it up in Jade's direction.

Jade stepped across the lounge and retrieved the phone from Mark's hand. With the screen unlocked, Jade easily navigated to the blue Ring app icon and scrolled through the events recorded for the last twenty-four hours. It showed no movement from the front door.

Jade shook her head in Karen's direction. Though it confirmed Mark hadn't left the house, Karen noticed the through-lounge led to the dining room and then to the garden beyond. With the house being a semi-detached, there was always a possibility Mark may have left through the rear of the property and evaded the camera overlooking the front of the house. Karen had to consider every possibility, even though she didn't enjoy suspecting Ruth's husband.

"Does Ruth have a laptop?" Karen asked.

Mark nodded towards the dining table. "HP laptop. It's Ruth's. She's got two laptops. She had one with her."

Karen remembered no laptop had been recovered from the scene. Had Ruth dropped it? Or had the killer taken it? Perhaps there was incriminating information on there the killer needed? Photos? Secret conversations? Had the person who killed Ruth been involved with her? Was there evidence of that on her laptop?

"We'll need to examine it. I'll also assign you a family liaison officer as your contact with the investigation team. We'll keep the liaison officer fully up to date with our progress. Any questions you have can be answered by them. They should be here any minute."

Mark sat silently staring at the floor, his body motionless. Karen sensed he was shutting down and crawling into a dark space in his mind filled with grief, unanswered questions, and disbelief.

"We'll be conducting a post-mortem fairly soon. So, if you're up to it, we'd like to take you to identify the body."

Mark nodded and shrugged before getting to his feet. "Just give me a few moments to change."

"We'll need to send an officer upstairs with you while you do that. We haven't searched your house yet and there may be evidence or information here that could help us with our investigation. The less you touch the better it is for us. I know it's awkward, but we need an officer present while you change."

Mark let out a sigh of resignation as he rose to his feet and shuffled out of the lounge, his footsteps slow and heavy as he went up to the bedroom.

"He looks a broken man," Jade whispered.

"I know, but take nothing at face value. I've been involved in lots of murder investigations where the partner has behaved in the same way, only to find they committed the murder. So, keep an open mind." Karen said, rising to her feet and heading to the front door to get some fresh air.

6

HE TAPPED his fingers on the desk and mulled over his thoughts. His plan hadn't gone the way he'd hoped. Ruth's journey from this world should have been quicker, with the air being squeezed from her and her body offering little resistance. But her loss of consciousness hadn't come quickly enough. He wondered if he had done something wrong. Perhaps he hadn't applied enough pressure to begin with, or maybe the position of his arm around her neck had been a little off.

The stillness and quietness of the room offered a complementary balance to the thoughts rushing through his mind like a raging river in spring. He wondered what could have been going through her mind in those final few moments. His research on survivor accounts spoke of fever dreamlike experiences. Others reported having out-of-body experiences and nightmarish scenarios which terrified them. Certain personal experiences detailed how their minds wandered and left their bodies behind.

Did Ruth experience any of those?

A strange and gripping fascination consumed his thoughts. A part of him wished he could experience it himself. He wanted to know whether he would feel the panic and the fearful realisation of death as he struggled for air. He imagined sweat from his brow stinging his eyes and his body fighting the urge to give up.

Many years of research led him to understand the finer details of someone dying of suffocation. The only thing lacking was his experience in applying the right hold with just the right amount of pressure.

He knew if he got it right, the sudden inability to breathe would trigger the body's panic response to anyone who suffered the misfortune of being his next victim. Their heart would race as the blood pressure and temperature rose. Their body would fight to get the remaining oxyhaemoglobin to their head. But this, of course, would use up oxygen and generate carbonic acid even faster, setting up a death spiral.

His eyes widened as an idea bubbled away deep within. His heartbeat quickened in excitement.

A plastic bag over the head. Was that what he needed to dispatch his victims sooner? It seemed to have worked with Ruth.

As he thought it through, he knew he was on to something. When the plastic billowed in and out, they would struggle to breathe. With no means of escape, vapour from their breath would condense around their mouth and nose. The oxygen around their head would be rapidly consumed and the surrounding space would fill with carbonic acid.

Yes. He imagined it now. Lifelike in his imagination as if real. Their heart pounding as their limbs thrashed because they couldn't get the clinging, damp wrap off their face. End-of-life regrets would fill their mind. He knew inhaling carbonic acid for a prolonged period would drive blood pH down, and synapses would stop working. The end-of-life regrets would mercifully cease as their mind entered unconsciousness. Heart rate and blood pressure would fall and the breath reflex stop. Their body would go slack as muscle tone released.

After about five minutes, their brain neurons would begin to die. After ten, not enough remained to resume life.

Sweet dreams.

Yes, he could see it now as an overwhelming urge gripped him to go out there and find another victim to practise on.

No. No. He reminded himself that these things can't be rushed. Doing things too quickly leads to mistakes. Mistakes leave clues. Clues get you caught.

Ruth wasn't meant to die so quickly. She should have been with him for longer. His fingers curled into a ball as he slammed his fist on the table. He'd wanted her to be compliant, but she'd carried a defiant streak. She had tried to reason with him. He'd let her drone on about this and that. Listened to her promises that if he released her, she wouldn't tell a soul. He laughed as he recalled the conversation.

He should have seen the warning signs when he'd tried to grab her and place a hand over her mouth. She'd made too much noise as her muffled screams had torn through the night air. The man shook his head, annoyed with himself as he flipped open his laptop and searched for the only folder contained in its hard drive. Clicking on it, he opened up a Word document and searched its contents. It gave him an opportunity to find out how to get it right the next time. Though he believed he knew everything, there was still so much to learn and there was only one way to do that, to learn from the best.

All this research made him thirsty. Luckily, he had brought a nice bottle of Merlot with him and poured himself a glass before bringing the edge up to his lips. Taking a small sip, he savoured the super-soft finish and the red fruity flavours. He closed his eyes to welcome and cherish the sensations swirling around his mouth. There were distinct aromas of plum and dark chocolate with slight earthy undertones. As he nodded, he marvelled at how rich Merlot could be. Some could be velvety and plummy, or rich and oaky, often layered with notes of clove, vanilla and cedar. He wouldn't call himself a connoisseur of wine, but he was partial to a small tipple every night.

As the wine did its job of relaxing his body and softening his thoughts, he glanced back at his screen and opened up another document. It would soon be time to have another go. He needed to be better prepared and, having spent the last few weeks tracking his victim, he knew it wouldn't be long until he could experiment again.

7

MARK TATE HELD his wife's hand as he sobbed uncontrollably. Tears dripped off his chin as he begged for his wife to come back. "Please wake up. Please. Wake up. Don't go!" he wailed as he leaned forward and stroked her dark hair.

Karen and Jade stood on either side of him and took one step back to allow him a moment of privacy. Jade glanced across at Karen as she found the moment hard to deal with. Jade's eyes were misty, her jaw muscle flexing as she fought to keep her emotions in check. Karen offered her a small sympathetic smile as if to tell her she understood. There was nothing to be ashamed of. After all, it was a basic raw human emotion. But Karen had faced this situation hundreds of times in her career. It never got easier, but it became more manageable.

Karen reached out and placed her hand on Mark's arm. He had already confirmed the identity of his wife before breaking down, and for the last ten minutes had remained rooted to the spot crying through red puffy eyes, wishing for a miracle to bring his wife back from the dead.

"Mr Tate, we really are sorry for your loss. We can take a seat in the relative's room? Jade can rustle up tea for us," Karen suggested, casting a glance in Jade's direction who nodded and left the viewing room.

Mark Tate was wrapped up in his own world, oblivious to Karen's voice.

"Mr Tate?" Karen asked again, squeezing his arm.

The physical contact had the desired effect as he jolted from his trance and turned in Karen's direction. "Who would do this? Find the bastard who did this," he said, his voice weak and soft.

"We will do our best to find the person responsible. Come with me and we can have a chat. I don't want to leave you like this," Karen said, placing her hand in the small of his back and leading him through the door into a small adjoining room with a table set to one side displaying flowers and a box of tissues, and several armchairs along two walls.

Mark Tate slumped into a chair, his body crumpling into what looked like a man of half his size. He stared ahead, transfixed on the bland and lifeless cream-coloured wall, tearing thin strips off a small scrunched up tissue.

Jade came in with three cups of tea on a tray and set them down on the small table before offering Mark one of them. Jade wasn't sure if he had the strength to hold it as his fingers trembled. She kept her hands close by in case he let his grip slip before she stepped back to pass Karen her cuppa.

Karen took a sip from her cup and welcomed the soothing warmth as it quelled her parched throat. "We'll be doing everything we can to find out what happened to Ruth. Is there anything else you can think of that might help us?"

There was an emptiness in Mark's eyes as he continued staring ahead. Karen was sure he hadn't blinked in minutes. Occasional sniffs broke the silence in the room.

Mark finally mustered up the strength to reply with a shake of his head. "I don't think so."

"I know we've discussed this already, but how did she sound when you spoke to her on the phone?" Karen asked.

Mark shrugged. "Her usual self. Happy. Full of beans. Excited about the art exhibition."

Karen placed her cup on the floor beside her. "And she didn't mention feeling bothered about anything? Nothing on her mind? No arguments or trivial disagreements?"

"No. She would tell me everything. Even the most trivial things. I remember her telling me, I don't know, maybe six months ago, about an argument with another motorist over the same parking spot. Ruth hated confrontation so shrugged it off and carried on driving looking for another spot. That was the kind of woman she was. So, if anything had happened in the past few days, she would have told me about it."

"Is it just the one car you have between you?" Karen asked.

"Yes. I remember her calling me from the Union Terrace car park. That's where she parked to go to the exhibition. We talked about her day. She asked me how my day was. I checked to make sure she'd eaten something," Mark paused, the slightest smile breaking from his lips. "She was always on the go and would forget to eat. Ruth always said I was like her mum, Angela, who always nagged her as a child to eat because she was so hyper and never sat in one place long enough."

Karen smiled at Mark's recollection.

"As I've already mentioned, we need to examine all angles. Were there any work associates or… perhaps former boyfriends she had mentioned recently?"

Mark narrowed his eyes in Karen's direction and shook his head as if disgusted at the suggestion. "No. No. She's not like that. She only had two boyfriends before we met. Nothing serious. And as far as I'm aware, neither had been in contact with her in all the time we were together."

"That's helpful. I need to look at this from all angles," Karen said, reassuring Mark. "Prior to going, did she say much about this art exhibition to you?"

"No. She knew I wasn't interested in abstract art," he sighed, getting frustrated with Karen's questions.

Karen sensed the tension in Mark's voice. "I know this is incredibly difficult, Mark. But we are doing everything we can to catch the person who attacked Ruth, and make sure it doesn't happen to…"

Mark tutted and jabbed a finger in Karen's direction. "Detective, I appreciate everything you are doing, but I don't give a shit about the other people it happens to, okay? My only concern was Ruth, and now she's dead. You're already too late to help unless you've found a way to turn back time?"

"And I'm sorry. I'm doing everything I can to ensure there isn't another person just like you who could soon be in the same position grieving for a loved one."

Mark tipped his head back and raised a hand. "Okay. Okay. I'm sorry. Of course, I don't want anyone else to experience what I've just been through. I am just exhausted and confused."

"I understand. Let's get you back. The family liaison officer is waiting for you back home. They can sit with you for a bit. I know it will be difficult for you but try to get some rest."

Mark nodded and dragged his weary body from the chair before following Karen and Jade out of the building.

8

JADE PULLED into the car park opposite Clarence Street and found a spot away from the rest of the cars.

"Why do you always do that?" Karen said, huffing as she unbuckled her belt and stepped from the car.

"What?" Jade questioned.

"Park so far away we have to walk even further."

"You might not know this, but a high percentage of damage to vehicles occurs in car parks. And with few witnesses, those accidents go unchallenged. I'm not having a pleb crashing into my car because they are useless at parking, leaving me to claim on my insurance." Jade dropped the keys into her bag. "They drive around as if they're blindfolded. I mean, how hard can it be to pull into a parking bay? Seriously? And yet these incompetent drivers go back and forth, back and forth, turn the wheel in the wrong direction, and have a dozen attempts before they get into the bay, and even then, they are so close to the white lines, you can't open your bloody car doors. Don't even get me on to 4x4 drivers!"

Karen burst out laughing. "Jesus, you do hate car parks, don't you?"

"No... I don't like stupid drivers."

"No shit, Sherlock!" Karen said as they crossed over the road and headed to the address which was next to York St John University. As Karen glanced around, she observed how busy the road was. With it being in the middle of the city, and a short distance away from York Minster, by day it had a buzzing vibe as students milled around in between lectures, and shoppers and visitors made their way from the car park.

Stepping through the doors of the exhibition hall, Karen noticed a serenity and calmness surround her. A few visitors strolled among the exhibits, pausing every few moments in silence to examine and reflect on the artwork. Karen had requested to speak to the organiser of the exhibition and having waited a few moments they were joined by a smartly dressed man in a crisp open-necked white shirt and a grey suit.

"I'm Howard Rutland-Pym, exhibition organiser," the man announced, extending his hand to greet Karen and Jade. "I understand you wish to speak to me. Is this in a personal capacity? Are you interested in the artwork?" he asked, fanning his hand out in front of him as he glanced across to the nearest display. "We have many fine pieces, ranging from just a few hundred pounds up to one thousand five hundred pounds. I'm sure there's something we can find to suit your taste. These pieces are a thing of beauty. Each one captures a different aspect of life and portrays it in such a unique fashion it takes your breath away," Howard said, his eyes widening in excitement as he locked in on Karen.

Karen held up her warrant card and introduced herself and Jade. "No, on this occasion we are here on business. We are trying to trace the last known movements of a woman who sadly lost her life. From what we can gather, this was the last place she may have visited before her death."

Howard stiffened as he pulled his shoulders back, niceties rinsed from his face as it took on a note of seriousness. "Gosh. That's tragic. I'm sorry to hear that. You're not suggesting someone visiting…"

Karen interrupted him. "I'm not suggesting anything. We are following up many lines of enquiry to build a picture of her last known movements. I spotted CCTV at the main entrance. Are those active cameras? And if so, were they working last night?"

Howard nodded. "It's a necessity. We are dealing with prized artwork. I'm sure many of the artists would be more than upset if someone walked in, lifted a piece, and strolled right back out of the front door without being spotted or challenged."

"How many visitors did you have here last night?" Karen asked.

Howard pursed his lips for a few moments and rolled his head from side to side. "In the region of eighty to one hundred visitors. And we sold a few interesting pieces. So, a very successful night."

"Do you mind if we look at the CCTV, please?" Jade chipped in, her tone flat as if bored listening to Howard harp on about his "pieces."

"Is that allowed?" Howard shook his head and tutted. "Of course, I guess it probably is. Isn't it? Or is there a rule about protection of data and you needing a warrant or something to see it?"

It was Karen's turn to tut this time. "No, we need nothing of the sort, but we need your cooperation... now!" Karen barked as she glared at the man.

Taking the hint, Howard cleared his throat, looked at the floor and marched off, asking them to follow through a set of rear doors.

Karen stopped as she entered the second room, her mind confused by the images hanging from the walls on either side. More abstract images which made little sense, but she noticed a few paintings with grotesque faces of tortured souls, blood, tears and what she could only describe as morbid abstract paintings that had gone horribly wrong with no theme or visible structure.

Howard looked over his shoulder and paused when he saw Karen taking in the scene.

"What's all this?" Karen asked, seeing the confusion on Jade's face as well.

"Ah, detective chief inspector, this is a different exhibition we're hosting for a more discernible audience. It's not to everyone's taste, so we keep this exhibition separate from the main one. People have expressed a high level of interest in person and online. Buyers who may have only seen one of these images through our online catalogue will happily spend one or even two thousand pounds to buy something they hadn't seen in person."

Karen wondered if Ruth had ventured into this exhibition as well.

A few moments later they were staring at a few monitors tucked away in a small office towards the back of the building. Karen instructed Howard to run the tape from seven thirty p.m., and it wasn't long until Karen spotted the image of Ruth Tate breeze in through the front doors, pay her entry fee and disappear into the exhibition. It at least confirmed Ruth had made it to the exhibition.

"That's the woman who lost her life last night," Karen said, tapping the screen as she looked at Howard, who looked mortified. He swallowed hard as he forced a smile, before flicking to another screen which showed the main exhibition hall. At various points over the next hour, they saw Ruth walk around the different pieces admiring them from a distance.

Karen narrowed her eyes when she spotted Howard, with a drink in his hand, come alongside Ruth as she studied a painting. She watched as they talked for a while before Ruth and Howard walked off and disappeared from view.

"What did you talk about?" Karen asked.

Howard shifted uncomfortably. "We just talked about artwork in general. What she liked. What she didn't like. Was she after a particular piece. Those kinds of things."

"Where did you go after this point?" Karen asked, nodding towards the screen before staring at Howard, searching for any sign of another uncomfortable reaction.

"I suggested other pieces which didn't attract as much attention, and I wanted to show her the way."

"Did she go into the *other* exhibition we just passed through?" Karen asked.

Howard shook his head. "I asked if she would be interested, but she declined, and left not long after."

Together, the three of them watched and it wasn't long before they spotted Ruth leaving at nine thirty-seven p.m. Karen allowed the tape to play for a further ten minutes in case they spotted someone following her. Karen pulled off a copy of the tape before she thanked Howard for his time.

Once outside, Karen blew out her cheeks and studied the area while she waited for Jade, who had popped to the loo in the foyer.

"Sorry about that. I was busting," Jade said, looping her arm through her handbag strap and throwing it over her shoulder.

"What did you make of him?"

"He was too smooth for my liking," Jade said. "I noticed how he was looking you up and down when you had your head turned away from him. He tried to be a charmer, but just appeared an arty-farty lech. All he needed was a cravat and he would have fitted the bill."

"Hm, that's what I thought too," Karen said as they spent the next few minutes walking around to better understand the area. "So, we know she was at the exhibition. She left at nine thirty-seven, and made her way to her car over there," Karen said, pointing to the car park where Jade had left the car. "That's a five-minute walk. Are you telling me someone abducted her in such a short space of time?" Karen asked. It made little sense to her. They had already seized Ruth's car for forensic examination, though Karen doubted they would find anything of significance.

"None of it makes sense," Jade replied, just as confused. "A successful woman, happily married as far as we can tell and planning to start a family. I can only think it was a random stranger attack. There was no sign of robbery and no sexual intent either."

"We can't be certain of the sexual element, Jade. Maybe it was one of the earlier intentions behind the attack, but something happened, which meant the attacker didn't follow through with it. Was he attempting to attack her in the car park but was disturbed? Maybe there were too many people around, so had no choice other than to abduct her."

"Risky. It meant he would have parked close by. We would have caught him on CCTV if that's the case."

"I bloody hope so. Let's get the footage back to the office and get the ball rolling," Karen said as she headed back to Jade's car.

9

KAREN RETURNED to her office and switched on her computer while Jade ran basic checks on Howard Rutland-Pym. Karen had an uncomfortable feeling about the man, though she wasn't quite sure what it was about him that bothered her. Maybe it was his smarminess and confidence or his lack of sympathy upon hearing about Ruth's death. It niggled her. It niggled her a lot. Call it a gut feeling, but he wasn't right. It was as if he'd had to force himself to sound genuinely upset. It just felt fake.

There was nothing back from SOCO yet and with nothing requiring her immediate attention, Karen logged off and headed to the main floor to see what the team had been doing in her absence.

"How are we getting on?" Karen said as she walked around the desks waiting for officers to shout out anything of significance.

Claire, who had seemed super-enthusiastic in the earlier briefing was the first to pipe up. "We managed to get the most recent phone records from Ruth's phone provider, O2. Other than her husband, there was one other number she appeared to call almost on a daily basis. I called the number myself, and it belongs to Nia Knowles, her best friend."

Karen nodded and headed to a whiteboard to add the name. "Was Nia of any help?"

"I'm afraid not," Claire said, with a shake of her head. "Mark had called her twice last night to find out if she had heard from Ruth and was devastated when I broke the news to her. I had a brief chat with her, but she wasn't making a lot of sense. Poor woman."

"Okay, thanks, Claire. I'll grab her address off you in a minute and I'll pay her a visit on my way home. Anything else?" Karen asked, looking around the team.

Ed rattled a sheet of paper. "I've been going through her emails on her laptop. The majority is work related, plus a few emails regarding items purchased at Argos and Amazon. There was nothing else that jumped out as suspicious. I'll look at the last seven days of emails and contact everyone to see if there's anything there."

Karen gave a thumbs up before stopping at Jade's desk. "Jade, can you get someone to start doing basic checks on Mr Arty-Farty Lech and Mark Tate too? We need to cover all bases."

"Yep, no problem," Jade replied, adding it to her list.

"Karen," Belinda said. "I started working through Ruth's contacts that Mark provided. He doesn't know all of them, but he gave me a fair few to start with. From the initial calls I've made, no one had a bad word to say about her. They said she was really charming, professional, thorough, and a delight to work with. I'll carry on working through the list, but do you want me to follow up with anyone face to face?"

"I don't think so, unless anyone jumped out sounding a bit sus?" Karen replied as she grabbed her marker pen and turned towards a whiteboard. "There are several action points we need to work on right away. I want a review of all the CCTV footage in the area around the exhibition hall in Clarence Street. Get on to the city CCTV control room and ask for their help. The university building beside the exhibition hall is also ringed with CCTV. They must have captured something. Find out. We believe she was abducted in the short distance between leaving the exhibition hall and the Union Terrace car park. That's literally a two-minute walk."

"Surely someone would have seen her being abducted?" an officer asked.

Karen agreed. "That's what I'm hoping for. She left at nine thirty-seven. We need to look for all vehicle registrations that were on the move ten minutes to either side of that time. Let's see what's thrown up before extending the time frame. There must have been cars either coming or going from the car park. Check for any reccurring vehicles that left and returned. Someone must have seen something," Karen said, tapping her pen on the whiteboard.

There was a ripple of murmurs from her officers as they agreed with Karen's assessment. The room eventually fell silent and as Karen looked around, she could see many were processing their own thoughts and ideas as they jotted down points they wanted to either remember later or action.

"Karen, I've asked Dan to get a list of all credit card trans-actions from the exhibition hall last night, both for those who entered and any who made purchases," Jade remarked.

"Okay. Thanks, Jade. Dan, you will need to trace every buyer and visitor who pays by card. Start with the men and then move on to the women. It's a shit job but whoever attacked her may have followed Ruth into the exhibition hall. Which reminds me, can someone look through this?" Karen said, pulling out a memory stick from her pocket. "This is CCTV footage from the exhibition hall."

Ty rose from his seat and took the stick from Karen. "I'll get on to that straight away."

Karen smiled and thanked Ty and the rest of the team. "For those of you on the late shift, I'll leave my phone on. If you get anything of importance, please call me. The rest of you need to get your arses back home. It's been a long day, and it's about to get busier. Get some rest."

10

THE ADDRESS for Nia Knowles took Karen back into town. The visit wasn't really on her way home, and she could have left it until tomorrow morning, but nervous energy still rippled through Karen's veins as it did at the start of any major investigation. This burning desire to find out everything and anything as quickly as possible separated her from her peers. She knew if she had left it until tomorrow morning, sleep would have been fitful and disturbed with a head full of questions.

Karen hit the button for Nia's apartment and waited.

A slight crackle and then a soft voice came through the speaker. "Hello?"

"Is that Nia? I'm Detective Chief Inspector Karen Heath from York police. I know it's late, but I wondered if you had a few minutes?" Silence followed her introduction, and she wondered if Nia had disconnected the call. She was just about to repeat herself when Nia replied.

"Um, sure. Take the lift and come up to the second floor."

The electronic lock buzzed. Karen pulled open the door and headed to the lifts on her left-hand side. Travelling up to the second floor, she stepped out into the hallway and spotted the correct apartment where she saw a mixed-raced woman lurking in an open doorway staring at her.

"Nia?" Karen asked, holding up her warrant card.

Nia nodded, and sniffed loudly, wiping her nose on the back of her long-sleeved T-shirt. She invited Karen in and together they walked in silence through the small apartment to the lounge, which overlooked the main street. Nia dropped into an armchair and tucked her legs beneath her, pulling the sleeves down on the T-shirt so they practically covered her hands.

Karen offered her a small smile and then glanced around the apartment. It was clean and contemporary with cream walls, white leather sofas, and a beech effect laminate floor. A few prints hung from the walls. A small alcove was stuffed full of books.

"It's a lovely place you have here. You work locally?" Karen asked.

Nia nodded. "I'm a senior finance administrator for an insurance company nearby. Can I get you a drink or something?" Nia asked, her voice still soft and timid.

Karen refused the offer. "I'm the senior investigating officer on the case involving the death of your friend Ruth Tate. I'm really sorry for your loss. I understand she was your best friend."

Just the mere mention of Ruth's name set Nia off again as her chin trembled and tears seeped from her eyes. She dabbed them away with the back of her sleeve as she looked away.

"I appreciate this is difficult for you. I know one of my officers spoke to you earlier today, so you know she was murdered. The investigation is still in its early stages and we're doing everything we can to build a picture of Ruth's life and find the person responsible."

Nia nodded as she cried silently.

"How long had you been friends?" Karen asked.

Nia stared at the ceiling. "I guess four years. Maybe five. We met at the gym in town, and both wanted to go on the same piece of equipment and stood there awkwardly not knowing who should go first..." Nia smiled at the recollection. "We started talking after that and just seemed to click. We bumped into each other a few times and then had a coffee, and from there we went out for drinks and got on well."

While Nia spoke, Karen studied her features. Nia had full lips and blemish-free, light brown skin. Her hair was pulled tight over her head and held in place at the back with a scrunchie, which allowed her wiry ringlets to cascade over her shoulders. With no make-up on, Nia had a natural beauty Karen admired. It was a quality she had seen in many Afro-Caribbean and mixed-raced women, and she felt envy for the complexion they had been gifted with.

The conversation ebbed and flowed between them but the more she heard, the more questions it raised. Nia was painting a picture of her best friend who had so much going for her, who didn't carry a grudge, and avoided arguments at all costs.

"Did you share everything?" Karen asked.

Nia nodded. "We didn't have any secrets. I'm gay, and she was always there for me when my relationships went wrong."

"So, did she share any problems or troubles she had experienced?"

"No. Nothing major. The odd worry she had spent too much on credit cards buying clothes, and that Mark wouldn't be happy. But it was more tongue in cheek than anything else. Ruth liked to treat herself to expensive clothes. That was her only vice, very much a labels queen. She didn't drink or smoke."

"How was her marriage?" Karen probed.

Nia shrugged. "Fine. Ruth and Mark were very happy. They were talking about starting a family at some point soon. They both just wanted to become established in their careers and save as much as they could so Ruth could take a career break for a year or two to enjoy motherhood... Whenever that happened." Nia bowed and shook her head.

"Did she mention anything about ex-boyfriends or any unwanted attention in recent weeks?" Karen was fishing and trying every angle but coming up empty-handed.

"Nope. I think she hadn't spoken to her last boyfriend in years. She hadn't mentioned anything since being with Mark. And I doubt she would have kept anything like that secret from me. I just know her too well... knew her too well."

Karen pulled out a business card from her jacket and rose. "Nia, you've been helpful. I know it's incredibly difficult for you to come to terms with Ruth's death. But we are doing everything we can. Here are my details. If you can think of *anything*, no matter how small or trivial, then please call me."

Nia thanked Karen as she left.

As Karen started her car, she wondered why would anyone want to hurt a woman who appeared to be perfect in every way?

11

KAREN DRAINED the last dregs of her coffee before entering the examination room at York Hospital mortuary. A PM was difficult at the best of times, but attending first thing in the morning always spoiled the rest of the day as she could never rinse the images from her mind.

Izzy's flame-red hair was pinned back and tucked into her gown. Her assistant stood on the opposite side of the table facing her, offering surgical instruments when Izzy needed them.

The strange atmosphere in the room took Karen by surprise. She wasn't sure what it was to begin with, but then realised the distinct absence of music which Izzy often insisted upon. Without it, the room felt colder and more clinical.

"No radio today?" Karen asked, stopping at the foot of the table.

Izzy looked up and gave Karen a wink. "Bloody fuse went on the plug, didn't it! You know what I'm like without music. Bear with a great big bloody sore head."

"Great," Karen said. "I'll make sure I don't stand too close. Those instruments in your hand make you a deadly person bordering on being unhinged."

"Karen, that's me most of the time, not just here."

"Remind me not to go on a night out with you. I'd hate to imagine what you're like when drunk."

"Put it this way, you'd be taking your life in your hands if you hung around with me. Half the tattoos on my body were done when I was drunk." Izzy laughed.

Turning her attention to the table, Karen studied Ruth's body. Other than the tone of her skin being rinsed of warmth and colour, she looked healthy and well proportioned. "What have we got?"

"Not a lot so far. There are abrasions on the back of her elbows and on the heels of her hands, possibly from where she was dragged backwards. As you know, her wrists were bound. I studied the indentations and marks. The edges are very defined."

"Defined?" Karen asked.

Izzy lifted one of Ruth's hands and turned it over to examine the back. "If her wrist had been bound by rope, the edges of the compression on her wrists would have been softer and less distinct. Ruth has very defined indentations and cuts. My guess would be her wrists were secured with plastic cable ties."

"Any sexual interference?"

"There was no evidence of forced vaginal or anal penetration, and no bruising to her thighs or buttocks. There is some debris beneath her nails, so I've taken scrapings for analysis. I've also taken bloods for a detox report for completeness."

"Okay. Thanks, Izzy. The debris from beneath her nails might help us identify if they held her anywhere first before being dumped. Any alien hair or clothing fibres?"

Izzy glanced over towards a metal table at the far end. "I bagged all her clothes up. Forensics can give them the once-over."

Karen came around the table and leaned in closer to inspect Ruth's face and upper torso. "And your initial assessment of the cause of death was compression of the neck. Is that still correct?"

"Yes," Izzy replied. "During a PM I need to examine all the tissues of the neck, superficial and deep, and track the force vector which produced the injuries. She was strangled as there was evidence of regional venous obstruction in the neck, recognised as pinpoint haemorrhages or petechiae, in the skin above the point of constriction in the neck." Izzy placed the tip of a metal probe under Ruth's jawbone. "See the red mottling? And interestingly, in Ruth's case we also had the rare occurrence of ear bleeding because of the petechia."

"Were there any impressions left by fingers?" Karen asked.

"I'm afraid not. There is further bruising to the front of her neck and that was from a limb being leaned on her throat, or it being wrapped around her, with her assailant being behind. We also have this extended bruising and inflammation to her right cheekbone. My view is she was probably struck with a blunt instrument, possibly even a fist."

Karen pointed to the slight purple-red discolouration along one side of Ruth's body. "Not as pronounced as I would have expected?" Karen said.

"Livor wasn't as pronounced as I would have thought either. I would assume they rested Ruth on her side after death. But she was moved in the following hour or two which didn't allow the blood to settle in the lowermost blood vessels. Immediately after death, the blood is unfixed and will move to other parts if the body's position is changed. After a few hours the pooled blood becomes fixed and will not move."

"Okay, that's good enough for me. I'll leave you to it."

"No worries," Izzy said. "Enjoy the rest of your day and I'll get the report over to you as soon as I can."

Karen left the mortuary and paused by her car. She wondered why Ruth had become a target. This had to be opportunistic. She couldn't think of any other reason so far. Karen got in her car and blew out her cheeks before she pulled out her mobile phone and sent Zac a text.

Really wishing we were still on holiday. I'm getting too old for this shit. xx

She signed off her text with her sad emoji face.

Zac's reply was almost instantaneous.

I know the feeling. I fear if we go on holiday again, we might not come back. xx

Karen smiled as his message tugged on her heartstrings. She would gladly not come back if she was with Zac and Summer. She fired off a reply before driving off.

I wouldn't want to come back if I was with you and Summer xx

12

THE TREE OFFERED him a shady spot to observe Leah, his body hidden from view by a fence and a natural camouflage wall of tall shrubbery. Hours of waiting and watching dulled his mind, but it was a necessary part of the plan if he was to fulfil his dreams. It had to be right this time. He'd messed up with Ruth. A schoolboy error. It hadn't gone to plan.

He soon realised it was a learning curve, a steep one, and he knew preparation was the key. In order to get it right, he needed to understand their routines. But there was the rub for him. If there was one thing he despised, it was routine. In fact, despise was probably too strong a word. He didn't understand how people could do the same thing day in and day out. It led to boredom, and without any stimulation, led to dull and uneventful lives.

And Leah Hayes certainly fell into that category. The last few weeks had been spent following her to understand her routines. Her life was so predictable it felt like a mind-

numbing chore to follow her. A part of him wanted to grab
her by the shoulders and tell her to get a fucking life. He
needed mental stimulation. Things that would challenge
him to think, to reason, to process outside the box. Leah
didn't appear to have that in her life and did little to stimulate his mind. But that would change soon.

Leah should have been his first victim, but Ruth had
presented the ideal opportunity when she'd left the art exhibition alone and headed towards her car at the far end of the
car park. Walking through the darkened space, he'd
followed, ducking behind cars to stay covert, each step
taking him closer to her. After checking his surroundings
and making sure no one was around, he'd closed the gap,
the anticipation and excitement rising to fever pitch.

Having mentally rehearsed where he would snatch her, how
he would take her, and what he would say, he'd been ready,
but she'd stopped in mid-stride. He'd dropped behind a car,
hoping she hadn't heard him approach. And then he'd
heard footsteps fading away. He'd risen and stared through
the side window of a car to see her disappear in the opposite direction. *Damn.* She'd been heading towards the shops
beyond the car park.

It had been another anxious wait until she'd returned ten
minutes later, and the opportunity had presented itself to
take her. He'd approached from behind and thrown his
hand over her mouth. She'd fought back, taking him by
surprise. Her screams had escaped his grip. Fearing the
noise would attract too much attention, he'd punched her
across the side of her face. Ruth had fallen to the floor,
dazed and semi-conscious. He'd dragged her through a gap
in the shrubs to his car, bundling her into the back seat and
tying her hands together.

Leah worked five days a week, Monday to Friday, nine to six p.m. That was the rule. He hadn't seen her break it in the nine weeks he had followed her. She would set off for a run around the edge of the racecourse at six forty-five a.m. on the dot. She ran the same route every day before returning home and stretching in her front garden for five minutes before showering.

The rest was clockwork, like it was an instruction manual for her life. Set off for work. Depending on her mood, either a forty-five-minute walk to her office, or on a rainy day a nine-minute drive to her office above Mickelgate News. A sandwich lunch at one p.m. from Carlotto's in Mickelgate. Chicken salad on granary, salt & vinegar crisps, and a bottle of orange juice. The same conversation between her and Carlotto, the owner, every bloody day. He should know. He had stood in the queue frequently. Carlotto would say, "how is my *bella signora* today?" Leah always replied, "better for seeing you today, my handsome man." Back at the office and leaves at six p.m., before heading home. She has her weekly Sainsbury's shopping delivered on a Thursday evening between seven and eight p.m. And only went out on a Friday or Saturday night, unless it's a special occasion, like her friend Alice's thirtieth birthday two weeks ago where they enjoyed a girl's dinner in town with a crowd of friends.

Yes, he knew everything about her, right down to her favourite shower gel, hair products, and cereal. Her bin offered a treasure trove into her life. He checked the time on his phone. Almost. And yes, three minutes later, Leah stepped out, threw her handbag over her shoulder, locked the front door, pushed against it twice… it was always twice to make sure it was locked, before she set off for work.

He smiled as he stepped back into the greenery. So
predictable.

13

WITH THE IMAGES of Ruth's body slowly dissolving from her mind, Karen sat alone in her office. A part of her mind was firmly glued to memories of her holiday. Shaking off the holiday blues was proving harder than she imagined. Life felt so good, but a niggle scratched away at her.

She'd been so used to fighting against the tide of life for much of her adult existence, that she'd tuned herself into looking for the "*what ifs*" in every situation. What if I missed a vital clue that leaves a killer roaming the streets? What if any happiness I have is taken away from me? What if my bosses see through me and see that behind this tough exterior shell, I have such a lack of belief in myself it gives me panic attacks? What if the love I've found slips through my fingers and Zac and Summer don't want me any more?

Karen reclined in her chair and sat dumbstruck. "Love," she whispered. It was such an alien word to her. She'd never *really* fallen in love before, and now her heart ached for Zac and the chance of being part of a family. She gasped as her heart slammed against her chest, taking her by surprise. Managing such powerful emotions terrified her. Her life had revolved around drunken one-night stands to satisfy her carnal cravings. A few snatched hours where feelings and emotions were left at the front door, along with her handbag for a quick escape the next morning. Love had never figured in her life and embracing it was something she needed to get used to.

Am I enough for him? Karen thought. Tutting, she sat up. "Get a grip, Karen. Enjoy the moment. Stop being such a dick."

Grabbing her mobile from her desk, she pulled up her WhatsApp conversation with Zac. Her finger hovered over the keyboard as she chewed on her bottom lip. Nervous butterflies tickled her belly. Staring at the screen, her mind froze. Her fingers felt disconnected from the rest of her body. The words were there, but she couldn't get them out. She sighed as she dropped the phone back on to her desk as her shoulders slumped. "What is wrong with you?!" she muttered as she rested her elbows on the desk and buried her head into her hands, groaning as she did.

"With me or you?" Jade asked, peering into Karen's room, her brow furrowed, a look of confusion spreading across her face.

Karen groaned again as she dragged her fingers down her face, pulling her bottom lids so far her face resembled a Halloween horror night mask. "How do I look?"

Jade pulled a look of fear and laughed. "If that's your morning look, you'll have Zac running for the hills. The cattle on the Wagstaff farm had better back ends than your face!"

"Not helping," Karen replied, standing and pushing her chair back.

"Anything I should know about?" Jade asked as Karen grabbed her phone and notepad before joining her at the door.

"Nope. The day isn't long enough to tell you everything and if I did, you'd get me sectioned under the Mental Health Act."

"Sounds like a normal day in the life of Karen to me," Jade laughed as she followed Karen to the main floor.

14

IN NEED OF AN UPDATE, Karen gathered the team. "Where are we with our different lines of enquiry?"

Ed was the first to begin. "I've been through Ruth's laptop and checked emails beyond the last week, and there's nothing there which stood out to me. The majority are work-related emails as well as offers from online retailers. Forensics recovered as much of her deleted data as possible and again there was nothing that raised suspicion or concern. She had lots of photos on there," he added, handing Karen a memory stick which she plugged into a computer linked to a large screen.

"Thanks Ed. Any joy in locating her second laptop?"

Ed shook his head. "The search team at the site didn't find a discarded laptop or her phone. The search area was a two-hundred-metre radius from where Ruth's body was found. We could look further?"

"I don't think we'll get the resources signed off. If a killer took both, they could have discarded those items in a ditch or a rubbish bin. Even kept as mementos. We just don't know. Though with electronic items, it is highly unlikely he kept them. They can leave too much of a digital footprint."

Ed agreed. "Ruth's phone last pinged a tower near to the Union Terrace car park. The phone could have been discarded somewhere in town or the SIM card destroyed."

Karen pressed a few buttons on a keyboard beside her, which brought up Ruth's photos from the memory stick. The team remained silent as Karen flicked through them. Ruth's face smiled back at them. There were various pictures of her with her husband in a restaurant. Other images showed her sitting in their garden enjoying the warm weather with friends. There were so many Karen couldn't view them all. A friend's wedding. A barbecue. An airport lounge. Hill walking. Karen stepped back and folded her arms across her chest. The photos painted a life full of adventure, smiles, and happiness.

"Wrong time and place?" someone asked.

Karen shrugged. "It might look that way. Look at the evidence so far. Clean laptop. Successful career. Happy marriage. Friends who didn't have a bad word to say about her. Good life," she said, pointing towards a screen.

"Cases like this are so hard to deal with," Jade remarked, with a shake of her head.

"You're not wrong there," Karen replied. "Stranger killings and stranger rapes are the hardest to solve. The clear-up rates are pretty low. But we have to try our hardest and know we did everything possible to track down her killer."

Dan chipped in next. "Karen, I've worked through a dozen or so card transactions so far for both the entry into the exhibition and for any purchases made by men. I've spoken to each individual and cross-referenced their names with the PNC and PND. Everything checks out and no one is known to us."

"Okay thanks, Dan. Continue working through the full list. We can't rule out the possibility our killer had an accomplice who stalked her."

Belinda wiggled her mouse to wake up her screen. "Forensics have come back with their initial findings of Ruth's clothing examined at the scene. Particles of dirt found on her clothes matched the scene, but they also found dust and fabric particles on her jeans that were not soil-related. The closest they could match it to were lint fabric, possibly the kind you would find with dressings. But they are running a further analysis."

Karen added it to the whiteboard.

Opening her notebook, Karen relayed the key points from the post-mortem this morning. "We have to focus on finding out where Ruth was murdered before her body was dumped north of Pilmoor. Whoever did murder her had access to transport. Jobbing Cross is a very remote location. A car. A van. So we need to look at vehicles which were in the area in the hours before her body was discovered. Izzy believes the body wasn't there for longer than twelve hours, so I need to know where she was before that. So it gives us a window to focus our efforts."

"I'll organise for signs to be positioned along Jobbing Cross," Jade said.

"Thanks, Jade. She was moved within the first few hours of her being murdered," Karen said, informing the team from the post-mortem findings. "That narrows our window further."

"How did you get on with visiting her best friend last night?" Belinda asked.

"It's everything we've heard already," Karen said with a shrug. "Popular. Fun-loving. Loved sports. Ruth was on the netball team at university. Apparently, she had plenty of male admirers while she was at Southampton university," Karen said turning to look at Ruth's picture. And Karen could see why. She bore a resemblance to the actresses Natalie Portman and Keira Knightley. Dark eyes, dark hair, high cheekbones, pronounced chin.

"So we return to the question of why her?" Belinda added.

Karen didn't have an answer yet. "Belinda, can you do me a favour? Can you check all prisoner release records for the last six months? Is there anyone who fits this MO?"

"Sure," Belinda replied.

Karen closed the meeting before heading off to the video room.

15

KAREN PUSHED OPEN the door to the video room to find Preet and Claire sitting in front of a large monitor sipping from their mugs and sharing a large bag of Sensations crisps. They looked up as she entered.

"Made yourself comfortable?" Karen said as she leaned over Preet's shoulder and dipped her fingers into the bag. Pulling out a few crisps, she popped one into her mouth and rolled her eyes before letting out a satisfying moan. "Sweet chilli. I've not had these in ages. These are so good."

Preet laughed. "You can never go wrong with a bag of sweet chilli crisps. They're moreish. I swear it's the reason I keep putting on weight."

"Of course, right? You're as thin as a stick. If you think you're putting on weight, I must be clinically obese."

Karen threw the rest of the crisps in her mouth and patted her hands clean. "How are you getting on?"

"As you said, there are a few cameras around the university building. We've not started on those yet as we focused our attention on one camera facing out over the entrance to the car park." Preet checked her notes before rewinding the footage back to a point she had marked. "The good news is we spotted Ruth entering the car park."

Karen leaned over between her two officers and watched the footage play out. Ruth's side profile came into view and crossed the street before heading towards the entrance to the car park. With her back to the camera, there was nothing in her posture or demeanour to suggest any cause for concern. Ruth walked at a normal pace, head bowed. She looked up briefly as she checked for traffic in both directions before entering the car park and heading over towards her right.

"She disappeared out of view for a few minutes before appearing here," Preet added, pointing towards the far right of the screen as Ruth appeared from behind trees obscuring their view.

Ruth weaved in between cars before stopping and turning a sharp right to head out of the car park.

"That's odd. Where is she going?" Karen asked.

"Not sure. But she appeared twenty-one minutes later." Preet wound the tape forward and then ran it at normal speed as Ruth reappeared for less than two minutes before the camera lost sight of her.

Karen tutted. "Was there another camera to pick her up?"

"No. We checked for thirty minutes either side of her first appearing. No cars entered or left the car park."

Karen furrowed her brow. "She couldn't have just disappeared. There must be a sighting of her on another camera?"

"Not that we found so far. There is still a lot of footage to go through. But whatever happened to her, happened out of sight. Looking at Google Maps, the car park is ringed by a fence and hedges. Maybe there was a gap in the fence?"

Karen made a mental note to check that out. "Any joy with the council control room. Did they spot any reccurring cars in the hour or two before her disappearance?"

"Sorry, Karen. Nothing there either," Claire added. "We've hit a bit of a brick wall so far. We'll start on the feeds provided by the university security team."

Karen thanked both officers before heading out of the room, a sense of frustration building within her.

16

THE MAN STAYED in the same shady area he had been in earlier. Taking a look at his watch, he registered it was precisely six thirty-five p.m. Leah would arrive in ten minutes. To make sure nobody could ever find out where he was, he'd left his phone at home. When the police launched their investigation, they'd be looking for cell site information on all the phones pinged close to where Leah was last seen.

He puffed out his chest, pleased with the progress he was making. It felt like there was an improvement in his mindset and the tactics he was using. Yes, he had done a few things wrong with Ruth. Perhaps he'd been a little hasty because so much was riding on this. He had gone through the same process for Ruth as he was doing now for Leah. Diligently following her. Building up a detailed profile of Ruth's life. He knew what she'd done day-to-day, he knew what she'd eaten, who her friends were, especially Nia who was her best friend, and where she'd gone with her husband Mark. Every aspect of her life had been explored. He had pored over pages of compiled information on her. But his impatience had let him down at the last minute.

It was an error he was determined to not make again. Emotion couldn't play a part in this. He'd learned that from studying others who were far more experienced than him. He had delved into their minds. Understood how they thought. Cross-examined their profiles to discover the universal quality they all possessed which made them deadly. To his surprise there were a few traits they all displayed. But the one which stood out to him was the complete lack of emotion. They were cold, calculated killers. That was what he needed to be.

He checked his watch again, six forty-four p.m. She would be here soon. He stepped out of the shadows and pulled the dog lead from his pocket, allowing it to dangle through his fingers. He crossed over the road and began pacing around, criss-crossing the road, occasionally looking around before continuing his erratic movements. Every so often he would take a sneaky look from the corner of his eye, waiting for Leah to appear.

And on cue, he spotted Leah a hundred metres down the road. He turned his back on her and trudged away. "Daisy!" he shouted. He waited a few more seconds before shouting again. "Daisy! Come on, girl!" he barked, his voice loud and intense. He walked a few steps before pausing and glancing around as if searching, before continuing. Deliberately, he turned and headed in Leah's direction, but crossed the road to keep his distance. When Leah was just a few metres away, he stopped and glanced up and down the street. He whistled before shouting Daisy's name again.

He spotted the confusion on Leah's face as she approached. "Hi, there. You haven't seen a brown and white spaniel further down the road, have you?"

Leah paused, a soft look of concern on her face. "Oh no, have you lost your dog?" she asked, looking at the loose lead hanging from his hand.

The man shrugged. "Unfortunately, yes. I take Daisy for a walk, well, more like a run because she never walks, along the edge of the racecourse. But she darted off into the hedges. Probably saw a rabbit. But I can't find her. She can be a little stubborn sometimes. She's only three."

Leah offered him a sympathetic smile as she glanced up and down the road. "Well, I didn't see her from the direction I've just come from. Are you sure she's not over on the grounds of the racecourse?"

The man glanced over towards the racecourse which skirted the end of the road, and the hedge he had hidden behind while watching her. "I'm going to head back over there now. She's a cheeky little thing. She's done this before. It's like a game of hide-and-seek for her. You're right. She's probably over there, nose buried in the bushes."

"I live a few doors away. I'm more than happy to come and give you a hand looking for her?" Leah offered, with a shrug of the shoulder.

He offered her his warmest smile but kept his distance to not alarm her. "That's very kind of you. I appreciate the offer. But I know what Daisy is like. She's a rescue dog and won't come to strangers because she's nervous of humans. She didn't have a very good start in life. Born on an unscrupulous puppy farm. When the RSPCA discovered her, she was one of a litter of seven. Daisy and her sister were the only ones alive. The mother had to be put to sleep because of internal injuries inflicted upon her by the farm owner."

Leah threw a hand over her mouth as her eyes moistened. "Oh my God, that's awful. That's so sad. It's a wonderful thing you've done to give her the chance of a normal life. Please, let me come and help you."

"I really appreciate it, but I'll head off now and keep looking for her. She knows her way home. So, I wouldn't be surprised if she's sitting on the front door mat looking pleased with herself. Have a good evening." He offered her a small nod and a warm smile before walking away, the smile growing bigger as he disappeared through the hedgerow and the racecourse beyond.

17

As KAREN MADE her way back to her office, ready to call it a day, she heard the familiar voice of Detective Superintendent Laura Kelly shouting her name from the far end of the corridor.

"Please don't make this a long conversation," Karen muttered to herself as she turned on her heel and offered Kelly her broadest, non-condescending smile. "Ma'am."

Kelly closed the gap, stopping just inches away, and leaning in closer than Karen was comfortable with.

Does this woman not know the definition of boundaries? Kelly was so close Karen could smell her boss's stale breath through the closed tooth grin Kelly had fixed on her face. Stepping back wasn't an option for Karen, it would be too obvious.

"I've been rushed off my feet today, back-to-back meetings. I feel like I was up and down those stairs a thousand times. Phew," Laura whispered, using her book as a makeshift fan to cool her face.

Yeah, and you smell like you need a shower. Your armpits are honking, Karen thought.

"I really wanted to catch up with you for an update on your new investigation. Any progress?" Laura asked.

"To be honest, ma'am, it's a bit of a mystery. I'm thinking this was murder committed by a stranger, which as you know, is the hardest to deal with."

Kelly furrowed her brow and narrowed her eyes. "What makes you think that?"

"So far, we are dealing with a victim who appeared to be well liked by everyone. A good circle of friends. Happily married. A successful career with a list of happy clients. We are struggling to find a motive," Karen replied.

Kelly nodded, but remained silent, giving nothing away.

Karen continued to fill the awkward silence. "We are still building up a full profile on the victim and her last known movements. We can confirm she entered Union Terrace car park after visiting an art exhibition. But she never left. Her car remained there. We believe she was abducted close to her car, but we have no CCTV footage to corroborate that. Having seen the video footage, I think there are strong grounds to set up a high-profile information gathering exercise at the car park."

Karen's phone buzzed in her pocket. She ignored it.

"Right. What resources do you need?" Kelly asked.

"I'm going to send a few officers over to the car park tomorrow, along with some uniformed officers, if that's possible? They can stop everyone who enters the car park to ask them if they've seen anything suspicious, and we can show them a picture of Ruth to see if it sparks any recollections."

Karen took a few moments to update Laura on the police notices being placed at the crime scene asking for further information, and the work being carried out to review university and council control CCTV footage from the night Ruth disappeared.

"Have you interviewed the husband? Any suspicions around him?" Laura asked.

Karen nodded. "We interviewed him at home, and I spoke to him again after he identified Ruth's body. He seems pretty genuine. I've assigned officers to look into his background and check his last known movements as well."

Laura checked her phone and swiped through a few recent alerts while Karen continued with the updates. "Crikey, I'm running a bit late. Is there anything else I need to be made aware of?"

"No, ma'am. Nothing urgent. I'm running late too. I can come and update you tomorrow if anything changes?"

"Perfect. I'll see you tomorrow." With that, Kelly turned and marched off.

Karen let out a sigh and trudged back to her office to grab her bag and car keys. Kelly had this knack of draining the energy from her. Maybe it was because she had to think hard about everything she told Kelly before the words left her mouth. Kelly was very matter-of-fact, direct, with little nicety. It was as if Kelly was always assessing her. But it wasn't just her. DI Anita Mani had said the same as had a few other senior officers. Maybe Karen was being paranoid, but the years of being judged

in the Met had left an uncomfortable chip on her
shoulder.

Karen pulled her phone out from her pocket and checked
the screen. She had a missed call and voicemail from Henry
Beavis, the reporter who had become a useful resource in
her last case involving the tragic death of the Lawson
family. Karen picked up the voicemail and listened to it as
she headed to the car.

*Hi, Karen. It's Henry here. Though you probably know that
because I assume you have my details stored in your
contacts list, and if you don't, why not?"* Henry laughed.
*"Anyway, I wondered if I could be of any help. I understand
you're dealing with a suspicious death, well more likely
murder. We worked well together on your last case, and so I
thought we could catch up over a coffee and see how I
could be of help? Anyway, call me back when you get a
chance. Bye for now.*

Karen rolled her eyes and smiled. He was persistent. She
would give him that. She dropped her phone into her
handbag and fished out her car keys. It was only a matter of
time before Henry would call again, though he would have
to wait for the exclusive.

18

KAREN PARKED a short distance away from Delrio's, Zac's favourite Italian restaurant. By the time she reached the front door, there was no sign of Zac. She checked her phone. Ten past eight. She was already ten minutes late and assumed Zac may have already taken a seat at the table and was enjoying a drink. Stepping through the front door, Karen scanned the sea of faces scattered around the restaurant but couldn't see him. Pulling the phone out of her handbag, she dialled his number.

"Don't tell me you're running late?" Zac said.

"Well, I was, and I'm here, but where are you?"

Zac laughed down the line. "My bad. It's my turn to be late. I'm parking up. Grab a seat and I'll be there in a fcw minutes."

Karen was showed to her table and ordered a glass of red, which arrived moments later. She let out a deep sigh and then inhaled the richness of smells that surrounded her. Italian herbs. Warm focaccia bread. Rich bolognese sauces.

There was something so warm and calming about the aromas. The chatter of a dozen conversations buzzed around her. Smiling faces. Laughter. Piped music. It all seeped into her pores as her shoulders finally relented and relaxed. She savoured the richness of her wine on her tongue, and the warmth as it tickled her empty belly. She closed her eyes to savour the moment.

"Don't fall asleep on me."

Karen opened one eye to see Zac pulling the chair back opposite her and sitting down. "I was enjoying the moment."

"I can leave you to it? Pick up a Chinese on the way home for myself."

Karen reached out her hand across the table. "Don't you dare. Besides, you're paying for tonight, and I fully intend to max out your bill."

"Cheeky mare," he replied, part rising to reach across the table to kiss her. "Mmm, you taste nice."

Karen's eyes sparkled as she smiled. Every bone in her body wanted to reach across and kiss him passionately. "I don't know about you, but I'm famished. I could eat a horse."

"I'm afraid that isn't on the menu," Zac said, running his finger down the menu. "Sorry, you're out of luck," he teased, as he called over a waiter. He placed their order and a drink for himself.

"How's your day been?" he asked, loosening his tie and blinking hard.

"Tiring. I haven't got much to go on with this case. It's still early days, but I haven't found a motive, nor have I found anyone who has a bad word to say about the victim." Karen spent the next few moments telling Zac about Ruth and her life.

"She sounds too perfect. That alone makes it suspicious," Zac offered.

"You reckon?"

"Yep. When you come across a victim who could put Mother Teresa to shame, I guarantee you there's more you haven't discovered about her."

Karen agreed with Zac's assessment. It was why she had decided to meet Mark Tate again tomorrow. She hoped he would offer further insights into Ruth's life.

"Have you still got the holiday blues?" Zac asked once the food arrived. They had both opted for spaghetti bolognese with a side of vegetables to share.

"I have, but I'm doing my hardest not to get pissed off about being back at work. I miss it."

Zac placed his fork down and placed his hand on the table, wiggling his fingers to attract Karen's attention. She reciprocated as their fingers entwined. "I know. I do too. Summer hasn't stopped talking about it. It's the happiest I've seen her in a long time. All that stuff with Michelle was getting to her. Michelle can't just be a mum. There's always an agenda with that woman."

Karen squeezed Zac's fingers reassuringly. "I know. Summer's a lovely girl. You should be really proud of the job you've done of bringing her up. Despite everything."

Karen smiled as her mind wandered back to their time away, cherry-picking the highlights. She laughed aloud, drawing looks of curiosity from the neighbouring diners. Zac stared at her in confusion.

"Sorry. I was thinking about the holiday. Do you remember when Summer was sitting on your shoulders in the pool and she thought she was falling back, so wrapped her hands underneath your chin and practically strangled you as she fell backwards?"

Zac rolled his eyes as he dabbed his lips with the napkin. "How can I forget? I couldn't breathe. I think Summer forgets she's not a six-year-old any more."

"What about when she tried the prawns pil pil?" Karen asked, jabbing a finger in Zac's direction. "You lied and told her it wasn't very spicy, but her face when she spat it out and drank everything in sight to quench the fire in her mouth. I thought she would never forgive you."

Zac's shoulders shook as he chuckled to himself. "Yep, that was a good one."

They finished their meal with profiteroles and crème brûlée before leaving and walking back to their cars, hand in hand, their bodies brushing against each other. They were in no hurry to be anywhere, savouring the moment of being together without the stresses and strains of work.

"Thank you for dinner," Karen said, stopping to wrap her arms around Zac's waist. She looked into his eyes and the dark warmth they radiated. Her skin tingled, her heart pounded, and her body ached for him. "Zac, I…" The words wouldn't come.

"What?" he asked, leaning in to kiss her deeply.

Karen cleared her throat. She was lost in him. A strange feeling she had never experienced. It was as if words couldn't express her innermost thoughts. "I was going to say that… The holiday was probably the best thing that's ever happened to me. I think it brought us closer together. Not just you and me. But it brought me closer to Summer as well. Thank you for being part of my life."

Zac nuzzled closer into Karen. "I'm liking this soppy Karen. I'm liking her a lot."

Karen playfully punched him in the chest. "Oi, don't take the piss. I'm not used to being in this kind of situation, let alone telling someone how I feel about them. It feels odd, but I know it's right. If I'm honest, I'm not used to feeling this vulnerable. I've always hidden it, and that's why so many people back in London thought I was a hard-nosed, cold bitch. It was my fuck-off shield."

"I'm not here to hurt you, Karen. That's not me. I'm grateful you've come into my life as well. You've saved me, and life feels normal again. Summer and I have you to thank for that. And now I've got you, I'm not letting you go."

"I was hoping you would say that," Karen whispered. "I want this and so much more. How about if I follow you home and stay the night?" Karen stared into Zac's eyes making her intentions known.

"Sounds perfect."

19

APPROACHING headlights lit up the street. He'd waited in his usual shady spot among the shrubs and bushes for the past hour confident of her imminent return. Leah had left an hour after he'd last seen her, heading into town to meet friends for a birthday dinner. It was one of the rare occasions where she'd gone out and out of curiosity and thoroughness to execute his plan, he'd followed at a discreet distance.

Leah had met three friends for an Italian meal in the city centre. Knowing her location, he had headed back and waited patiently for her return. The night air still carried warmth, but he'd thrown on an extra layer to be sure he stayed comfortable. He glanced around his darkened surroundings as leaves on the ground rustled. He had company tonight. Not sure what, but he suspected mice, rats, and other four-legged creatures were scurrying around searching for grubs and other juicy morsels.

It was time to move as the car neared and approached Leah's house. Grabbing the lead from his pocket and a small torch from the other, he appeared from the shadows and skirted the edge of the hedge line. Glancing over his shoulder, he checked to confirm it was Leah's car. *Perfect*, he thought, as it pulled into its usual spot.

"Daisy!" he shouted, followed by a whistle. He threw the light from his torch in a sweeping arc across the darkness ahead of him. He heard the car door open and close behind him. "Daisy. Here girl," he shouted again as he moved off towards the hedge line of the racecourse again, his stride becoming erratic for effect.

"Hi, there. You still haven't found her?" Leah asked, a heightened sense of concern tinging her voice.

The man stopped, looked at the ground, and shook his head in defeat. "I thought she might have returned home, so I headed back to check. When she wasn't there, I came back and have been looking for her ever since."

"Oh my God, you must be beside yourself. Have you got any other friends or family who can help you search?" she asked.

The man shook his head. "No. I relocated here recently for a job. I'm from Norfolk and still have my sister and her family living there, and my mum lives with them too. My guess is Daisy has got lost because she is still unfamiliar with the area."

Leah looked hesitant as she glanced up and down the street. "I can pop back home, throw on a coat, and help if you would like?"

The man offered her an appreciative smile. "That's really kind of you, but I wouldn't want to take up any of your time. It's dark and it's late. I'll keep looking for her for the next few hours. I'm sure I heard her bark somewhere off in the distance," he said, pointing towards the racecourse. "She's probably confused because it's such a large piece of open land. There are no reference points for her."

"Give me one minute to grab a coat, and I'll help you for a bit," Leah said, walking briskly back to her house.

"Seriously, I really don't want to take up any of your time," the man shouted after her.

"It's really no bother. One sec," Leah shouted as her brisk walk turned into a gentle trot.

He smiled as he turned and walked back towards the hedge line, lurking close to the bushes where he had stood moments ago. If he could get her through here and on to the open ground skirting the racecourse, he could seize the opportunity. A minute or two later, he heard hard footsteps approaching. He glanced over his shoulder to see Leah zipping up her jacket and greeting him with a concerned smile.

"I thought I would go through here and on to the racecourse for a few minutes. If I shout and wave my torch, Daisy might see it."

Leah shrugged. "Will the torch be enough? It's going to be pitch-black over there."

Sensing the fear in her voice he needed to think fast. "Well, how about you wait here on the pavement, and I'll dart through the bushes? You never know, but me calling Daisy might bring her to us from a different direction."

"Sure."

He stepped through the bushes before reappearing on the ground surrounding the racecourse. "Daisy!" he shouted, repeating her name several times for effect. "Daisy! It's Daddy!" he shouted again. Looking over his shoulder to make sure the coast was clear, he threw himself to the ground and yelped. "Fuck," he shouted before groaning loudly.

"Are you okay?" Leah shouted from the other side of the hedge.

"Yes," he shouted back, tossing his torch to one side. "I think I twisted my ankle on a dip in the ground, struggling to get up."

The loud rustling of bushes signalled Leah's arrival as her silhouette appeared in the gloom. She picked up his torch and crouched beside him. "You sure you're okay?"

An exasperated sigh left his lips as he staggered to his feet and feigned a limp, throwing in the odd ouch as he gingerly made his way across the grass. "I'm not sure what else I can do to find Daisy. I know there's a local dog owner's Facebook group I can post on. I'll try as soon as I get home. Perhaps someone might have seen her this evening."

"That's a good idea," Leah said.

"How about if you lead the way back on to the street as you have the torch? I don't want to damage my ankle any further," he suggested.

Leah obliged, shining the light from the torch on the ground ahead of her as she made her way towards the line of bushes.

This strategy had worked better than he imagined. Adrenaline coursed through his veins, and his pulse throbbed in his temples. He pulled back his shoulders and puffed out his chest, an air of supremacy washing over him.

As she reached the foliage, he quickened his pace and stepped in behind her wrapping his arm around her neck to apply a sleeper chokehold. A muffled cry tore from her throat as her hands clawed at his arm. Leah leaned back for leverage, her body folding backwards as her legs fought to keep her upright. Further muted squeals punctured the night air as he continued to apply pressure. Timing was crucial and something he was keen to experience. Too much pressure for too long would restrict air instead of blood flow and she would die. It could take as little as three or four seconds for her to pass out, but more likely up to ten seconds. He counted silently, only his lips moving. Eight seconds, and then her body fell limp, falling into him as she slumped to the ground.

The man stood over her, his heart banging so hard in his chest his ribs hurt. He knew he had just seconds before Leah would wake. Pulling the cable ties and gaffer tape from his coat pocket, he secured her arms and legs before applying a strip of gaffer tape to her mouth. He slipped his hands under her armpits and dragged her backwards through the bushes, appearing on the pavement seconds later. He glanced up and down the deserted road. There wouldn't be anyone out at this time of night and he hadn't spotted any lights being switched on in nearby houses.

He retrieved his car keys from his pocket and unlocked his car. Her dead weight proved harder to shift than he had imagined and as he neared the car, Leah woke, her squeals catching him off guard as she tried to wriggle from his grip. It was a challenge, but he finally dragged her on to the back seat of his car before pulling away. As he drove off, a small smile broke on his face as he threw one last look at her house.

20

THE KEY RATTLED in its lock as he pushed open the door. After stepping into the darkened room, he glanced around to see where she was.

Leah flinched as her limbs scrambled across the floor like Bambi on ice. Her eyes were fixed wide in terror, her breath catching in her throat as she backed herself into a corner.

The man threw his keys on the table and walked over to Leah, crouching down before offering her a smile. "It's good to see you awake. I've brought you a bottle of water and a croissant for breakfast. It's the least I can do to help you enjoy your stay. I'm sorry I had to go to great lengths to bring you here."

Leah's eyes never left his as she pulled her knees up to her chest and looped her bound hands over them.

He was just inches away from her as he ran his fingers through her dark brown hair. "You really are a thing of beauty, which is why I had to have you. Leah, I know so much about you. I've been studying your habits for several weeks now. I know what you like to eat and where you like to go. I've heard the same conversation between you and Carlotto dozens of times. I even know what hair shampoo you use." He raised a brow and smirked, feeling proud of himself.

"THIS WAS YOUR FAULT. You liked routine too much which made my job *so* much easier. Though you will be pleased to know I have little use for you. Call it an experiment. Yes," he nodded, "capturing you was nothing more than an experiment."

He had been confident enough to leave her here last night, removing the gaffer tape from her mouth and the cable ties from her ankles. There was nowhere she could go and no amount of screaming that would attract any attention. She was all alone and yet she didn't know that.

Leah licked her dry, cracked lips. "Please… Please don't hurt me. I promise I won't say anything if you let me go."

The man stood and stretched before walking around the room, his shoes echoing on the bare floorboards. He stopped by the boarded-up window and stared at his reflection in the glass. He turned his head from left to right to admire his features from different angles before letting out a satisfied breath. "This is nice, isn't it? You and me. It gives us a chance to talk. I've spent all my life talking to people, much in the same way you have. It's human nature after all. The spoken word gives us an opportunity to express what we think and what we feel."

He stepped away from the window and came back over to Leah, standing a few feet from her. He felt nothing as he stared at her. No guilt. No sadness. No excitement. No desire for her. *Perfect*.

"I find it fascinating to witness the patterns in my life and in the lives of people I see. I often recognise reccurring situations, issues or dramas that are happening for those around me. Some call it same shit different smell, some believe this is the burden of their lives they have to bear, while others dig a little deeper and ask why does this keep happening in my life? That's the thing, Leah," he leaned over and locked eyes with her, "The power of the spoken word has profound effects. We live in a world where words are cheap and actions are what seem to get our attention, but what if we all took responsibility and truly embodied the understanding of how our words create our reality? Huh?"

"Please. Please. I don't understand. I don't know what you want me to say." Leah's voice was soft and timid as she cowered further into the corner.

"Interpretation, Leah. Interpretation," he replied firmly. "It's how we take the spoken word and turn it into action, and action becomes a reality. It's like a piece of art. Two people could stand side by side and form differing opinions about it. One may like it, and the other might hate it."

The man straightened up and stepped back into the middle of the room before raising his arms either side of him. "Look around you. What do you see? This room is a living piece of abstract art. To me it represents sanctuary. Protection. Sensibility." He paused and raised a brow before shaking his head when she didn't reply. "To you, it probably represents… hell." He checked the time on his watch, again careful not to bring his phone, which could give his location away.

"I wish I could say you'll be here for a while, but I don't have any use for you. I can reassure you now I'm not here to rape or torture you. I'm not about to demand a ransom for your release. The fact of the matter is I wanted to take you. There were only ever two parts to this experiment. I've completed the first. The second won't be as pleasant for you."

Walking towards the open door, he paused and looked back at her. "You really should eat. Not long now." He closed the door behind him and turned the key in the lock as he heard Leah's bare feet slapping across the floor towards the door, her fists slamming into the wood, her cries for help echoing in the surrounding corridor. As he walked away, he heard her sobbing pleas fade into the distance.

21

KAREN STOOD by the rear patio doors, cradling her mug of coffee in both hands. Her mind drifted as she stared at the grassy lawn beyond. Feeling warm and snuggly in Zac's dressing gown, she could smell his manly scent on the fabric. It still felt surreal, and Karen needed to remind herself that she was in a much better place now. The panic attacks and racing for the ladies' toilets back in London had all but gone. Her heightened state of awareness, which led to sleepless nights, upset stomachs, and raging headaches were gone too.

She'd spent so much time wondering what others thought of her. It was as if she'd spent much of her recent career under the spotlight of suspicion and doubt. Her colleagues, team, and senior management scrutinised her every move. Karen gritted her teeth as the spectre of Skelton's face flashed through her thoughts. He was the one who had plotted and instigated her demise. Skelton was the one who'd tripped her up at every opportunity and she had been blind to it. Karen tutted as she tried to push those thoughts from her mind. Taking a sip of her coffee, she savoured the bitterness.

It was those she'd trusted who'd nearly ended her career. But as she stood there, catching the reflection of herself facing the glass, it still felt like unfinished business. Sally Connell. Just recalling the name sent shards of anger through her. The head of a major OCG, she had evaded capture by slipping out of the country. There was always the risk she could return, enter the country undetected, and either re-establish herself as a major player in the criminal underworld in London, or seek revenge for the death of one of her brothers.

"Why am I even wasting my mental energy thinking about it?" she whispered.

"Thinking about what?"

Karen jolted and looked over her shoulder. "Shit. That made me jump. I didn't even know you were there."

Zac padded barefoot through the kitchen and came in behind Karen, wrapping his arms around her waist. He nuzzled his face into her neck. "That's because you were away with the fairies. What were you thinking about?"

Karen sighed. "Nothing much. I was reflecting on my life back in London and all the troubles I went through."

"I hope you're not thinking of ever going back?"

"I have more reasons to stay here than I do to go back to London." Karen took another sip of her coffee.

"I hope one of those reasons is me?" Zac asked.

Karen turned in Zac's embrace and studied his features. She adored his warm dark eyes, his stubbly beard, and his tight jawline. She'd often thought he must have Italian ancestry in his blood, though Zac had never looked into it. "You're the biggest reason I'm staying here. You can be annoying sometimes, but no one is perfect." Karen smiled as she kissed him softly on the lips.

"Perfect would be boring," Zac replied, releasing Karen from his grip before heading to the kettle to rustle up a coffee for himself.

Karen followed, draining the last of her coffee and placing the mug in the dishwasher.

"Are you heading straight into the office?" Zac asked, slowly stirring his coffee.

"That's the plan as Laura has organised a press briefing for later, but I first want to head back over to the crime scene at Jobbing Cross. I'd like to look over the area again on my own and see what else springs to mind. I often find once we've cleared the scene and there's no more police activity, I get a different perspective. It's odd, but I sometimes feel like I'm seeing the scene play out through the eyes of the victim. As if I'm there? I know it sounds daft."

"Ouch." Zac licked his lips after sipping hot coffee too quickly. "It doesn't sound daft at all. I think it builds empathy for the victim. It makes you more focused and determined to seek justice for them."

Karen shrugged. "Yeah, maybe. Anyway, is it okay to grab a shower?"

Zac placed his mug on the worktop and pulled Karen into him. "Of course. But how about we get hot and sweaty first?" Zac suggested, loosening the cord on her dressing gown and slipping it off.

Karen pressed her naked flesh against his. "You come up with the best ideas."

22

As KAREN PARKED up at Jobbing Cross, it crossed her mind that she hadn't seen a single person, or any other vehicle pass her. Opposite her were farmers' fields for as far as the eye could see. Behind her was dense woodland. A shiver ran down her spine as she imagined how scary the place would be in the middle of the night, miles from anywhere and with poor phone reception.

A yellow police notice beside the road outlined the date and time when Ruth's body was found and the contact number for anyone with information. Karen stepped over the large tree trunk that lay on its side and walked the short distance to the site. She paused and looked down at the spot before looking up and surveying the horizon.

"Why here?" she said as she walked around the area. The ground was dry and firm beneath her shoes. With little rain over the summer, large fissures had developed. An opportunist murderer may have driven miles before stumbling upon this location. It wasn't uncommon for murderers to dump their victims away from the actual location where they were murdered to confuse the police.

One thing was likely though—the direction from which the car had travelled.

There was only one residential property along the length of this road, a boarding kennel for dogs. A visit to the owners by her officers had confirmed CCTV overlooking the main entrance. Her team had reviewed the footage and concluded no vehicles had passed on the night Ruth had been brought here. Karen concluded the vehicle hadn't travelled from the direction of Little Hutton, Sessay, or Hutton Sessay, instead travelling from the Brafferton end of Jobbing Cross. The insight had opened a new line of enquiry for her team as they scoured the area for any domestic CCTV or roadside cameras.

Karen thought back to Ruth's last moments. She could only imagine how terrified the poor woman had been. With asphyxiation, she knew the death wouldn't have been painful or horrific, or drawn-out. Perhaps that part was a blessing because being brought out here in the middle of the night and then being murdered would only have created more anguish, fear, and pain.

But what did it say about the murderer? There was no attempt to hide the body or bury it. It was in plain sight for a walker, runner, or farmer to discover. It suggested a bold-ness and a lack of fear. Karen sensed the way in which the killer presented the body carried meaning, though she wasn't sure what yet. Ruth's body hadn't lain in a crumpled heap, her limbs broken and disfigured. It had been posi-tioned purposefully. Thoughts and ideas tumbled through Karen's mind, colliding with one another, desperate to find a connection.

Karen paused for a moment and tucked her hands in her pockets as she let her eyes wander across the peaceful land-scape. The location and the positioning of the body suggested someone who was methodical and thought through the crime. Above all else, Karen wondered if there was a hint of confidence in their actions. Karen was certain the perpetrator wasn't scared of the police.

She was interrupted when her phone vibrated in her pocket. Expecting it to be Henry because she hadn't returned his call yet, she let out a sigh of relief when Ty's name popped up on the screen.

"Hi, Ty. Is everything okay?"

"Where are you?" he asked.

"I'm just at the crime scene. I wanted to get a few things straight in my mind. But I'm heading back to the office now."

"Oh, right. Has it helped?"

"I think so."

"Karen, a search of Ruth's deleted text messages found a text confirming the account set up on the website Plenty of Fish about fifteen months ago."

Karen's eyes narrowed as she leaned up against her car. "That's interesting. Perhaps Ruth wasn't as perfect as we first thought?" Ty remained silent, and she wondered if he thought the same. "Were there any other messages connected to Plenty of Fish? Maybe notifications around communication with other members?"

"There were a few. Mainly notifications about various users sending her winks."

"Did she reply to any?"

"Not that we could see from her text or chat history."

"Good work, Ty. Keep looking. In the meantime, see if you can find contact details for Plenty of Fish. I doubt they'll release any chat history from within the website portal, confidentiality of members and all that bollocks, but we can apply for a warrant if necessary."

"Will do. Are you still heading back here?" Ty asked.

"Not just yet. I'm going to pay Mark Tate and Nia another visit."

23

"HAVE you found the person who did this?" Mark Tate said as he flung open the door seconds after Karen pushed the doorbell. A painted lattice of red lines filled his eyes and dark saggy bags hung beneath them. His stubbly jowls looked heavier.

"Not yet, Mr Tate. Do you mind if I come in?"

Mark nodded and stepped to one side, allowing Karen to walk through the hallway and into the lounge.

Mugs half full of cold tea filled the small table beside one armchair. Scrunched up tissues were tossed close to the bin, and a stale, heavy odour hung in the air.

"How are you coping?" Karen asked, but judging by the look of his dishevelled state, and the untidy lounge, he was struggling.

"I'm coping. It's hard. One minute I think she's going to walk in the door, and the next I can't believe she's… gone." Mark dropped into the armchair and rested his hands on his thighs as he stared across the lounge towards the front window.

Karen took a seat on the sofa. "I know. I wish there was something I could say to make things better, but we are doing our best to find out what happened to Ruth." Karen let the silence settle between them for a few moments in case Mark had anything to say. He stared straight ahead, transfixed, eyes wide, and not blinking. She watched the rise and fall of his chest. Steady. No short, sharp intakes of breath from being upset or feeling anxious. It was as if he was meditating.

"Is the family liaison officer providing you with all the updates you need?"

Mark Tate nodded once, his eyes not shifting.

"I don't know if this is of any help to you, or not the right time, but we can put you in touch with a counselling service specialising in families who've lost a loved one. I'm more than happy to do that for you, Mark?"

Mark shook his head once. Slow and measured.

He wasn't coping in Karen's eyes, but there was only so much she could offer.

"Mark, I've got something I need to ask you. It might appear insensitive, but it's not my intention. We recovered a few deleted text messages on Ruth's phone from fifteen months ago. One was about an account set up with Plenty of Fish. And there were several other text notifications from other members reaching out to Ruth. Are you aware of that?"

Mark snapped his head in Karen's direction. His eyes pinned wide in shock. "What? Plenty of Fish?" His eyes scrunched up in confusion as he grimaced. "No. There must be a mistake. Why would my wife be on Plenty of Fish?"

Karen shrugged. There could be many reasons, but she needed to gauge Mark's reaction.

"Text notifications? What, people contacting Ruth?" he asked.

Karen nodded. "That appears to be the case. She set up an account in the name of Blossom473. Several members sent her wink notifications. I hate to ask this, but was your wife having an affair?"

Mark shook his head. "No. No. We were happily married. We loved each other."

"Did she ever say she was unhappy with her life or with your marriage?" Karen asked.

"No, never," Mark replied emphatically.

"Did you ever have any arguments?"

"Of course, we did. Every couple does." He shrugged.

"Heated arguments?" Karen probed.

"No. We disagreed over normal things like spending too much on food, shopping, or clothes. Or one of us coming home drunk after a night out with friends. But that was it. We both hated confrontation. I don't get it. Why would you think she's having an affair? Why would she set up a Plenty of Fish account? None of this makes sense," Mark said firmly as he rose from his chair and walked across to gaze out the front window, arms folded across his chest.

"It could be nothing. We are peeling back the layers of Ruth's life, and we have a duty to investigate everything, even if it might be painful for anyone close to her. I'm sorry this upsets you. But I had to ask," Karen said, before getting to her feet as well.

Mark dropped his head to his chest as he slowly banged a fist on the windowsill. "I know. You're only doing your job. I'm sorry for being abrupt with you. It's... Well, I'm just shocked. There must be an explanation behind it. It's not in her nature to meet random people off a dating website."

His words appeared sincere, but Karen noticed a hint of doubt and lack of conviction in his voice. "Okay, Mr Tate, thank you for your time. This wasn't an easy conversation for you, but... Well, you know."

Mark Tate nodded. "Yes. You had to ask."

24

"I'M HERE to see Nia Knowles," Karen said to the middle-aged woman on reception at Barrow Insurance Services, who wore a badge on her blouse saying her name was Cheryl Peterson, Senior Receptionist.

"And who shall I say is here and the nature of your visit?" Cheryl asked.

Karen pulled out her warrant card and held it in clear view for Cheryl to see. "We were hoping she could help us with an enquiry we're following up on. It's a personal matter."

Cheryl eyed the details and cast Karen a broad but fake and insincere smile before hitting a few buttons on a dialler pad in front of her.

"I have a Detective Chief Inspector Karen Heath in reception for you, Nia." Cheryl cut her call seconds later and turned towards Karen again. "She'll be with you in a minute. Please take a seat over there," Cheryl said, nodding towards several chairs lining one wall between the reception desk and elevator.

Karen stood instead, taking in a few framed photos hanging on the wall above the chairs. Nothing eye-catching other than pleasant prints to while away the monotony and boredom for visitors who waited to be seen. Just viewing the pictures reminded her of a visit she had made to an office in Canary Wharf several years back. Interestingly, the firm, a banking subsidiary of a large international investment bank, had on display impressive, framed photographs of the construction of the very building she'd been standing in from its start when it was nothing more than one of several small docks which formed one of the largest docks in the world.

She recalled being fascinated as she'd moved from image to image, seeing the dock drained and the water pumped back into the River Thames, to when the first pilings went in and the eventual construction of the whole building.

"Detective chief inspector," Nia said, coming up behind Karen.

Karen was shaken from her reverie as a solemn-looking Nia paused beside her. "Hi, Nia. Can we talk?"

Nia looked around and shifted uncomfortably as she caught Cheryl's intense stare. "Um, yes. Just not here. We can use one of the meeting rooms," she said, pointing to a row of doors at the other end of the reception area. Nia led the way and slid the sign on the door to occupied before closing the door after Karen. Pulling one of the leather chairs away from the table, Nia sat down, the plush leather squeaking beneath her as she settled in.

Karen took a seat opposite her. "I wasn't expecting to hear you were back in the office when I called you. I thought you would be at home."

Nia played with the lanyard draped around her neck. "I couldn't sit at home, I had to keep myself busy. I can't stop thinking about Ruth." Nia tried to smile in Karen's direction, but it appeared as an awkward grimace.

"I understand. It's never easy coming to terms with the loss of someone so close to you. But I need to talk to you. Other than Ruth's husband, as far as I can tell, you were Ruth's closest friend and knew her better than most."

Nia nodded.

"We've been looking into Ruth's life in a bit more detail. You mentioned Ruth and Mark were happily married when we last spoke. Has it always been the case?"

Nia took a deep breath and exhaled.

Karen watched, studying Nia's eyes, which bounced around in their sockets like a set of overexcited ping-pong balls. It was as if Nia was trying to figure out what to say. "It's okay. You can say whatever you want. I'm not here to get you into trouble or anything like that."

Nia's shoulders dropped. "They went through a bit of a rough patch a few years ago. Ruth said that they were constantly arguing. It got so bad they kind of separated. And Ruth went to stay at her mum's for a few weeks to give them a bit of space."

"Do you know what they were arguing about?"

"I think lots of things, but mostly around money. Ruth told me Mark was spending a lot of money, but then whenever she spent a bit to treat herself, he would get annoyed."

"Did those arguments turn physical? Did Ruth ever say he had assaulted her in any way?" Karen probed, leaning forward in her chair.

Nia shook her head. "Not as far as I know. If that happened, she would have told me."

"You said Mark was spending a lot of money? Did Ruth mention what he was spending the money on?"

"Yes," Nia replied, with a roll of her eyes. "He was spending more money than they were making. Mainly on online betting. Dogs and casino offers. It wasn't good. Ruth accused him of having an addiction, and of course, he denied it. He told Ruth he had it under control, which he clearly didn't when the credit card companies got involved because he started missing payments."

"Was he still gambling?" Karen asked.

"I don't think so. After they separated, he kept turning up at Ruth's mum's house begging her to come home. Eventually, he got help and joined a gambling addiction group and things have been okay since then. They took out a loan and paid off all the cards before cutting them up. Well, Ruth made him do that," Nia replied.

"And he was okay with that?"

"As far as I know."

"Nia, did Ruth ever meet other men either to socialise with, date, or have sex with?"

The question alarmed Nia as she sat back in her chair, eyes wide, mouth open. "No. She wasn't like that."

"Do you think she could have had a secret life even you weren't aware of?" Karen suggested.

Nia shook her head, too shocked to even reply.

"We recovered deleted text messages connected to the website, Plenty of Fish. Ruth had set up an account on there and was receiving messages from other members. Were you aware of that?"

Nia wiped her moist eyes as her chest heaved. "No. She was never like that. There must be a mistake."

"Okay, Nia, thank you for your time. If there's anything else you can think of, please call me." Karen rose from her chair and made for the door with Nia a few steps behind. She pressed the button on the elevator and watched as Nia disappeared down the corridor, head bowed, her steps small and fast.

25

KAREN BREEZED through the doors to the main floor and headed towards Bel and Ty. Ty was writing up notes, and Bel was scooping out the last remains from her pot of yoghurt, licking the plastic spoon with so much effort it bent under the pressure.

"I've just been to have a chat with both Mark Tate and Nia. We seem to have differing accounts of Ruth."

Ty dropped his pen on his pad while Bel continued to lick her spoon as if it was a large lollipop, her pink tongue almost touching her chin.

"If it means that much to you, Bel, I'll get you another yoghurt from the canteen. Not only does it look gross, but it's bordering on indecency," Karen laughed.

Belinda ignored Karen's jibes and continued to lick the spoon to annoy Karen further.

"Anyway," Karen said, turning towards Ty and ignoring Belinda's slurping noises. "Mark knew nothing about

Plenty of Fish, obviously. But it knocked him for six. To be honest he looked a mess when I turned up. Mark couldn't believe his wife would do anything like sign up to a dating site and meet other men behind his back, regardless of intent."

"Well, she's hardly going to broadcast it and slap up an enormous banner in their lounge," Ty remarked.

"Exactly. But he painted the perfect picture of their marriage. A few difficulties around money which he glossed over as minor issues. This is where it gets interesting, because when I spoke to Nia, she said Mark had a gambling addiction which caused a lot of problems between them. They separated for a short while with Ruth living at her mum's until Mark got the right help and sorted himself out."

"There has to be more to it," Ty added.

"Were you able to take a look at the account?" she asked.

"I could only go so far. I registered with some dummy details to become an unpaid member, but you can only do basic searches. The account had hidden the profile picture and it's only available to paid members *if* the account holder chooses to share their pictures with whoever they're talking to."

So her husband couldn't find her if he were suspicious? Karen wondered.

"We could check his bank and credit records to determine if he had been gambling up to when Ruth was murdered? Maybe he was doing it on the quiet?" Ty suggested.

Karen agreed and thought it was a good idea to do an in-depth financial sweep of the couple. She gave Ty the go-ahead to do that for her. "Despite their close friendship, Nia was not aware of Ruth being on Plenty of Fish and assumed it was a mistake."

"So the husband's saying they didn't have a lot of difficulties other than those most married couples deal with, and we have the best friend saying financial difficulties almost spelt the end of their marriage. If that doesn't sound suspect, I don't know what does," Belinda chipped in.

"Nice of you to contribute, Bel. Are you finished having your *moment*?" Karen teased.

Belinda stared towards the ceiling as if contemplating the predicament before nodding. "Someone is being thin with the truth. I reckon it was the husband."

Karen smiled and rolled her eyes. "Thanks for that, Sherlock."

"Well, look at press conferences we've seen over the years from different forces around the country. How many times has the husband sat at the front with the SIO looking heartbroken and pleading for any information leading to the capture of his wife's killer. Then we all find out he did it," Belinda argued.

"Which is why we can look more closely at Mark. Ty is looking at the financials, and you can look at his connections," Karen replied.

"Maybe he found out about the Plenty of Fish account and attacked her. He may have set up his own account in revenge, and Ruth found out, and they fought," Bel offered.

"If he attacked her, why tie her wrists? There are lots of things for us to consider, and we need to keep an open mind… Belinda." Karen tapped her finger on Belinda's desk to push her point across.

"Well, as you said, someone isn't telling the truth," Ty summed up. "I'll get cracking on the financials straightaway."

Karen looked at the time on the phone. "Shit. I've got the press briefing shortly and need to dash. Time to do my hair and apply a bit of lippy. I don't want to scare everyone away. Wish me luck," Karen said as she hurried off.

26

Detective Superintendent Laura Kelly hovered outside the door to the press room. In between checking the time on her phone, she glanced up and down the corridor keen to not keep the press pack waiting.

"Sorry, ma'am," Karen said as she appeared through the doors leading from the stairwell.

Kelly offered her a smile. "It's fine. We are still waiting for David Cornwell, who'll be our press officer today. I'm going to do a brief introduction, before handing over to you. Does that work for you?"

"Fine with me. Is there anything you want me to say or not say?"

Kelly shook her head. "Nothing in particular. The usual. Don't say too much and don't say too little."

"Understood."

Ten minutes later Karen, Kelly, and David were seated at the top table overlooking a large gathering of reporters, journalists, and photographers. Several pictures of Ruth Tate were fixed to a whiteboard beside them. Karen used a few minutes while the assembled crowd settled to cast her eye over who was attending. From the far left, she spotted Henry Beavis throwing her a broad, cheesy grin. Karen sighed inwardly. He was persistent. She'd give him that.

Kelly asked for silence before continuing. "Thank you all for coming here today. The serious crime unit is investigating the abduction and murder of Ruth Tate three days ago. Her body was discovered at a remote location north of Pilmoor. We are working with friends and family to build a timeline of her last known movements. I'd like to hand over to the senior investigating officer on the case, Detective Chief Inspector Karen Heath." Kelly nodded in Karen's direction.

Karen glanced down at her notes, let out a long slow deep breath and then cast her attention towards a sea of eager faces. Several photographers clicked away as Karen began.

"Ruth Tate was a happily married and successful businesswoman. The impact on her family and friends has been devastating. As Detective Superintendent Kelly stated, we are working hard to understand what happened to Ruth in the final few hours of her life. At the moment, we are still determining whether she was murdered by someone she had known or met, or whether this was an opportunist and tragic case of being in the wrong place at the wrong time."

Karen checked the few scribbles she had made to her notes before walking into the conference room to make sure she had missed nothing. "I also want to add we are making an appeal to the public for any information or sightings of Ruth Tate on the night she disappeared." Karen gave the day and time as to when Ruth was last spotted on CCTV.

She watched several reporters look down at their notepads and scribble down the facts. "We are asking members of the public to come forward if they were in the area close to the Union Terrace car park around nine thirty p.m. that evening, or in Jobbing Cross in the early hours of the following morning. All information will be treated in the strictest confidence, and if they wish to remain anonymous, then they can call the Crimestoppers helpline."

Karen glanced at Kelly who nodded once to suggest "that's enough."

Kelly turned her attention to the assembled group. "We'll take a few questions."

One reporter shouted out, "Is this a random murder women should be concerned about?"

"Not at all. As always, we always ask women to be vigilant if they are alone. At night, we advise them to stay in well-lit areas, and always have their phone close to hand in case they need to report anything suspicious."

Henry jumped up from his seat rather than raise his hand, his exuberance catching those around him off guard as they jolted in surprise. "In murder cases, the police would always look at next of kin to begin with. Is Ruth's husband under suspicion?"

Karen tightly gripped her pen until her knuckles turned white. *Dickhead.*

"We are keeping an open mind, and her husband has cooperated with our investigation so far. Please understand he is a grieving husband who has lost his wife," Kelly replied firmly.

Henry sat down as another reporter raised his hand. "Charlie Whitehead, *York Times*. Was there a sexual element to the murder?"

"No," Kelly said, glaring at him.

"Was it a botched robbery?" Whitehead pushed.

"As I said, we are keeping an open mind. The motive behind the murder remains unclear," Kelly replied as she closed her folder. "That will be it for the moment. We will update you all in due course as the investigation proceeds." Kelly stood as several small conversations broke out among those gathered, the collective murmur drowning out Kelly's last few words.

Karen noticed the tightness in Kelly's voice and knew her boss was becoming irate as she watched her step off the podium and disappear through a back door. Karen raised a brow. David pursed his lips in response.

As the various members of the press filtered out, Henry made a beeline for Karen as she collected her paperwork.

"DCI, you've been avoiding my calls."

"Henry, I can't sit there with my feet up on the desk having cosy chats with you because you fancy calling me." Karen wanted to tear a strip off him for his question which was inflammatory and unhelpful to the investigation, but she bit her tongue, knowing she couldn't lose her rag while other members of the press were still milling around.

"DCI, I want to help. We worked well together on the Lawson case. I saw your team conducting door-to-door enquiries in Ruth's street. Did they find much?"

"Henry, you know I'm not at liberty to tell you."

Henry nodded and then stepped in closer to avoid being overheard by the others. "I did my own digging and spoke to a few neighbours. A resident from the far end of the street has seen Mark Tate walking past his house frequently in the early hours. Don't you think that's suspect?"

It was in Karen's eyes, but she wasn't about to let on, and remained po-faced. "Maybe he suffers from insomnia?"

"Come on, DCI. I'm not stupid. I bet your officers didn't discover that did they? Anyway, this resident who shall remain anonymous said he only recognised Mark because he had seen Ruth's husband in the twenty-four-hour bookies in town a few times and Mark would always wear a bright red hoodie with a big Under Armour logo on the chest."

"Okay, Henry. I'll look into that, but I need the address of this eyewitness. And if there's any credibility in the information, I'll make sure you get recognised for it. Sound fair?"

Henry nodded, before writing the address on a scrap of paper and handing it to her, giving her a wink and strolling off.

Karen watched him saunter through the doors, clearly pleased with himself. Maybe Henry would be of use later. She made a mental note to get her team to follow up on that statement before they went home for the night.

27

HOLDING his battery-powered lantern above his head to cast light into the gloom, he unlocked the door and stepped into the darkened room. Scratching and scurrying on the floor revealed Leah's location as she hurried to the corner like a trapped rat. Walking over towards the desk, he rested the lantern upon its surface and turned to study her. Fear raced through her wide eyes. Knotted hair, dirty clothes, and tear-stained cheeks left her looking like a homeless charity case. The soles of her bare feet were grubby and black.

He dragged a chair across to the other side of the room and placed it in front of a full-length mirror fixed behind a shatterproof glass casing. The beginning of the end was near.

The smell of urine grew stronger as he inched closer to her, a dark wet patch in the crotch of her jeans confirming she hadn't made it to the bucket in time or had chosen not to. He didn't care either way.

"You may wonder why I have kept you here," he said, fanning his hand out in an arc around him. "This place is heaven to me, but I appreciate it may be hell for you." He reached down and grabbed Leah's arm before dragging her across the room towards the chair. Leah screamed and cried, the soles of her feet desperate to get traction on the hard wooden floor, but weakness robbed her of the will to fight. Placing his hands underneath her armpits, he hoisted her up on to the chair before cutting the cable tie from around her hands and re-securing her wrists behind her.

Leah's breath came in ragged gasps as she looked around. "Please. Please I haven't done anything wrong. Just let me go. I swear I won't say anything." Tears tumbled from her eyes as snot trails dripped from her nose.

"It's too late for that. This is where you and I part company. It's been a useful experience. I wouldn't say it's enjoyable or thrilling. Nor am I sad to see you go. For me, it's part of the journey."

Leah screamed and wailed, the sound bouncing off the walls and the dusty bare floor. She thrashed in the chair, her head tossing from side to side. She screamed again as the cable tie cut into her wrists. Her screams reached fever pitch, loud and sharp enough to pop an eardrum. Leah coughed and spluttered as she sobbed uncontrollably.

"Scream as loud as you want, there's probably no one around for miles. I chose this place as my sanctuary so I can't be disturbed, and you can't be found." He circled around her like an eagle eyeing up its prey from above, waiting for the moment to pounce when it was least expected. She wasn't paying attention to him. Lost in her broken thoughts, she continued to thrash and scream. He continued circling. Waiting. Watching. The longer he left it, the more Leah thrust her head back and forth with her eyes rolling back into their sockets, as if an evil spirit had possessed her mind. It felt satanic, even ritualistic, as the circling continued until the switch flicked and he stopped behind her.

He watched his reflection in the mirror as he wrapped his arm around her neck and squeezed hard, pulling up and back to apply the greatest amount of pressure. His attention turned towards Leah's distorted expression staring back at him. Leah's strangled screams tore from her throat as her face reddened. Her eyes bulged. Spittle flew in all directions. Her feet scraped across the floor, pushing her body back as she desperately tried to ease the pressure on her neck and get air into her lungs. He squeezed harder, all the while watching Leah's reflection as the life was drained from her. "It will soon be over," he whispered into her ear. And as promised, her resistance petered away. Her body stopped thrashing and convulsing. Her limp figure slumped in the chair. She had gone. He squeezed for a little longer to make sure before releasing his grip and stepping away. Pulling back the sleeve on his jacket, he checked the time on his watch and made a mental note. Nine ten p.m.

It didn't take him long to wrap her body in a bed sheet, there were plenty in the storeroom. Standard issue. Not much forensics could take from it. The company manufacturing them had gone out of business a long time ago. The need to dispose of her body as quickly as possible meant there was less chance of picking up any incriminating DNA or forensic evidence. The drive to the disposal site was uneventful but long. He had planned the route in advance, sticking to small B roads to avoid being noticed on any CCTV or ANPR cameras. Again, preparation and planning were key, something he was fast learning.

Parking up, he switched off his headlights and waited a few moments. He checked in his rear-view mirror to make sure there weren't any approaching headlights in the distance. There was nothing ahead of him either. He had chosen this spot deliberately and had scouted the location several times in recent days. On those occasions he had parked up the road and had walked the rest of the way before stepping off the road and hiding in the shadows waiting and watching. He had chosen the spot well because on the four occasions he had been here before, only one car had passed by.

Opening the car door and stepping out, he tuned into his surroundings. An eerie silence greeted him. No planes overhead. No distant murmur of traffic on a motorway or even the hoot from an owl. Perfect. He came around to the rear and flipped open his boot before hauling Leah's body out and throwing her over his shoulder. Her dead weight didn't make the task easy as he staggered through the undergrowth to a clearing before dropping her body on the ground with a heavy thud. He unfolded the sheet and removed it from around her before positioning her body. He placed her legs together, feet touching, before moving around to readjust her arms. He stepped back and checked the positioning. Scooping up the sheet he returned to his car, started the ignition and pulled away.

He felt nothing. Perfect.

28

THE EARLY MORNING call from the station had Karen and her team rushing to a new scene north of the city. The discovery of a deceased female had alarm bells ringing as Karen closed in on the address. Her journey took her down a narrow single lane track to Brieryend Wood where she pulled in alongside other police vehicles and unmarked cars. Two white vans from scientific services confirmed Bart Lynch, the CSI manager, and his team were already on site. Izzy's car was a few vehicles ahead and patrol cars occupied the rest of the space close to the scene.

Another remote location, Karen thought as she flung her car door open and stepped out. *He's making it hard for us.* Karen was getting fed up staring at farmers' fields wherever she went. This location was no different. In front of where she stood was a vast expanse of ploughed fields for as far as the eye could see, and behind her was Brieryend Wood. Scenic, picturesque, calming and relaxing. All words that could describe this gorgeous location on any other day. She could imagine herself taking a packed lunch and heading out for an afternoon walk with Zac and being surrounded by nature, the birds in the trees, and enjoying the warmth of the sunshine on her face. Not today, though.

Ed and Preet approached, shaking Karen from her thoughts. "Morning you two," she said, turning to face her officers and the woods behind them. "What have we got?"

"Leah Hayes, aged twenty-nine," Preet said checking her notes. "A jewellery buyer for a high-end and luxury export business. Strangled with open wounds to her wrists. SOCO are examining her. No sign of robbery. Her handbag was beside her with her house keys, driving licence, purse, et cetera. No phone."

Karen nodded as Preet continued with the update.

"It looks as if Leah's bag was laid out beside her, rather than casually discarded. You'll see when you have a look."

"And you think it's our man?" Karen asked.

Preet nodded. "We think so from the positioning of the body, the wrist wounds, and the strangulation."

Karen headed across the road and signed in with the scene guard before getting kitted up in a white Tyvek suit and blue booties. Stepping on the silver inspection plates Bart's team had laid out, she headed over to where the blue tent had been erected.

Several SOCOs milled around the tent in quiet discussions as they recorded evidence. Karen pulled open the flap of the tent and peered in to find Izzy kneeling beside the victim. She stood by the bare, blackened feet of the deceased, her eyes drifting up the victim's body taking in its position, what she was wearing, and stopping at her face. Matted hair, tear-stained face with blackened trails of eyeshadow streaked down her cheeks. But her lips looked odd. It took a few seconds for Karen to figure out why. Freshly applied lipstick.

"Morning, Izzy. How are you getting on?"

"Morning, lovely. There's not much for me to do here. Compression to the neck. Bruising on both sides of the trachea. No evidence of indentation from fingers. I would say it's very similar, if not identical to Ruth's. I can't see any other physical injuries contributing to her death at the moment."

"Time of death?" Karen asked, her eyes darting up and down Leah's body.

"I'd say within the last eight to twelve hours," Izzy replied, packing her bits away and standing up with a groan as she straightened up her tight back and stepped around Karen. "I'm getting too old for this game. PM tomorrow afternoon," she added, squeezing Karen's arm.

Alone and without distraction, Karen could take in the scene clearly. Someone had indeed positioned Leah in much the same way Ruth had been. On her back. Legs straight, feet together. Lipstick applied, and hair fanned out around her. The right arm extended ninety degrees to her right, while the left had been positioned at around forty-five degrees. *Odd.*

She diverted her attention towards Leah's handbag. A distinctive brown Louis Vuitton bag with the LV logo emblazoned across it. Karen had never owned one but had envied them every time she walked into the high-end stores on Oxford Street, London. Selfridges was her downfall. Though she could never afford much in there, she punished herself often as she wandered around the aisles looking at the shoes, handbags, scarfs and coats. Leah's handbag was around twelve hundred pounds from memory. If it had been a robbery, the handbag would have been long gone and flogged for five hundred quid online.

"We can rule out a random one-off stranger killing then," Karen said as she stepped out of the tent and met up with Ed and Preet.

The pair nodded in unison. "I've sent officers to both ends of the lane to seal it off to traffic," Ed said.

"Thanks, Ed. What else have we got close by?"

"We've got a farm about one mile down the road," Ed continued, pointing to his right. "I'll head over there shortly. The River Derwent runs behind this wood. The Derwent is a popular location for fishing. There is a place up the road where quite a few fishermen park up before heading to their familiar spots."

"Is that Howsham Bridge I went over to come here?" Karen asked.

Ed nodded.

"Get officers down there. Fishermen often turn up in the evening to set up, and then spend the whole night fishing for roach and perch before heading off in the morning. We might catch a few packing up."

"The fishing aficionado!" Ed remarked.

Karen laughed. "Not really. I lived in Epping when I worked back in London. I had Epping Forest on my doorstep. Vast place. A dumping ground for many bodies during the fifties and sixties. Rumour has it a few gangsters who had fallen foul of the Krays met their last resting place there. Anyway, I digress. One of the Epping Forest constables told me about the roach and perch fishing, so I imagine it would be the same here."

"What next?" Preet asked.

"Well, we have her driving licence, so we know where she lives, and we have her house keys. That's where we are heading next."

29

KAREN SNAPPED on a pair of latex gloves before retrieving Leah's keys from a clear evidence bag.

"What happens if there's a house alarm?" Preet said, taking a step back to look for any signs of an alarm box. "I can't see one."

Karen slipped the key in the white double-glazed front door and unlocked it before glancing in Preet's direction. "We are about to find out." Karen nudged the door open and braced herself for the piercing shrill of an alarm and then breathed a sigh of relief when silence greeted her. She stepped into the modern hallway. Birch laminate floor and white walls offered a clean and contemporary welcome. "You check upstairs, and I'll have a look down here."

Preet headed upstairs leaving Karen to head into the lounge. The clean lines continued. White walls with several mirrors positioned to give the illusion of space and grey crushed velour sofas. Everything looked expensive, from the large ultra slim TV hanging above the fireplace, to the silver vases lining the windowsill for decorative purposes more than anything else. First impressions confirmed no presence of a disturbance as she walked through the lounge come dining room and then on to the kitchen at the rear. Polar white glossy kitchen cabinets with black marbled worktops offered an opulent feel to the kitchen as Karen ran her gloved finger along the smooth work surface. Everything was clean and tidy, and even the recent post sat in one corner of the kitchen table in a neat pile. Karen thumbed through a few of the envelopes.

Family portraits were positioned at regular intervals along the wall as she climbed the steps. Karen paused. There were pictures of Leah with who Karen assumed were her parents, as well as a few more with friends while on holiday. One captured Karen's attention. Leah was in a fashionable, skimpy bikini, with two other girlfriends draping their arms around her and posing for the photograph. She had a slim body, but it was her features that stood out and struck a chord with Karen. Leah's features were similar to Ruth's —dark hair, dark brown eyes, high cheekbones and a distinct chin.

Karen continued on to the landing and felt her feet sink into the plush, dark grey carpet. The smallest of the bedrooms served as an office, while the other two were swish and stylish with dark grey bedding and light grey walls. Beds in both rooms had numerous cushions presented on them as if dressed for a magazine shoot.

"Anything?" Karen asked as she wandered into the main bedroom at the front of the house. Preet was sitting on the side of the bed looking through the bedside cabinets.

"Just the usual stuff. Headphones, phone charger, a couple of store cards, and a vibrator," Preet said, raising her eyes in Karen's direction.

"Yep, just the usual stuff," Karen said, grinning as she opened up the wardrobe doors. Expensive shoes lined the bottom, and Leah's clothes were all presented in colour order. The more Karen looked through the house, the better the picture she built of Leah's life. Leah had expensive taste. Perhaps it was to be expected because of her work. A chest of drawers in the rear bedroom contained dozens of sample necklaces, rings, and bracelets. Many were unusual and individual pieces Karen had never seen in high street stores. *Gorgeous*, Karen thought.

With a quick search of the property concluded, and the request put in for SOCO to attend, Karen grabbed Leah's keys and headed out into the street with Preet in tow. Karen spotted at least three BMWs near Leah's house. Karen pressed the car fob and glanced up and down the road. The indicator lights from a small black BMW 1 Series flashed twice a few yards away. They both wandered over towards the car and peered in through the side windows. Everything appeared in order with no signs of disturbance to the glovebox or door bins.

Karen dropped the keys back in the bag and then folded her arms as she looked up and down the street. Leah's house was close to the end of Whin Road. Beyond it was the boundary of the racecourse. "Let's secure the car for forensic analysis. The house was locked, and the car parked on the road. So where was she abducted?"

"We can start door-to-door enquiries. If it had been a violent abduction, then surely her neighbours would have heard something. I can see a few Ring doorbells from where I'm standing," Preet said, glancing at the houses on the opposite side of the road.

"Unless someone forced her against her will and told her not to make a noise or else. But that feels weak in my opinion. It takes balls to abduct someone in the middle of a residential street," Karen remarked. "Preet, can you stay here and organise the door-to-door enquiries while I head back to brief the team?"

"No problem. I'll call it in and also arrange for recovery to take Leah's car."

"Thanks, Preet. I'm not sure if she was abducted from near her home or car, so we need to figure out what her last known movements were. We'll need to contact her next of kin for formal identification too," Karen said before heading back to the office.

30

KAREN RACED into the incident room and rallied her team around her as a matter of priority. Officers dropped what they were doing, logged off, or cut short their calls to gather around the whiteboard as Karen pinned up crime scene photos and images of Leah printed off from Facebook.

"Right, team. Following the discovery of a body this morning, I believe she was killed by the same perpetrator who abducted and murdered Ruth Tate." Karen turned to the whiteboard and tapped on the new photographs. "Leah Hayes earlier on this morning," Karen added as she looked at the crime scene photos. "We cannot ignore the fact the two cases are linked due to the similarities. Both Leah and Ruth bore striking similarities in appearance. Both were strangled and discarded in remote locations with their arms posed unusually."

"Why were the bodies dumped and not buried? If a murderer wanted to cover their tracks, they would have done a better job of hiding the bodies?" an officer suggested.

"Because I believe the murderer wanted their bodies to be found. I'm not sure why, but both locations offered the perfect opportunity to have the corpses buried beneath the undergrowth where they may not have been discovered for weeks, months, or even years." Karen stepped to one side to allow her team to study the photographs.

"I think we can rule out a stranger killing now," Claire said, folding her arms across her chest and leaning back in her chair as she squinted at the images from where she was sitting at the back.

Karen nodded and agreed. "There isn't an opportunity for us to do door-to-door enquiries at the scene. It's a very narrow and isolated lane. There's a farm close by and Ed is organising a visit. There's also the River Derwent which runs very close to the crime scene. He's going to see if there were any fishermen who were there overnight."

"What do you want us to do?" Ty asked, his pen hovering above his notebook, ready to take instructions.

"I want a full victimology built up on Leah Hayes. Her parents need to be tracked down. We need to understand her background, her social media profiles, and someone needs to speak to the phone providers to find out who she's been communicating with. Then we want to download her phone records and any cell site data. Though her handbag, and I hasten to add it was an expensive handbag costing more than a grand, was beside her and contained all of her personal effects, her phone was missing."

"That tells us he is forensically aware," another officer pointed out.

Karen picked up a marker pen and added it to a profile outline they were building of their suspect. "Exactly. He's either done a lot of research, been linked to a forensic-related field, or has offended before these two murders."

"I hate to suggest this," Claire chipped in, "But could he be ex-job?"

Karen pointed in Claire's direction and raised a brow in agreement, adding that point to their profile outline. "God help us if he's ex-job. The bloody press would have a field day. Shit."

There wasn't much the team wanted to find out about the scene, having reviewed the uploaded body cam footage from the first officers attending. But over the next few minutes, theories and ideas were tossed around the room especially when cases were high-lighted from around the country of serving or former police officers involved in the abduction or murder of women.

Karen turned towards the board and added a few more points which needed addressing. "Next of kin. I believe her parents live in Kent. Jade, can you do that for me? We need a formal ID."

"I'll see if I can organise officers from Kent to visit her parents to give the news. We need her parents to travel up today, as we need the identification done before the post-mortem tomorrow," Jade remarked.

"Agreed." Karen opened her folder and pulled out the forensic report on Ruth Tate. There wasn't much news to share, but she informed the team they had found no semen traces in or on Ruth's body and there was no sign of sexual interference either. The toxicology report confirmed the presence of alcohol, but the BAC (blood alcohol content) was less than one per cent.

"What about Ruth's car?" Belinda asked.

Karen grimaced. "That came back clean as well. Hair fibres found on the driver and passenger seats belonged to Ruth and her husband Mark. There were no other unaccounted hair fibres, blood or semen traces."

Silence fell around the room as officers processed information from the fresh case.

Belinda chewed the inside of her mouth as she listened before catching Karen's attention. "I spoke to Henry Beavis' contact, the resident who had seen Mark Tate during the middle of the night."

Karen's eyes widened as she clicked her fingers in Belinda's direction. "Oh, good. Anything of interest?"

Belinda pulled a face. "Not really. Craig Muirhead, at number four, said he had seen Mark walk past on at least four occasions over the last three months. It would always be between eleven thirty p.m. and two a.m. Craig sleeps at the front of the house, and there's a dodgy manhole cover on the pavement in front of his house which rocks whenever someone steps on it. He said it makes a clanking noise." Belinda looked at her notes before continuing, making sure she hadn't missed anything. "Anyway, it always wakes him up, so he gets out of bed to check in case there's someone lurking outside his house. That's why he's spotted Mark."

"Any idea how long he's out for?" Karen asked.

"Yes. About two to three hours on each occasion. Craig assumed Mark was sneaking out to the twenty-four-hour bookies while his wife slept."

"Okay. Let's get cracking on pulling together everything we need on Leah's case. I'll update the super," Karen said as she grabbed her notepad and rushed from the main floor. Her phone rang as she entered the corridor. "Really?" she muttered when she saw Henry's name appear on the screen. "Henry. I can't talk at the moment. I'm busy."

"I know, Karen. You've got your hands full with the second case. Leah Hayes, right? What have you got so far?"

Karen stopped and stepped to one side of the corridor and checked to see if she was alone. "Henry, how are you getting this information so quickly?"

The line fell silent for a few moments before Henry spoke up again. "I'm a good reporter. I have my sources."

"Well, I hope it's no one from my team or they'll be on traffic duty before the end of the day," Karen whispered through gritted teeth.

Henry laughed. "That's your problem not mine. Anyway, what can you tell me? I'd like to put up a newsflash on our website."

"Nothing at the moment, Henry. We are still processing the scene and the next of kin haven't been informed yet, so if you print anything you'd better grab your passport and go on an extended holiday because I'll kick your arse from here to Dunnet Head. And if you don't know where that is, then look it up. I'll let you know when we have anything," Karen said, cutting the call off. "Bloody cheek," she muttered, stuffing her phone back in a pocket and heading off to find Kelly.

31

KAREN HADN'T EVEN MADE it to Detective Superintendent Laura Kelly's office before she was stopped on the stairs by a uniformed officer informing her Nia Knowles was in reception. Surprised by the unexpected visit, Karen headed back downstairs and made her way towards the public entrance in another block. Coming through the main doors, Karen spotted Nia sitting to one side, her hands balled into fists and pressed between her thighs.

Nia jumped up the second she saw Karen approach.

"Is everything okay?" Karen asked, noticing the look of concern etched on Nia's face. Her eyes looked sorrowful with a pained expression which twisted her features.

"Not really. Is there somewhere we can talk?"

"Of course, come this way," Karen said, placing a hand on Nia's back and guiding her towards the first interview room. Karen slid the sign on the door from vacant to occupied before closing it behind them. She offered Nia a seat on the other side of the table. "Can I get you a cup of tea or water?"

Nia pursed her lips and shook her head. She squirmed in her seat, her shoulders pulled forward, her arms tucked into her sides.

"What is it you wanted to see me about?" Karen asked, sitting back in her seat, keen not to crowd Nia and make her feel uncomfortable.

Nia crunched her eyes closed and drew in air through her clenched teeth. "Plenty of Fish was my idea," she blurted out. "It was to help me get back into the dating game. Not Ruth."

Karen narrowed her eyes in confusion. "Right. I'm a little confused."

Nia groaned. "Oh, this is a nightmare. I'm rubbish at dating. I get so nervous. And every date I go on always ends in disaster. So, one night for a laugh Ruth set up a profile. We both had far too much to drink, and it was a silly idea. But she was adamant it would be fun. Then she told me about the winks."

Karen let out a deep sigh before she leaned forward and rested her elbows on the table, burying her head in her hands. *Oh, shit.*

"I know, sorry. I'm really embarrassed now, but I'm so socially awkward and hate small talk," Nia added, trying to justify her situation. "I'm not a very interesting person, so Ruth said she would jazz up my profile and handle all the messages to pave the way before I met anyone. And to be honest it made sense to me. I could hide behind the chats until I felt confident enough to agree to a date."

"Nia, why didn't you tell me this earlier? You've side-tracked the case."

"I know. I'm so sorry," Nia repeated. "Ruth knew I've had a few terrible relationships. As you know from our earlier conversation, I always called Ruth when my relationships were falling apart. That was why we did this. It was a good way for me to keep my distance until I was confident enough to meet someone."

"Right, so ignoring the Plenty of Fish mix-up, had Ruth ever been with someone else or met anyone else while married?" Karen asked.

Nia bowed her head and shook it.

Karen stood and pushed her chair back before opening the door and standing to one side. "Okay, Nia. That's cleared that up. Thank you for coming in."

Nia rose from her chair and shuffled around the desk to the doorway. She paused and looked in Karen's direction. "I'm really sorry."

"So am I," Karen snapped.

32

"I WONDERED WHERE YOU WERE," Karen said, tossing her sandwich packet and bag of crisps on the table opposite Jade. Karen pulled out a chair and sat down heavily on it before running her fingers down her face and groaning.

"What's the matter? Don't tell me the super has pissed you off again?" Jade said with a wry smile.

Karen shook her head. She didn't know whether to laugh, cry or pull her hair. She stared at the ceiling and blew out her cheeks. "Some people just need a high five. In the face. With a chair." Karen closed her eyes and quietly whispered, "I must not let it affect me. I must not let it affect me. I must not let it affect me."

Jade choked back a laugh. "You crack me up. Someone has really pissed you off."

"One word. Nia." Karen rolled her eyes, clenched her jaw and tightened her lips.

"Ruth's best mate?"

"Yep. The one and only. I didn't even make it to see Laura. Nia was waiting for me in main reception. So, me being a nice person, I wandered over to not keep her waiting. What did I get?"

"Don't know, but I guess I'm about to find out."

"I don't even know where to start. You know we found evidence of deleted messages relating to an account on Plenty of Fish and an exchange of messages?"

"Yes…" Jade replied slowly.

"And we thought Ruth may have been seeing people behind her husband's back?" Karen continued, slowly dropping each sentence.

"Right. Where is this leading?"

"Well, it only turns out Nia is rubbish at dating. So, one drunken night when she was out with Ruth, Ruth set up a Plenty of Fish account to help Nia for a laugh. Nia was too nervous to do it herself."

Jade's jaw dropped as the revelation hit her squarely between the eyes. "Oh… Shit."

Karen nodded slowly. "Exactly. I've now got to tell Mark Tate, "Oh, remember when I was asking you about Plenty of Fish and whether your wife may have been seeing other men behind your back… Well, we got it wrong, she was an innocent party in all of this." Not only has he had to deal with the loss of his wife, but also the suggestion she may have been interested in casual hook-ups. What a shit show."

Jade sat back in her chair shocked and speechless. "The poor bloke. He's going to be livid."

"Tell me about it," Karen sighed, staring at her sandwich before pushing it to one side, having lost her appetite. "Focus, Karen," she said, desperate to shake off the dark cloud hovering above her.

Jade drained the last of her Coke before screwing the lid back on it. "We really don't have a lot to go on now. So far, we haven't been able to find any connection between Ruth and Leah on the socials. They didn't mix in the same circles. They both had successful businesses. Ruth was married. Leah was single."

"That's what makes it so challenging. I think we need to not look at it from the victim's angle, but the perp's. He's picking them for a reason," Karen replied, tapping her fingers on the table.

Jade agreed as she loaded her plate, cutlery, and empty bottle on to the tray and pushed it to the end of the table. "I received a call from the officers who had seen Mark. It turns out he suffers from insomnia brought on by stress from battling his gambling addiction. Even though he doesn't gamble now, the need to want to gamble still lurks in the background. When he can't sleep, he goes for a walk and heads to the bookies where he stops outside and faces the urge to go in head-on. It's a kind of exposure therapy for him."

The more she heard, the more Karen realised Mark Tate was slipping down her list of suspects.

"Oh, we've got the details back from cell site triangulation," Jade remarked, leaning back and rubbing her swollen belly having eaten too much. "Cell site data for Mark's mobile phone placed him as being at home, with multiple calls made late into the evening to various numbers in his contacts list including York Hospital as he endeavoured to find out where Ruth was. Further cell site analysis for Ruth's phone confirmed it had last pinged towers just before nine forty-five p.m. on the night she was abducted."

With nothing reported after that time, Karen suspected someone had removed and destroyed the SIM card and discarded her phone.

"I know we've drawn a blank with Ruth's phone, but can you get the team to pull in the data for Leah's phone? I still need to find out where she was in the minutes and hours before her abduction."

Their conversation was interrupted when Claire appeared. "Karen, I've been talking to an old friend of mine, DS Don Groves. I told him about our cases. And you won't believe what he just said."

Karen and Jade exchanged a glance of joint curiosity.

"It's happened before."

33

KAREN HASTILY ORGANISED a meeting with the team while Claire asked DS Don Groves to join them. Nervous energy prickled Karen's skin as her thoughts somersaulted.

I've got a good feeling about this, Karen thought when she saw Claire appear through the doors at the far end of the room followed by a short, rotund individual with closely cropped, white hair which thinned to almost nothing on top. He had drooping jowls and heavy lids that partially cloaked his eyes. Karen's first impression was he looked tired and worn out as he trudged slowly behind Claire to the front of the room.

"Karen, this is DS Don Groves. I think we all need to hear what he has to say," Claire said, before stepping back and looking for an available seat.

"Good to meet you, Don. I'm DCI Karen Heath," Karen said, shaking his hand.

"Ma'am."

"No need here. I prefer to be called Karen."

Don shifted on the spot, feeling uncomfortable about not addressing his superiors by their titles.

"I don't know how much Claire has told you so far, but we are dealing with two abductions and murders that we assume the same individual committed. Claire mentioned this has happened before? Could you share your insights with us?" Karen asked, before taking a step back.

Don nodded before taking his position in front of the whiteboards. He glanced over his shoulder and lingered on the photos before returning his gaze to the assembled officers. "This isn't a simple thing to talk about. Bruce Carson, the Tick-Tock Man, and our murderer, not only baffled us but took us into a bleak period in the force's history. He's banged up now and serving life in Full Sutton with no chance of parole for a long time. He abducted women, kept them for only twelve to twenty-four hours and then strangled them before dumping their bodies very uniquely."

Don ran a hand over his head as he puffed out his cheeks. "I'm not sure where to start because there's so much to tell you, but he laid out his victims very similarly to how you've found your victims. Legs together, arms positioned at unusual angles. During the later stages of the investigation we figured out that the arms were positioned in a certain way to tell us what time he'd killed his victims."

There were a few noticeable gasps from the assembled officers. Karen spun around and looked at the images of Ruth and Leah. It was so obvious now she knew. Ruth was killed at approximately three a.m., and Leah was killed at approximately ten past nine in the evening. *Shit.* As Karen looked at her officers, she could tell they had worked it out too as they began nodding at each other.

"So, is this a copycat?" an officer asked.

Don shrugged. "I don't know. There was the suggestion during our interview the Tick-Tock Man may have had an accomplice. But Carson did not deny or confirm it. But there's something else worth mentioning."

Silence fell over the room. Every officer gazed at Don, hanging on his every word.

"Bruce Carson is the brother of Janice Slattery. If the surname Slattery doesn't ring a bell, and it probably won't, Janice was married to ACC Scott Slattery of North Yorkshire Police."

Eyes widened and jaws dropped as the revelation sunk in. Karen's face turned ashen. "Was ACC Slattery connected or implicated in the case?"

Don shook his head. "He knew nothing about it. But it was the reason we found it so hard to track Bruce Carson down. He was often going around to see his sister Janice, and would stay for dinner, drinks, the usual things families do. Carson had spent a lot of time picking ACC Slattery's brains on police procedure, forensic processes, and how our investigations were conducted. He just came across as an excited member of the family who found the whole being a police officer thing fascinating. Slattery didn't see any harm in talking about these things. As far as we are aware he never spoke about individual cases."

"So Carson was always one step ahead of you," Karen remarked. "He knew what you were about to do before you'd even done it."

"Pretty much," Don shrugged. "This all happened twenty years ago. He was caught at the age of thirty-six and sentenced to serve twenty-five years before being considered for parole. He killed three women in the space of nine months." Don stared up towards the ceiling as he pulled more facts from the darkest recesses of his mind. "Stacey Davies, Fiona Williams, Frances Jolly. All successful women which was a lot rarer twenty-five years ago. The bastard was forensically aware," Don growled. "There was no DNA left at the scenes, CCTV quality was okay, but not of the HD 1080p or 2K clarity of today, plus there wasn't a huge network across the region, and there were no witnesses. Carson worked in an art gallery and preyed on the women who attended. He charmed them. Got their details and then stalked them."

The similarities were astounding in Karen's mind as an image of Rutland-Pym flashed through her thoughts. She made a note of his name on her pad and drew a circle on it to follow up. The more Don revealed, the more terrifying it sounded. Back then, detailed DNA analysis and CCTV trawls didn't have the advanced technology or resources of today, so everything took longer. Their investigation had to rely on good old-fashioned detective work, which sometimes crossed the line as collars were felt rather aggressively and secretive bribes were made in exchange for information.

Don continued. "He broke into each property just to intimidate his victims. Items of clothing recovered from his safe linked him to the three victims. However, he was linked to the unsolved cases of a further eleven women strangled over an eight-year period. There wasn't enough evidence to convict him, and the cases remain unsolved."

"And what happened to ACC Slattery?" Jade asked.

"It was a big dark blot on the history of our force. Slattery took early retirement and resigned in shame. He moved to France with his wife."

Karen turned to Don, "So, Carson is in Full Sutton."

Don nodded. "Yes. I was just a young trainee detective at the time, but every officer on the case took this personally. They are still haunted by it to this day, including me." Don stuffed his hands in his pockets and stared at the floor for a few moments. "A criminal psychologist assessed him before he went to trial. They deemed Carson a psychopath of the highest degree. But you wouldn't know from talking to him. He was coherent, polite, and had well-formed opinions on life. But there was a coldness in his eyes, and I'll never forget that look for the rest of my life."

Silence fell around the room once again, every officer lost deep in thought. Some stared down at their notepads while others gazed towards the windows, mesmerised.

Karen took a step forward and stood shoulder to shoulder with Don. "Thank you, Don. This has been helpful. Can we pick your brains again if need be?"

"Yep. Though I can't think of anything else that could be of use to you. But that's because it was such a long time ago." Don thanked the team for their attention before leaving.

Karen looked around her officers. "I'm not even sure where to start now. But, Ed, can you track down the files around Carson? They are probably archived and sitting in boxes in a basement somewhere. We could be dealing with a copy-cat, but it could also be Carson's accomplice, if there was one. Let's pull out everything we can find around the case. Press articles, family statements, suspect interviews, physical evidence, and PM reports." Karen left her team to it as she headed off to update Kelly.

34

THE TEAM HAD CLEARED a large table towards the far end of the room to accommodate more than a dozen storage boxes identified from the archives.

For the past few hours people whether detectives or support staff, had taken bundles of paperwork to trawl through. Stacks of grey Manila folders, the contents held in place by rubber bands, perched on many of the desks. Not wanting to waste any time, Karen had mucked in too by finding a spare desk to work from.

Tiredness claimed a few officers as they propped up their heads with their hands, others walking back and forth from the kitchen to grab another coffee. The scale of the job took Karen by surprise. Forms and paperwork she had never seen in her career lay scattered on the surrounding table. It amazed her how technology had made information gathering and storage so much easier. It was easier to search records, witness statements, and evidence stores using a single keyword. A task impossible to do if they'd still been operating a paper-based system. She wondered how officers had done their jobs back then.

The smell of pizzas and Chinese takeaways filled the room as several officers came in laden with bags and boxes. It pumped renewed energy into everyone as they took a break away from their desks to stretch their legs, rest their eyes, and fill their bellies.

Karen grabbed a spring roll and shoved the whole thing in her mouth, etiquette and grace going out of the window. She moaned in contentment as she savoured the taste. "Oh my God, this tastes so good," she said, reaching for another. A few officers mingling around her nodded in agreement, scooping chow mein and special fried rice off their plates.

Karen moved over towards the warm smell of pizza. Grabbing a pepperoni slice, she went and stood by Jade and Belinda. "How are you getting on? My eyes are melting into their sockets."

Jade finished her mouthful and wiped her mouth. "I can't believe the amount of paperwork. Can you imagine having to fill in all of this crap?"

Belinda laughed and agreed. "I know. It's any wonder they could go out on enquiries. Most must have been chained to their desks. I doubt they had support staff, evidence officers, or collators back then."

They all agreed before falling silent as they enjoyed the food.

"Carson had a certain type. And looking at Leah and Ruth, our victims carry very similar features to his three victims. What's your hunch? Copycat or accomplice?" Belinda asked.

"I'm more inclined to think it's a copycat," Karen replied as her eyes drifted off towards the far end of the room, her mind fuzzy with so much detail. "*If* he had an accomplice, what has that individual been doing for the past twenty years? We need to check prisoner release records. Have we looked for any individuals released in the last twelve months with a similar MO?"

"If he had an accomplice, perhaps they slipped out of the country not long after they caught Carson. And it's only now they have returned and carried on what Carson started?" Jade speculated.

That was a possibility Karen had considered while reviewing the case files. From what she had seen so far, there was very little evidence to go on. Don had been right. Without witnesses, forensic evidence, or modern-day camera CCTV footage, information was thin on the ground. The bundles of notes contained lots of reports from the officers involved, much of it circumstantial or speculation. But Karen noticed a sense of urgency and panic in the accounts that had been recorded by the investigating team. They'd been jumping on anything and everything, perhaps out of sheer desperation.

"Every document in these files has to be read and checked. I would imagine 90% of it is going to be of little use to us. But we need to focus on the possibility Carson did have an accomplice and, for whatever reason has started up again," Karen instructed. "It's a shit job, but we need to do it."

Ed overheard Karen's conversation and joined her. "I think I know why it may have started again." Karen, Jade, and Belinda were all ears as they listened to him. "Something Don said piqued my interest. I've checked my files. Ruth was murdered on the anniversary marking Carson being sent to prison twenty years ago."

Jade raised a brow startled by that fact. "Coincidence or homage?"

Ed shrugged. "I don't believe it's coincidence. I'm leaning more towards homage. Whether that's a copycat or an accomplice, I'm not sure."

Everyone filtered back to their desks and spent the next few hours going through more files with Karen returning to her office in the early hours of the morning to update the database, her body exhausted, her mind frazzled, and her eyes bloodshot. It wasn't until she heard a voice in the background and her body jolted that she realised she'd fallen asleep at her desk.

"You need to get yourself off to bed, love," the cleaner said, offering Karen a sympathetic smile while standing in the doorway to her office.

"Shit. What time is it?" Karen asked, glancing around in confusion, her mind disorientated.

"Two thirty in the morning. Go home and get some kip," the cleaner added, before stepping into the hallway and switching on her Hoover.

Karen rubbed her tired eyes and stretched her back before logging off and lifting her weary body from the chair. She couldn't believe no one in her team had woken her before leaving. As she shuffled down the corridor, the drone from the Hoover hammered into her brain like a pneumatic drill. If she was lucky, she could get a few hours' sleep before being back.

35

HE SHOULDN'T HAVE BEEN out so soon, but he needed to satisfy a compelling urge to continue with his experiments. The more he did it the more he understood. It was the perfect way to witness the abject fear a victim experienced when all hope was lost. He had seen it in both Ruth and Leah. Powerful reactions. Denial. Impaired memory. Shock. Numbness. An overwhelming sense of helplessness.

One thing he'd been keen to avoid was both women suffering from Stockholm syndrome, a peculiar psychological condition involving abductees becoming attached to their kidnappers. His intention had never been to keep them long and risk such relationships being formed. He'd wanted to keep them on their toes and in an emotional and mental state which would leave them confused and unsure long enough to conduct his experiment.

Mission accomplished.

He walked past her house. A faint flickering light from the through-lounge indicated she was still awake. A fox wandered in and out of nearby gardens looking for tasty treats, glancing up as he approached, before ignoring him in hurrying away. He stuck to the line of trees that shielded him from view and he'd chosen soft-soled trainers to dampen his footsteps.

He glanced up and down the road to make sure there weren't any other late-night walkers around before crossing the road and dipping down into the gap between her semi-detached house and the neighbouring property. A tall fence surrounded the back garden and made it impossible for him to look over. Not put off, he ran his fingers along the fence panels until he found the gate and tried the handle. It didn't budge. He reached over the top and felt around for a bolt. It took a few moments before the tips of his fingers felt the cold metal. He hoped there wasn't a padlock keeping it in place. Millimetre by millimetre he edged the bolt across and to his surprise, it slid all the way. Trying the handle again, he eased the gate open enough for him to squeeze through.

It was too dark to make out the garden, but he wasn't there to admire her horticultural talent. He stepped towards the rear patio doors and stood to one side waiting for the pounding of his heart to settle before peering through the kitchen window. Empty. Light from the TV flickered on the walls of the dining room. He peered around from his position and beyond the dining table he saw the TV towards the front of the house and there she was, dressing gown on, her legs curled up underneath her, her head resting on the pillow while she watched a movie. He wasn't sure what it was, but it must be good for her to stay up this late. She would normally be in bed by ten thirty p.m., but it was fast approaching midnight. Unusual for her.

As he retraced his steps and secured the bolt on the garden gate, he was sure of one thing. She spent a lot of time alone. On the five other occasions he had followed her or observed her house, she hadn't had a partner come to stay, nor had she had any visitors. Taking her would be easy.

36

THE FLOOR SWAYED as Karen walked along the corridor to her office. The ceiling lights burned her retinas and the drone of the air conditioning sounded like an RAF Typhoon jet doing a low-level pass over her head.

Turning into her room, Karen dropped her bag beside her desk and fell into her seat with a heavy thud that pushed the air from her lungs.

"Jesus, you look like shit," Jade remarked as she appeared in Karen's doorway.

"I'm shattered. Today is the kind of day where I wish vodka came out of my shower."

Jade laughed. "You were still at your desk when I left not long after midnight. You didn't even hear me shout good night!"

"I must have been dead to the world at that point. Can you believe it? I fell asleep at my desk. The overnight cleaner woke me at two thirty this morning." Karen let out an almighty yawn and scrunched her eyes.

Jade threw a hand over her mouth to stifle a laugh as she rocked back on her heels. "Oh my God, I did that a few times back in London. It looks like you're going to need a caffeine intravenous drip. Come on. We've got work to do."

Having both made a strong black coffee, they stood in front of the two whiteboards. One had Ruth's and Leah's images on it. The other had images of Carson's victims. There was a strong commonality between all five women. Dark hair, attractive, and successful in their own professions. Only one was married. The rest were single.

Ty joined Karen and Jade as they discussed the profile of each victim. "I'm going over the text and cell site data on Leah's phone. On the evening she disappeared, her signal was picked up in town. Text messages confirmed she met friends for a birthday dinner at Lucia in Grape Lane. We are contacting the restaurant this morning to find out if they have any CCTV both within the restaurant and overlooking the street."

Karen nodded her thanks but stuttered her words, still too tired to engage her brain and spit out a cohesive sentence.

Jade took over as she looked at the information they had already compiled about the potential killer. "If it's a copycat, then we need to build a better psychological profile. Can you and Bel compile a list of all visitors who have visited Bruce Carson in prison over the last twelve months? And… I know we went over a lot of files last night, but can you look at Bruce Carson's friends, families, and acquaintances? Check to see if we already know any of them."

"On it," Ty replied as he dashed off.

Karen took a few hefty glugs of coffee before deciding she needed another. "I'll arrange for us to visit Bruce Carson this afternoon. Let's see what he has to say. We can try to find out if he did have an accomplice, but I'm still thinking a copycat is a more likely scenario."

Jade headed back to her desk leaving Karen to make her way to the kitchen for another strong coffee. She stopped by Dan's desk en route. "Dan, can you do me a favour?"

Dan sat upright in his chair, pushing his broad muscly shoulders back and sticking his chest out. "Yeah, sure. What do you need?" His tone was light and excitable.

That's what she liked about Dan. He was always full of beans, mega enthusiastic, and willing to help and do anything regardless of how busy he was. If she could bottle his enthusiasm and sell it, she would make millions. But he was forever popping pills and supplements to help him with his weight training. His bottom drawer was filled with supplements like maca, creatine, BCAAs, and protein shakes. She had no idea what they did but was sure it contributed to his zest for life and his boundless energy.

"Can you cross-reference our victims with Carson's? Look for any crossover. I know we're talking of a twenty-year gap but check anyway. Friends, family, workplace, areas they lived in. Anything like that."

Dan jotted down all those points. "What are you hoping to find?"

"I'm not sure. It's probably a dead end," Karen replied with a shrug. "I want to make sure we've looked at every single angle. And while you're at it, I know we did a basic check on Howard Rutland-Pym, but can you do a more detailed review of his background? It might be nothing, but he runs art exhibitions and Bruce Carson worked in an art gallery. There's something about Rutland-Pym that doesn't sit comfortably with me. Is there more to Rutland-Pym than we are aware of?"

"I'll see what I can find," Dan said.

Karen thanked him before returning to her desk and dialling DS Don Groves. Don answered after a few rings. "Don, it's Karen here. Thank you for your help yesterday. It was incredibly helpful."

"My pleasure. I don't want us to go through the same thing the force went through twenty-odd years ago. It took us a long time to recover. The public were baying for blood when they discovered Carson was ACC Slattery's brother-in-law. They were convinced the ACC was complicit. So, Slattery had no choice but to resign and save the force from the added media attention."

Karen listened, and every time she heard Don talk, she could sense the sadness in his voice and the enormous burden which still rested on his shoulders. "That's why we need to move quickly on this. If we need you again, would you be able to help us with the investigation?"

Don fell silent on the other end of the line and Karen guessed he was battling with his thoughts before he spoke again. "Sure. I'll square it with the boss. Give me a shout if you need anything."

"I'd appreciate that."

Don sighed. "Just talking about it yesterday with your team opened up a few wounds. I remember the atmosphere around our team being so tense. I think our nerves were jangling more than Carson's. We were working 24/7 on this. Every scrote for miles around was getting an unwelcome visit from us. Day or night, it didn't matter to us. We were dragging the poor sods out of their beds in the middle of the night. There was so much pressure for a result from the chief constable and the local MP at the time." Don tutted down the line and muttered something incomprehensible. "We even arrested a sex offender with a long history of sexual offences. They charged him with three murders. It was a weak case because we had so little evidence. They threw the case out of court. Looking back now, the bosses were looking for a scapegoat, someone to take the hit. Nowadays, the CPS wouldn't waste the ink in their pen to review the evidence we had back then."

"Well, I will not allow my team to make the same mistake," Karen said. "I'll be in touch, Don." Karen hung up, shocked by how they had handled the case back then.

There was too much riding on this case and with two victims and few leads, she needed more insight and knew exactly who to call. She scrolled through a contacts list before dialling the number.

"Gabby Ritchie."

"Gabby, it's DCI Karen Heath here."

"Karen, it's been a while. I heard you moved to York. Decided for a quieter life?"

"Hardly. I think it's as crazy as London."

Gabby was Karen's contact in SCAS. SCAS was short for the Serious Crime Analysis Section at the National Crime Agency. SCAS worked on identifying the potential emergence of serial killers and serial rapists earlier in their offending. The organization had been set up following the review of the Yorkshire Ripper enquiry which had highlighted the need for a national database to hold details of such offenders. Karen had had dealings with them in the past and had formed a good working relationship with Gabby.

"Karen, crime is crime wherever you are, I guess. At least it's a nice part of the country with some breathtaking scenery."

"Breathtaking and remote which makes it even harder to find the victims let alone the killers."

"I assume this isn't a social call?" Gabby asked.

"I'm afraid not. I'm working on a double homicide and I could do with your input." Karen went on to explain the nature of both cases and the similarities in MO to that of the Tick-Tock Man. "We are not sure if it's an accomplice or a copycat. But I could do with your thoughts on this once you've had a look into it."

"Sure. Can you send me over everything you have regarding the victims, the nature of the murders, the positioning of their bodies, and any initial thoughts on the kind of suspect you're dealing with?"

"No problem. If he is a serial killer then we need to stop him before he kills again. I don't believe this is his first rodeo. It takes some balls to abduct someone, keep them captive and then strangle them in cold blood, before dumping their body. The fact he didn't hide the victims' bodies suggests an air of confidence."

"Or a change in behaviour. He likes to murder and then panics about disposing the body and doesn't want to waste time burying it," Gabby suggested.

"Then why go to the effort of positioning them to let us know what time he killed them?" Karen said.

"I'm not sure. Leave it with me and I'll get back to you."

"Okay, thanks, Gabby. Speak soon."

She grabbed her jacket and handbag. She was about to face the gauntlet of Full Sutton with Ed.

37

KAREN DROVE the short distance to HMP Full Sutton prison and parked in the visitor car park. It was an imposing prison housing over six hundred category A and B prisoners, many of whom were some of the most dangerous criminals in the country. Karen had visited it occasionally while working in London and it always left an uncomfortable feeling in her. A robust and tough prison that also contained a section nicknamed the "Beast Wing", it housed men convicted of the most despicable sex offences. With tight security, the prison proudly boasted of no prisoner escapes since its opening in the late eighties.

As she signed in at reception with Ed, her thoughts turned towards the update from the mortuary. The formal identification of Leah Hayes had been a difficult one. Her parents, Andrew and Carol Hayes, had travelled up from Kent first thing that morning. A family liaison officer had met them there and understandably Leah's parents had struggled with their visit. Her mother, Carol, upon seeing her daughter, had collapsed in grief.

The FLO had called Karen with an update as Karen had been wrapping up a few things in the office. Karen had listened to the FLO's account. Andrew had gone through periods of quiet reflection, to flashes of anger, and then floods of tears. All typical reactions Karen had seen first-hand. In part, she was glad she hadn't been there to witness it. Especially the part where grieving parents begged the attending officers to find and bring to justice those responsible so they could lay their loved one to rest knowing no other family would suffer the same tragedy.

Karen had sent a text earlier to Izzy apologising for her absence. The post-mortem was well underway with officers from her team in attendance on her behalf who provided updates at regular intervals. Karen, expecting a similar outcome to Ruth Tate's post-mortem wasn't surprised to hear there was no evidence of defence wounds, stab wounds, blunt force trauma injury or any similar outcome. Compression of the neck confirmed the cause of death.

Karen and Ed went through the security scanners, placed their personal possessions in safe storage, and waited in the reception area for someone to take them to the formal inter-view rooms. It was while she was there, she noticed articles and drawings on one wall highlighting the work on building a new mega prison which would house nearly one thousand five hundred inmates. The plans looked impres-sive, and the new facility would sit alongside the existing prison. Karen read a list of features with interest. Billed as the UK's first all-electric jail, the site would be powered by solar panels and heat pump technology.

"That's gone down like a lead balloon with the locals," Ed remarked, standing beside her.

"Really?"

"Yep. Huge objections from the local community. But they need it. The prison is already overcrowded."

Their conversation was cut short when a member of the prison staff called their names and led them up a few floors and through a series of locked gates to an area which was set aside for police and legal representatives to meet with prisoners. Karen heard the familiar sound of jeering and heckles as they neared the main prison population. A few gates and an open corridor separated them from prisoners who loitered outside of their cells glaring at the visitors with hatred etched on their features. One prisoner pointed at Karen and Ed before running his finger across his neck while screaming obscenities at them. Others made whooping noises like a troop of monkeys from a tropical rainforest in Asia. It was bone-chilling and uncomfortable to listen to as the tension rose.

"Charming," Ed said, staring back, unperturbed by the prisoners' aggressive behaviour.

Karen threw Ed a sardonic smile as she followed the prison officer to one of the vacant rooms.

"Same old, same old. News travels fast," Karen said, placing her notepad on the table.

The prison officer rolled his eyes. "Briefs get a lukewarm reception but visits from the police always get a frosty one."

Karen was used to the hostility. It came with the territory. After all, prisoners were there because of the police and justice system. "I know. The last time I was up here was in 2019 after the big riot in 2018."

The officer nodded. "Yep. It took a hundred officers to bring it under control. A hundred to take down one inmate. Bloody ridiculous. I swear, we're too soft on them. Carson won't be too long. Good luck. You'll need it," he said, jangling his keys around his index finger before leaving the room.

The guard's parting remark left Karen surprised and unnerved.

38

IT WAS AN UNCOMFORTABLE WAIT, one not made easier by the muted heckling as it filtered through the open door. Karen tapped her fingers on the table, a growing agitation unsettling her stomach. She stiffened and pulled her shoulders back when she heard footsteps approaching and the jangling of more keys. She stared towards the open door, waiting to catch a first glimpse of Bruce Carson.

A large black officer appeared and filled the doorway, offering Karen and Ed a polite nod before he stepped through and moved to one side. Bruce Carson appeared next, his hands cuffed and flanked on either side by two further prison officers who each held his arm. They guided him around towards the solitary chair which sat across the table from Karen. A large Perspex screen attached to the table kept him at a safe distance from her.

Bruce Carson rested his cuffed hands on the table and cast a shifty eye between Karen and Ed. He remained silent, expressionless, his breathing slow and steady.

Fast approaching sixty, he was smaller than Karen had imagined. But it wasn't his physique that troubled her. It was his face. Closely cropped salt-and-pepper hair with thin lips made him look like a hardened thug from the streets of East London. But it was his eyes she was drawn to. They were soulless and cold. He had a drooping right upper eyelid, a depressed cheekbone, and a twisted nose. It was as if the right-hand side of his face had suffered a partial stroke or an injury. Karen's muscles tightened and her pulse quickened as she locked eyes with him. For whatever reason, she couldn't look away. Her mind willed her, but the message didn't reach her eyes. It was as if there was this magnetic force drawing her in, which unnerved her.

Karen finally offered him a thin smile. "Bruce Carson, I'm Detective Chief Inspector Heath, and this is my colleague Detective Constable Hyde."

Carson inhaled and slowly released his breath as if already fed up. "As much as I would like to stare at you all day and imagine all the things I could do to you, I'm sure you have more pressing issues to deal with."

Karen forced a nod. There was something very chilling about Carson which Karen found unsettling. "I do have other pressing issues, but I need a few things from you."

Carson let out an almost unnoticeable sigh as his body remained still as a statue. "Of course. Your two victims. The cases must be puzzling you otherwise you wouldn't be sitting here now passing the time of day with me."

Karen noticed Carson's eyes move away from her face and to what she thought was her chest. She was about to continue when Carson interrupted her.

"You have elegant lines. Your neck. Beautiful. Strong, firm, just perfect."

Karen shot a look to Ed, who appeared alarmed, before she continued, framing her words. "At the time of your capture, there was speculation you had an accomplice. Tell me, after twenty years why would your accomplice decide to continue your work?" If she hoped for a reaction, none was forthcoming. No eye flicker. No licking of lips. No shifting in the chair. No averting his gaze. *Damn.*

"Interesting choice of words, Detective Chief Inspector *Karen* Heath. Tell me, was the pain you carried in London too much for you? Is that why you ran away to York? Does the shame and guilt gnaw away at your innards like a hungry rat?"

Karen felt a heaviness spread from her chest that left her skin tingling. She raised a brow as her eyes widened. *He's really good at pivoting to gain the upper hand.* Karen cleared her throat as her hands twitched.

"Bruce, this isn't about me. And as much as I would like to sit and talk to you all day and imagine how miserable your existence is here, I'm sure you have more pressing issues to deal with, like staring at the four walls of your dingy cell."

"Touché, DCI. Very good," Bruce replied, his voice monotone and measured.

"Perhaps you have a sad twisted fucker who idolises you so much that on the twentieth anniversary of you being sent down they reawakened the legend you are."

"Possibly. There was no accomplice. As I said in my interviews, I acted alone."

"Did your brother-in-law help you?" Karen hadn't intended to ask but it came out.

"Scott was very helpful. He told me everything I needed to know. The idiot basked in the glory of being so knowledgeable. I put him on a pedestal, and he duly obliged, loving the attention. But as I've said all along, I acted alone."

He was good. Karen had met many killers in her career, but a psychopathic killer was next level stuff. Bruce Carson fitted the profile perfectly. In all the time she'd sat there, he hadn't taken his eyes off her. He hadn't flinched nor looked around the room or towards Ed. Carson hadn't even looked at his hands, which remained in the same place since taking his seat. His breathing—controlled and measured throughout the interview. His eyes—cold glass marbles that hardly blinked. She imagined how terrified his three victims must have been.

"Are we done now?" Carson asked.

"I think so," Karen replied. "Just one thing. Why did you do it?"

"It's just something I wanted to do. There's immense satisfaction when you place your arm around a woman's neck, and you see the fear in their eyes as you squeeze every... last... drop... of... air... from her body. It's something quite remarkable. It makes you realise how fragile life is. Don't you agree, detective chief inspector? I mean, imagine what it would be like if I wrapped my arm around your beautiful neck and squeezed so hard your heart threatened to tear from your chest. Your skin became sweaty and clammy. Your head felt like it was being squeezed in a vice and those little black dots appeared in your vision signalling the end was near."

Karen sat back in her chair and smiled. "Keep imagining it because it will never happen. But if it helps you to while away your hours here, then I'm glad I've been of use to you." Karen nodded towards the prison officers who hoisted Carson from his chair and led him from the room.

"I'll see you again real soon, Karen," Carson said before he disappeared into the corridor.

39

"THAT WAS ONE SCARY INDIVIDUAL," Ed said, blowing out his cheeks and running a hand through his hair before clipping in his seat belt.

Karen nodded as she stared through the windscreen. She had met many killers in her career, but Carson was near the top. He was cold, calculated, calm, and very sure of himself. He displayed not an ounce of regret, shame, or guilt while he sat there. That in Karen's mind was the true mark of a psychopath. He was playing games with her, and Karen knew that. He had done everything to unsettle her and almost succeeded. She had drawn on all of her experience to compose herself and stay focused. The hairs on her arms stood on end as icy-cold shivers raced down her spine.

"Do you reckon he acted alone?" Ed asked.

"I'm not sure. He came across as a very controlling individual. Would he be willing to delegate anything to an accomplice? That would allow errors to creep in, and until the point of his capture he had been meticulous in his approach." Karen thought about Carson. There was no way he would allow anyone to act on his behalf. In his twisted and warped mind, he was supreme.

"So it puts us back in the camp of our perp being a copy-cat?" Ed said.

"Yes, that's what I'm thinking. The case was well-documented, and there are plenty of people like Carson who are idolised by nutjobs out there. It only takes one unhinged individual to be inspired by Carson to act out their fantasies. And when they get a taste for it, they can't stop," Karen said, pulling her phone from her bag and taking it off silent mode, before scrolling through her emails and alerts. Spotting a missed call from Jade, she hit the redial button.

"Jade, we've left Full Sutton, and will be back in half an hour."

"How was it?" Jade asked.

"It was fine. Well, not fine. Carson is one disturbed individual. I swear, if he'd lunged at me, I would have shit my pants."

Jade laughed down the line. "Not the invincible DCI Karen Heath. You've got cast-iron knickers."

"Yeah, which leak! You need to see Carson to realise how dangerous he was and still is if they let him loose. Anyway, anything urgent?" Karen asked, grabbing her keys from her lap.

"The door-to-door enquiries on Leah's road haven't given us much. We have obtained copies of Ring doorbell footage from surrounding houses. We haven't spotted anything yet. We've also spoken to Leah's employers. They were very upset and spoke highly of her. A well-respected team member, great at her job, with a fantastic eye for detail."

"Socials?" Karen asked.

"Clean." Jade remarked. "We double-checked to see if there was any crossover between Leah and Ruth. There are a lot of pictures on her Facebook page and Insta to do with high-end jewellery. There are also quite a few pictures of her being overseas, I assume on buying or sales trips. She's always alone in them. Everyone we've spoken to including her neighbours said she was a lovely, kind and very thoughtful person."

"Anything else?" Karen prodded.

"One of her neighbours, Angela Evans, even said Leah had seen her struggling with her shopping and had hurried across the road to help her. There doesn't appear to be a boyfriend on the scene either."

The update helped Karen to fill in the gaps in what they knew about Leah so far. "Well, let's hope we can grab CCTV footage from the restaurant. We need to firm up a timeline of her movements that evening. On another note, while we were waiting to see Carson, we checked the visitor's log and spoke with the deputy governor. Carson isn't a popular man. In the last twelve months, he had one visitor on two separate occasions. A professor of psychology. I'm not certain about the reason, but we have his details."

"Carson has tight visiting restrictions," Jade suggested.

"Yes," Karen replied. "The deputy governor mentioned the only other person to visit him since being sentenced was his sister, Janice Slattery. Janice visited him about eighteen months ago, and it was a fiery confrontation that ended with prison staff having to lead Janice away when she tried to attack her brother. The DG confirmed, other than that, he's had no other visitors. Jade, can you do me a favour and arrange a call with Janice Slattery for later on today if possible and failing that then tomorrow?"

"Will do. See you shortly."

Karen hung up and then punched in the number that prison staff had provided for Professor Kenneth Bryant. Her call was answered on the second ring.

"Good afternoon, Professor Kenneth Bryant," the professor said with a firm and precise tone.

"Professor Bryant, this is Detective Chief Inspector Karen Heath from York police. We are doing routine enquiries on a double homicide, and we understand from prison records you have visited Bruce Carson in Full Sutton twice over the last twelve months. Is that correct?"

"Um, yes. Correct. Is there a problem?"

"No problem. We've visited him and are heading back to the office shortly. Could I meet you a little later when I've got more time to talk to you about Bruce Carson?"

"Of course. It would be my pleasure. I'll send you my address. I'll be here all afternoon and evening. I look forward to talking to you then," he replied, his words well rounded, his tone sounding like a typical academic.

"Brilliant. I'll see you soon. Thank you for your time," Karen said, hanging up. "Right, let's go back. The super has organised another press conference, and as usual I'm the last to know about it," Karen groaned as she eased out on to the roadway, and sped away.

40

"LADIES AND GENTLEMEN, please take your seats," Detective Superintendent Laura Kelly said in a firm but loud voice.

The room fell silent as reporters edged past each other to get seats as close to the front as possible. Photographers filtered to the edges of the room to get unobstructed views of the front stage. Kelly, a press officer, and Karen shuffled in their seats and repositioned the microphones and voice recorders a few reporters had placed on the table. Jade, Belinda, and Preet stood towards the back of the room.

Large posters had been attached to a noticeboard behind the front table. The smiling faces of Ruth Tate and Leah Hayes reflected happier times.

Kelly looked po-faced as she looked down at her notes. "Thank you for your attendance today. We are dealing with a double homicide investigation, which we hope will receive your full support and cooperation. Following the discovery of Ruth Tate's body near Pilmoor, the body of twenty-nine-year-old Leah Hayes was found early yesterday morning in Brieryend Wood, close to the River Derwent. We are treating this as a murder enquiry and have strong reason to believe the same individual was also responsible for Ruth Tate's death." Kelly paused and glanced around the room. As she did, photographers snapped away, the clicking of their shutters breaking the silence.

"As a result, we are pulling in extra resources and ensuring we do everything possible to apprehend the person responsible."

"Do you have a suspect?" asked Henry Beavis, a familiar voice from the middle of the audience.

Not giving Laura a chance to reply, Karen jumped in straightaway. "The investigation is moving at pace. We will share everything we can when it's appropriate."

Henry smirked before dropping back into his seat.

Another reporter from the back of the crowd raised her hand. "When can we expect a further update?"

"As soon as we have something to tell you," Laura replied firmly. "But for now, I would like to appeal to everyone. Do you know anyone, friends or family, or people you've just noticed recently who are acting strangely? Are they acting out of character? Are they going out at odd hours and coming back without an explanation? I would also like to ask if anyone was night-time fishing on the River Derwent close to Brieryend Wood in the last few days, and they heard or spotted something unusual, to please get in touch."

Laura paused as reporters jotted down the salient points. "Both Ruth Tate and Leah Hayes were much loved and admired by friends, family, and business acquaintances. We are keen to find out why someone would want to harm them. So, please come forward with any information, no matter how small. You can either contact our incident room hotline or contact Crimestoppers should you wish to stay anonymous. Both numbers are on the leaflet handed out to you when you arrived." Laura turned to Karen. "Have you got anything else to add?"

Karen nodded. "These crimes have taken the lives of two wonderful women. Two sets of parents have lost a daughter, and a husband has lost his wife. They both had so much to live for. Their loss has devastated their friends and families to a degree most of us would barely understand."

Henry stood up again. "The investigation into Ruth's murder has been ongoing for a while now. What progress has been made so far?"

Karen gritted her teeth and let out a long, deep sigh. Henry was trying her patience, and he knew that. He was desperate for her to react. "As we pointed out earlier, Henry, we cannot offer specifics. The team are working on several lines of enquiry, but I can't say more than that. Our focus is on apprehending a very dangerous individual, and as the investigation unfolds, we will go into those details further."

Henry folded his arms and looked around at his gathered colleagues. "You're asking for our cooperation and support, but you're not really giving us much information. We don't know how the crimes are linked or the profile of the perpetrator. How can we be of help then if you're leaving us in the dark?" Henry's comments elicited nods and grumbles from the assembled audience.

Laura stepped in again. "We are not here to enter the blame game. We need to reach out to the public and ask for their help and I believe we owe it to Leah and Ruth to work together. I appreciate you want more information, but this is still very early in the investigation and as soon as we have built up a profile of a likely perpetrator, we'll share that with you."

"Is it possible the perpetrator committed more crimes in the past that have not been linked to the current cases?" a female reporter asked.

"Not only are we throwing all our resources at our current cases, but we are also looking at any recent, similar and unsolved cold cases," Laura replied.

"This individual may have murdered other women and gone undetected by the police?" the reporter questioned. "Is that a failing by the police? Could you have prevented the deaths of Ruth and Leah?"

Jesus, you're going to start a panic, Karen thought, as she glared at the reporter.

"Not at all. Whether they were solved or unsolved, we would always look for similarities with past cases in any murder investigation of this nature. We would leave no stone unturned." Laura's steely stare unsettled the reporter who looked down at her notes. "Thank you all for coming."

Karen and Laura watched the reporters and photographers file out of the room, hushed conversations rippling among them.

"I thought for one minute that bloody female reporter was going to turn on us," Laura fumed as she gathered her notes together and stepped off the stage and headed to the back door. "Hurry and get a result, Karen. At the next press conference, I want to announce we have someone in custody."

41

KAREN CHECKED the address one last time before dropping her phone in her bag. Professor Bryant's office was above a Sainsbury's local on the corner of Bootham Row. *If I was looking for an office, this would be a perfect location*, Karen thought with a sly smile. *Sainsbury's for food and the Bootham Tavern for alcohol. I'd be sorted.*

Karen took the stairs up to the first floor and searched for the professor's office, eventually finding it down the end of the corridor. She knocked on the door and waited a few seconds before it was opened by a man that Karen could only describe as a smarter version of Doc from the *Back to the Future* movies. His eyes were sticking out on stalks, his hair was white and wiry with a few flecks of grey and his movements animated. He had dimples in his cheeks and on his chin, and he wore a dark navy suit, white shirt, and pale blue tie. His broad smile was warm and confident.

"Professor Bryant?" Karen asked.

Bryant nodded and extended his hand. "Detective Chief Inspector Heath?" he asked for clarity.

Karen nodded.

"Please, come in. Take a seat." Bryant guided her into the room and allowed her to take a seat, before he came around to his side of the desk, settling in and sucking in a sharp intake of breath that puffed out his chest.

The room was smart and functional. A leather topped desk, two plush chairs for visitors, and his leather chair on the other side. Various framed certificates and awards hung on a wall to Karen's left, as well as pictures of Bryant standing at a podium delivering a speech or lecture, Karen assumed. She spotted two other framed photographs of Bryant standing alongside uniformed officers, but from where she was sitting the words beneath each photograph were too small for her to see.

"Thank you for taking the time to see me. As I mentioned on the phone, we're investigating two homicides at the moment."

Bryant's face took on a serious note. "Yes, I've seen the press conferences. Very tragic."

"Indeed. What I'm about to say is confidential, and I need your reassurance nothing I say here today will leave this room," Karen said.

Bryant nodded. "Of course. As you can imagine my work is reliant on confidentiality. So, whatever you wish to discuss will remain between the both of us."

Karen nodded and thanked him. "We visited Bruce Carson today because we identified similarities between our current two cases and those involving Bruce Carson. Can I ask about the nature of your visits?"

"Of course. I have studied his case since his arrest. It's fascinating. I've spent the last twenty years of my professional career studying the mindset and psychological profiles of serial killers in the UK and further afield. I've travelled to interview psychopaths in America, Germany, France, and Italy. I guess you can say it's my pet project, but it's fascinating to meet these individuals face to face and understand the workings of their minds, how they see the world around them, and why they committed such crimes. Erskine, Mackay, Bamber, Dennehy. I've met them all. Carson was another subject to study." Bryant rapped his fingers on the table. "Maudsley is an interesting character. He currently holds the world record for the time spent in solitary confinement. He's housed in a bulletproof Perspex cell specifically built for him. Some of the people I have met would be considered psychopaths."

"You sound very knowledgeable and passionate about your work," Karen commented.

"Absolutely," his tone was enthusiastic as he waved his hand in a grand, eccentric fashion. "My research and the papers I've written over the years have been discussed at medical conferences, university lectures, and online sites. I've stood on stage and spoken about my work to audiences in their hundreds." Bryant picked away at stray cloth fibres on the sleeve of his jacket.

"My team has been looking at the old case files connected to Carson. There was a suggestion he may have had an accomplice. Is that possible?"

Bryant looked over Karen's shoulder and stared off into the distance for a few moments before returning his gaze towards Karen. "Unlikely, but possible. I wasn't involved in his case, and investigations weren't as thorough as they are now. So it's possible he may have had an accomplice no one is aware of, but psychopaths and serial killers aren't individuals who like to share their work with others, or the notoriety they gain, or the fame and attention they attract. They are selfish by nature. Is that the angle your team is investigating?"

"It's one line of enquiry. But the obvious question is why an accomplice would pick up the baton now twenty years after they sent Carson down."

"Sure. I appreciate you can't go into the finer points of your investigation, but is there any evidence of robbery or sexual interference?"

Karen shook her head and said, "Someone killed Ruth on the twentieth anniversary of Carson's incarceration. That's why we believe this case has a connection with him. No robbery. No sexual interference. No torture. Someone abducted them, kept them for less than twelve hours, strangled them, and dumped their bodies. Their arms positioned at angles to signify the time of death."

Bryant raised a brow. "Now that's interesting. Perhaps it was something the investigating team at the time missed."

"In your conversations with Carson did he ever hint at having an accomplice?" Karen asked.

"I'm afraid not."

"So what did you talk about?" Karen probed.

"All manner of things. My work with him was to understand how his mind worked and why he did it."

"And what did you find out?"

"That he felt nothing. No remorse, no guilt, no excitement, nothing. He has a one-track mind. It was as if a switch had flipped each time. He could walk along the street and pass a hundred women and he wouldn't bat an eyelid. And then out of the blue he would spot someone and, for whatever reason, would go after them. He couldn't explain why, but the more he stalked them the more he wanted to understand why his mind had drawn them to him. It was fascinating to listen to." Bryant paused as he studied Karen's reaction. "And for whatever reason, his brain was selecting dark-haired, attractive women with successful careers. It was like a drug once he latched on to them. He needed to find out everything about them. What they did from the minute they got up to the minute they went to bed. What they wore, who their friends were, what they ate, even down to what hair shampoo they used."

"Nothing sexual?" Karen asked.

Bryant pulled a face. "He didn't see them as sexual objects at all. Certainly not on the conscious level. But there was something working at a deep subconscious level that was drawing him to a particular type of woman."

Karen glanced up at the wall and saw the time. "Right, it's getting late. This is helpful, but I must dash. Perhaps we can carry on this conversation in the coming days?"

Bryant offered his broadest smile as he jumped up from his chair, startling Karen. "It would be my pleasure. I'm more than happy to assist you in your investigation should you feel it's necessary and would find my insight helpful. I've worked with the South Wales and Kent police forces who called me in to assist them on investigations of this nature."

"Thank you. I'll bear that in mind." Karen shook his hand and left, feeling a strange confusion wash over her. Her visit hadn't answered many of the questions still swimming around in her mind.

42

KAREN HUNG up her coat and fired up her laptop as Jade followed in and sat in the seat opposite her.

"Janice Slattery was a hard woman to convince. I was on the phone with her for over twenty minutes before she agreed to talk to you this morning." Jade took a sip from her coffee and cupped the mug in both hands.

"Thanks, Jade. Why didn't she want to talk to me?"

Jade shrugged. "She didn't want to talk at all. Not even to me. Janice said she didn't want the past dragged up again."

"I don't blame her. And to be honest talking to Janice may not help anyway, but we need to for completeness. If there was an accomplice involved, Janice may have her hunches. If it's a copycat, then it's a dead end." Karen clicked on the icon for Zoom and checked the time on her screen. There were still a few minutes to go, but Karen dialled anyway. She figured Janice would be sitting waiting for the call.

It took a few moments for the call to connect, and Karen put that down to Janice's connection in France. From what they could see on Google Maps the Slatterys had a small property in a remote location outside of the village. Janice Slattery popped up on Karen's screen. The woman's face looked older than Karen had imagined. She looked tired with heavy crow's feet around her eyes and her lips turned down at the ends. Her brown hair had been pulled tight into a ponytail, revealing grey roots.

Karen greeted her with a small smile. "Good morning, Janice. I'm Detective Chief Inspector Karen Heath from York police. Thank you for taking the time to speak with me."

Janice nodded once but remained tight-lipped.

"I know this is difficult for you and I won't take up too much of your time, but we are dealing with two murders carrying similarities to those committed by your brother."

"This is very difficult for me," Janice began. "It's been a tough time for many years and moving here to France was our opportunity for closure and to move on. I don't think you realise how much remorse, shame, and guilt we both carry every day. From the minute we wake to the minute we go to bed, the memories of what my brother did haunt us."

"I understand, Janice. And I'm not here to burden you with more troubles or pain. We've been reviewing the murders committed by your brother. Notes made by the investigation team claimed there may have been an accomplice. Did your brother have any close acquaintances or friends you had suspicions about?"

Janice shook her head without giving herself any time to think about it. "No," she replied flatly.

"Could there have been an accomplice you or your husband weren't aware of?"

"Detective chief inspector, I'm not my brother's keeper. I used to speak to him three times a week, and he would come for dinner twice a month. I have no idea what he got up to in his own time."

Whichever way she turned the feedback remained the same. It was unlikely Carson had an accomplice. But Professor Bryant had said it remained a possibility, which meant she had to keep exploring it as an option.

"How is your husband?" Karen asked.

A pained expression spread across Janice's face, which only intensified the crow's feet. "Scott has significant health problems now. Grief and guilt have taken their toll on him. Having to leave a job he loved broke him. He did what was right but paid a high price. He went through a long period of suffering anxiety and depression. The stress led to high blood pressure and a heart attack." Janice bowed her head and sniffed. "He's never been the same again."

"Janice, I'm sorry. We understand you visited your brother about eighteen months ago. Why did you see him after such a long time?"

Rinsed of emotion, Janice stared at Karen through cold, steely eyes. "I needed to look my brother in the face and tell him in person what he had done. What he had destroyed and how cowardly he had been for taking three lives... and possibly more. I needed to tell him that as far as I was concerned, he was no longer my brother. I hope he rots and dies in prison, and even then, it wouldn't be good enough for what he has done."

Karen glanced over the top of her laptop in Jade's direction who widened her eyes in surprise.

"Janice, I know this is something you want to put behind you, but in the next day or so, if you can think of any friends or acquaintances known to your brother then I would appreciate you letting me know."

Janice didn't agree or refuse. She stared at Karen for a few moments. "We felt so foolish after he got captured. Bruce had taken a keen interest in Scott's job. After Sunday dinner, the three of us would sit there and work our way through one or two bottles of wine and we would talk about life, work, plans, anything really. Bruce was always asking if there were any juicy cases his force was working on whenever he came around. He kept asking Scott how the teams conducted investigations because he was so fascinated with their work. Nothing confidential, and he didn't see the harm in it." Janice shook her head and sighed. "That's how he could stay one step ahead of the investigation. I feel so sorry for those women who lost their lives. And Scott will always carry the guilt he had unknowingly played a part in their deaths."

"Janice, thank you for your time. I really appreciate it. Pass on my best wishes to your husband, and I'm sorry we had to drag up the past, but I hope you understand."

Janice nodded once before disconnecting the call.

"I feel so sorry for her. She sounded broken," Jade said.

Karen shut the lid on her laptop and put it back in her drawer. "I can't imagine what they've been through over the last twenty years. Yes, Slattery was an idiot for saying too much, but at the time he thought there was no harm in it. After all, they were family."

"Where does that leave us?" Jade asked, rising to her feet and heading to the door.

Karen leaned back in her chair and stared at the ceiling. "No further on, Jade. If Carson did have an accomplice, then it could be anyone. And other than paying homage to the fact Carson has been in prison for twenty years, I can't see any other reason he would have killed again. That's why we need to keep an open mind."

Karen's phone pinged. She leaned forward and grabbed the phone from her desk and checked the screen before opening the message and smiling. Karen hit the call button.

43

"YOU THINK YOU ARE HILARIOUS, don't you?" Karen growled down the phone.

DI Tommy Nugent, her old friend from when they'd both served in the Met together, laughed. Now settled in Dorset as a detective inspector, they had reconnected on a recent case and had kept in touch ever since, with Karen and Zac spending a weekend with his family.

"Well, I thought you might miss sunny Dorset, so I thought I'd send you a picture," Tommy replied.

Karen put her phone on loudspeaker and looked at the image again. It was a glorious picture of West Bay beach with a large expanse of the Jurassic Coast cliffs towering in the background. The sun shimmered off the sea, and with blue skies, it looked tranquil and relaxing. "I am, but I didn't need you pissing me off by sending that."

"Yeah, right. You love it," Tommy said.

"Anyway, what are you doing on the beach? Have the seagulls all ganged up together and robbed a tourist of their chips?" Karen teased.

"Ha ha. Very funny. It's my day off. Erin had a ton of stuff for me to do around the house, but Carol was pissing me off as usual."

Carol was Tommy's mother-in-law, and they had a love-hate relationship. On her recent visit, she and Zac had got on well with Carol, much to Tommy's annoyance. Karen couldn't see what all the fuss was about as Tommy had chewed her ear off about Carol this and Carol that. He never had a good word to say about her.

"I'm sure you exaggerate and make things up."

"Do me a favour, Kaz, she was playing up for you. Made me look bad. You come and live down here. You wouldn't last a week under the same roof as her," Tommy hissed. "An hour this morning. That's all it took. I had to get out and come for a morning stroll. I know she's got early dementia, but she keeps calling me Daniel for fuck's sake. Do you know who Daniel is?"

Karen stifled a laugh. "I'm sure you're about to remind me."

"Daniel was Erin's boyfriend when she was nineteen years old. Apparently, the sun shone out of his arse, and he could do no wrong. I'm sure she calls me Daniel to wind me up."

"Tommy, you're just paranoid. It's a wind-up, that's all."

"I swear, I'm not. Do you know something? When Erin and I first started dating, Carol always wound me up by comparing me to Daniel and how he was *so* perfect. Golden balls Daniel could walk on water and part the bloody sea."

"Oh, you poor boy. You're letting a pensioner get to you. You were always a sap from our days in Hendon, and you still haven't toughened up."

"Oh, shut up, Kaz. You are as bad as her. Anyway, while I'm enjoying a stroll on the beach, how's things with you?"

Karen told him about the two cases she was dealing with and the links to a case over twenty years ago.

"Sounds like a juicy one. I don't think it's an accomplice. I reckon it's a copycat. There are cases like that up and down the country. It doesn't take much to tip an unhinged individual over the edge. From what I've read, most of them are sad, insecure, and unsociable loners. Doing something like this increases their self-importance and ego for the first time in their lives. In their sad and twisted little minds, they experience power and control for the first time, and once they get a taste for it, they can't stop."

Karen raised a brow, impressed by Tommy's assessment.

"Are you not getting much from forensics?" Tommy asked.

Karen swivelled in her chair and looked out of the window at the bank of trees behind her building. "Not really. I read the report on the second crime scene this morning. It was clean. No evidence other than trampled grass and drag marks. We have the same issues in York as you do down there. Outside of the major towns the areas are remote. A criminal can easily hide their tracks and avoid being seen by anyone or anything due to the remote areas outside of major towns. It's a nightmare."

Tommy laughed. "It's not like being in the Met, is it?"

"No it's not. I have to do proper old-fashioned policing sometimes. Anyway, Tommy, I need to dash and get an update from the team. Keep in touch, mate, and stop sending me photographs."

"No chance. I'll keep sending them. I'm about to go grab myself a ninety-nine ice cream with the full works. Sprinkles, flake, and strawberry sauce. Might even stretch it to a double flake," Tommy laughed. "Stay tuned for my next instalment. Take it easy, Kaz."

Karen hung up and smiled.

An hour later Gabby called from SCAS.

"Hi, Karen. Sorry it's taken a while to get back to you, but I've been running some searches in the database and waiting for it to spew out something of value."

Karen grabbed her pen from her desk and opened to a fresh page in her notepad. "Shoot, go ahead. What you got for me."

"I've come up with a name for you. Carl Munro, aged forty-two. A serial killer on the loose. So far, he has evaded capture. In his teens he developed an obsession with serial killer stranglers like Ronald Dominique, known as the Bayou Strangler, the Stockwell Strangler, the Vienna Strangler, and the Cleveland Strangler. A highly dangerous individual who has moved around the country and been very difficult to track."

Karen's eyes widened as she scribbled down the information. "Last known whereabouts?"

Gabby sighed down the line. "Whereabouts unknown. He could be anywhere in the country and York would be as good a place as any to find him. We have linked him to murders in Canterbury, Tenby, Forfar, Lancaster, and Grimsby."

"Jesus. Talk about spreading yourself thinly," Karen said.

"Exactly. He has also been linked to attempted abductions in Maybole, Alnwick, and Crediton."

"What makes you think he could be on our patch?"

"I flagged several things up on the system. He has a certain type. He mainly abducts single females between the ages of twenty-five and forty-five. Dark-haired, attractive, and most were financially independent. He never kept them for longer than a few hours and strangled *every* victim."

"Any sexual element, Gabby?"

"Yes. Half of his victims had been sexually assaulted with evidence of scratches inside their vaginas, but no semen traces."

"Not penetrated with the penis?" Karen asked.

Gabby clarified. "Unlikely, something else. An instrument, fingers with long nails, or something like that."

Karen tapped her pen against the paper. "How does he get around?"

Gabby paused for a moment as she scanned through the details on her side. "He's mainly used an unregistered camper van. Two-tone, blue and grey. The usual checks confirmed no recent entries on social media and no banking transactions. None of the victims had cash on them. So we believe he took their money."

"Neither of our victims were robbed or sexually assaulted," Karen pointed out, unsure Munro fitted the profile.

"Mixing up the MO is not unusual for a serial killer, who does it partly out of boredom and partly to confuse the police. He moves around and parks in remote locations where he won't be discovered. Woodlands are a particular favourite of his."

Karen rolled her eyes. There was woodland in every direction leading out of York.

Gabby continued, "He's laid out many of his victims in a certain way. Almost decorative and artistic at times."

"Does that suggest something about his background? His profession perhaps?"

"Quite possibly. He studied engineering at university, then had his own metalwork business for a while. His parents, Fiona and Logan Munro, are divorced. Fiona is from the UK, and Logan is from the US. Logan was with the United States Air Force before retiring and for a while was stationed at RAF Lakenheath in Suffolk, but as a family they spent most of their life stationed in the US. Fiona was a florist and created floral displays for weddings and wreaths for funerals. Here is the interesting thing," Gabby continued, "Several of his victims were laid out with their hands criss-crossed across the chest like they would be positioned in a coffin."

Karen furrowed her brow and nodded, soaking up the insights. "That's interesting."

"Munro chops and changes his MO when he latches on to a new serial killer he admires. Following information from a member of the public, police raided an abandoned cottage in Forfar. They found pictures pinned on a wall of various news articles linking to a particular serial killer in Germany, Leo Schultz, who shaved his victims' heads and wrapped them in white bed sheets before strangling them."

"And he copied Schultz?" Karen asked.

"Yep. Within a month of discovering the cottage, two local women were murdered, their bodies wrapped in bed sheets and their heads shaved."

"So if it's Munro, he might have latched on to Bruce Carson's notoriety and copied him?"

"Yes, but he'll often add his own twist," Gabby replied. "I can't say for certain if he is on your patch, but there's nothing else popping up on the system at the moment that matches your cases. The most prolific serial killer we are tracking down is Munro. We are waiting for him to pop up again while running a nationwide search from him."

Karen and Gabby continued to discuss the case for a while, agreeing to share information as investigations continued.

44

WITH THE REMNANTS of a smile still lingering after Tommy sent a few more pictures from his walk, Karen left her office and made her way towards the main floor to update the team on her conversation with Gabby and a potential new suspect. She immediately tasked an officer to liaise with city CCTV control to run a search for any two-tone camper vans spotted within the city perimeter in recent weeks. Not an easy task, but they were equipped with software that could be programmed to identify a certain shape and size of vehicle.

The press conference yesterday had garnered mixed reviews. The incident hotline had recorded a steady stream of phone calls from members of the public either expressing concern for their safety or suggesting names of people who had been acting suspiciously in recent weeks. Every call had to be taken, and it was a time-consuming process, but it could take just one call or an off-the-cuff remark to give them a new lead.

The press reports weren't complimentary. Several pieces posted online and in local newspapers spoke about the "New Suffolk Strangler" roaming the streets of York and how the police were "baffled" and no nearer to identifying a suspect. Articles that were biased annoyed Karen. Most had been pretty light on the pleas for public awareness and information, but heavy on conjecture about methods, who might be next, motives, and why women should be worried. Referencing that last point alarmed Karen more than anything else. She could do without the press whipping up fear among women and taking everything out of context.

The problem was Karen needed the press and public on their side, and she could only do that if the press team offered regular updates.

She scanned the incident boards to find any new updates or information since yesterday. Though she tried to focus, her mind kept flitting back to recent conversations with Janice Slattery and Professor Bryant. The more she thought about it, the stronger her belief they were dealing with a copycat. With no tangible leads or evidence pointing towards an accomplice, she wondered if they were chasing a dead end. She wasn't comfortable dispelling the theory completely, but she was pushing it to the edges of the investigation and would park it there unless fresh evidence came to light.

Preet called Karen's name as she approached.

Karen turned towards her. "Yes, Preet."

"One of the junior officers has been doing a bit of digging for me. It turns out Howard Rutland-Pym has a caution under his name. Making lewd comments to women in Kent four years ago. They didn't file any further charges against him, and he got away with a caution."

"What comments?"

"About how attractive they were. What was their favourite colour of underwear? Asking them out for drinks with the suggestion he could get a glimpse of them. And also asking them what their sexual preferences were."

"Jade thought he looked pervy when we went to meet him. I would say he isn't worth pursuing at the moment, but because Ruth Tate was last seen alive at one of his exhibitions and he was seen on CCTV talking to her, I think it gives us grounds to call him in for a chat. Can you take Ed with you and bring him in now and see what else you can dig up on him?"

Preet headed off, grabbing Ed along the way.

Karen turned towards her team. "Any further updates than what's on the system or on this board?" Karen asked, throwing a thumb over her shoulder.

"I've checked for any crossover between Carson's victims and ours. There were no connections with friends, family, or work. We can cross that line of enquiry off the list, and I might have something on the ex-offender front. Give me a sec to hunt out the info," Dan said.

"Thanks, mate," Karen replied.

Ty chipped in next. "I spoke to Denise Appleby, Leah's friend who organised the meal. Denise is devastated at Leah's loss and is carrying a huge amount of guilt because it was the last time she saw her alive."

Karen understood Denise's feelings. It was a natural reaction.

"Denise confirmed Leah arrived at the restaurant at around eight p.m. There were four of them at Lucia. They had something to eat and a few drinks. Leah left before the rest of them around ten thirty p.m. I've got a copy of the CCTV, but it only covers the inside. There is CCTV across the road at Thirty-Three One restaurant, so I've got a copy from them. Grape Lane is a very narrow road. Barely wide enough for a car, so it might offer us something. It's also the hub for lots of bars and restaurants, so we are making enquiries with them as well."

"Thanks, Ty. Can you get on to that as a matter of urgency?" Karen asked.

Claire offered further information. "Leah and Ruth were in a business networking group for women who met regularly to support each other, share marketing strategies, and business leads. Sandra Lessing is the organiser of Women in Biz. It might be worth you having a chat with her as well?"

Karen shrugged. "Yeah, maybe. I doubt it will be of much use, but can you call her and let her know I'll pop in and see her on my way home this evening?"

"Will do," Claire replied, picking up the phone to call Sandra.

"Dan, you said you might have a lead to do with an ex-offender?" Karen asked.

Dan nodded, having waited for his turn. "Joel Bartram. Released three years ago and lives within two miles of both Ruth and Leah. According to prison records he was a fantasist. Obsessed with strangling women and listening to their screams."

"What did he do time for?" Karen asked.

"Burglary and robbery. Sentenced to nine years, did five. He attacked and robbed three women from behind. Each attack becoming more violent. His last victim was nearly choked to death. He was cautioned for stalking a woman two years ago. A neighbour of his. I asked for a unit to pay him a visit, but there was no one in. They checked with neighbours who said he keeps odd hours. Sleeps a lot during the day but is out at night, coming back in the early hours."

Karen clapped her hands. "That's more promising. Let's try him again later on today, and if no joy, Jade and I will give him an early morning wake up call. Thanks team." Karen headed back to her office, with the first hint of optimism geeing her up.

45

Two hours later, Karen and Jade entered the interview suite armed with extra information her team had provided on Rutland-Pym just moments before. Howard Rutland-Pym had reluctantly agreed to come in to be questioned and now sat on the other side of the table looking a forlorn figure. The man's brashness, arrogance, and smarminess, which Karen had seen earlier, had been replaced by sullenness as he eyed both officers.

With Rutland-Pym denying the offer of legal representation, Jade did the formal introductions before handing over to Karen.

"Thank you for coming in, Mr Rutland-Pym. We have a few questions we'd like to ask you." Karen looked down at her notes, allowing the silence to continue and unnerve Rutland-Pym further.

"I don't see why I've been called in. As I said to your officers, I cannot see what Ruth Tate's death has to do with me."

Though he attempted to regain control and speak with confidence, his body language suggested otherwise in Karen's opinion. His fingers were interlocked in a tight grip with rounded shoulders, and Karen felt the vibration of his leg bouncing up and down beneath the table.

"We understand you were cautioned for making lewd comments towards women in Kent four years ago. Is this something you do often?" Karen asked.

Rutland-Pym's eyes widened in shock. "I... I don't know how that applies to your case?"

"We are following up on enquiries. I'm wondering if you progressed from making lewd comments to attacking women. It wouldn't be difficult for us to track your last known movements before discovering Ruth's body."

Rutland-Pym cleared his throat. "Listen, yes, I admit I made lewd comments which I shouldn't have, and the police suitably reprimanded me. Since that time, I have not approached, propositioned, or made lewd comments towards any other women."

"Well, we only have your word. What were you talking about when Ruth visited your exhibition? We have you on CCTV sharing a glass of champagne, and you appear to be standing very close to her."

"I was making general chit-chat as I wanted to know her taste in art. I asked whether she was window-shopping or looking to buy. Those kinds of things. Nothing untoward if that's what you're thinking?" Rutland-Pym furrowed his brow as he searched Karen's and Jade's eyes.

"Here's what I think. You talked to Ruth and attempted to charm her. She spurned your advances and left. We've identified you picking up her glass, examining it before placing the flute to your lips. That's odd behaviour. Don't you think?" Karen asked.

Rutland-Pym squirmed in his chair. His words came out in an indecipherable mess.

Karen continued. "That annoyed you and you followed her out, staying out of view of the CCTV cameras positioned around the area. At some point when she left the car park, you pounced, abducted, and strangled her."

"No. No!" Rutland-Pym protested. "I didn't do any of those things. You're trying to coerce me into confessing to something I didn't do."

"Not at all. It's a suggestion. What concerns me is you were the last person to see Ruth Tate alive and the last to speak to her. That, with your caution and odd behaviour with her glass makes me a little suspicious. Especially considering the caution took place in Kent, which is where Ruth's parents come from. I wonder if you perhaps met or spotted Ruth for the first time in Kent and were fortunate enough to cross paths again in York." Karen let the suggestion settle and watched as Rutland-Pym shifted in his chair, his face reddening, his bravado melting quicker than the polar ice caps.

Karen continued to push. "Perhaps you planned this all along, looking to play the long game. You developed such an obsession with Ruth that you followed her movements since you first met her."

Rutland-Pym continued to protest.

"Do you have much contact with your brother, Jeremy?" Karen asked.

The mention of his brother's name sent Rutland-Pym reeling. He pushed back in his chair and threw his arms up in the air. "Enough. What has my brother got to do with this?"

"I don't know. You tell me. We've learned your brother is in E Hall, Barlinnie Prison, Glasgow. E Hall is the segregated wing housing over two hundred sex offenders. He is serving seven years for downloading snuff videos of women being strangled as well as indecent child porn."

"Did his bad habits rub off on you? Is that what it is? We can seize your laptop and search for deleted history. There's not much we can't do. Perhaps you were so fascinated by your brother's obsession it rubbed off on you, and you took it one step further."

"I swear. I didn't touch Ruth Tate. Yes, I found her attractive. She was charming, elegant, and sexy. So of course, I wanted to talk to her. But that's as far as it went. I showed her around the exhibition, and she left a short time later. No, I didn't follow her out. I needed to stay there to manage the exhibition. I swear," he repeated. "I'm not lying."

Karen glanced across at Jade and spotted her sergeant raising a brow. "Okay, Mr Rutland-Pym, I think that's it for the moment. Please make sure we have up-to-date contact details for you in case we need to talk to you again. And with your permission, we would like to download GPS and cell site data linked to your phone. We would also like to look at your laptop, and once we've examined it, we will return it to you."

Rutland-Pym nodded and bowed his head. "Whatever. Do what you need to do. I've not done anything wrong."

Karen stood and ended the interview. "Well, you'll have nothing to worry about then."

46

WITH PHONE IN HAND, Karen stepped outside to enjoy the late August sunshine. Though her office was light, bright, and breezy, it was nice to stretch her legs and pad around in the grass. It was something she couldn't do in London with its busy streets, bustling pavement, and gritty air. She found a peaceful area behind her building where she could be alone. It was a spot where she had taken lunch and enjoyed the downtime.

She kicked off her shoes and wiggled her toes in the grass. There was something quite calming and special about being connected to the ground. She had read green was a soothing colour which helped to calm the mind and reduce tension, and when walking barefoot on grass, the level of endorphins, the body's natural happy hormones, increased by over sixty per cent. She agreed as it lightened her mood, calmed her mind, and relaxed her body.

Karen recalled a conversation with her friend Debbie back in London as they had walked barefoot on the grass in Regent's Park. According to Debbie, who was into nonconventional medicine and holistic therapies, walking on grass prevented insomnia, reduced inflammation in the body, improved mental well-being, helped with heart health, and was great for the eyes. Karen wasn't so sure about the last point, but Debbie was insistent that according to the science of reflexology, when we walk, we put the greatest pressure on our second and third toes. These two have the maximum nerve endings, which stimulate the functioning of our eyes.

Swiping the screen on her phone, Karen smiled at the memory as she dialled Professor Bryant's number.

"Hello, Professor Bryant here."

"Professor Bryant, it's DCI Karen Heath. I'm not disturbing you, am I?"

"Of course not. I'm awaiting my next patient, so I have a few minutes spare. How can I help?"

"I wanted to pick your brain about something. You mentioned Carson was a psychopath, and now I'm leaning away from the idea Carson had an accomplice and more towards a copycat killer. I know we throw the terms psychopath and sociopath around a lot. I'm trying to get in the mind of this killer, so I wondered if you could help me to understand the difference between a psychopath and a sociopath?"

"Of course. It would be my pleasure. Both character types surround us in most walks of life. It's quite prevalent in industry to be honest, but from a criminal perspective, psychopaths and sociopaths share several characteristics including a lack of remorse or empathy for others, and a lack of guilt or responsibility for their actions. They have a disregard for the law and a tendency to display a degree of violence."

Karen listened as she walked around the grass, feeling the blades tickle the soles of her feet.

"A core feature of both is a deceitful and manipulative nature which can often be so subtle it's hard to notice."

"Which of the two is more unbalanced?" Karen asked.

"Oh, without doubt sociopaths. They are less emotionally stable and highly impulsive. Bordering on erratic. They are more likely to act on compulsion and will lack patience, so they won't be much in the way of planning their crimes."

"More impulsive than psychopaths?"

"Without a doubt, detective chief inspector. Psychopaths are the opposite. They will plan their crimes down to the smallest detail and take calculated risks to avoid detection. The clever ones will leave very little in the way of clues and they make fewer mistakes because they don't get carried away."

"Agreed. From what I've experienced, we have to work harder to catch them, which can be frustrating in any case involving a serial killer."

Bryant paused for a moment before continuing. "Psychopaths are born that way, whereas sociopaths are made. If you're looking for a sociopath, their behaviours are often because of something like a brain injury, or abuse or neglect in their childhood."

"Based on what you're describing, professor, I'd say our individual is a psychopath. He is leaving very little evidence for us. There's a strong element of planning in the abduction and disposal of their bodies. I'd say he displays an air of confidence."

"I would agree with you there, detective chief inspector. They can be charming, which allows them to lure potential victims easily. It's also worth noting psychopaths who become serial killers experience a cognitive dissonance where two minds coexist, one a rational self, able to successfully navigate the complex intricacies of normal and acceptable social behaviour, the other a far more sinister self, capable of the most unspeakable and violent acts against others. Dr Jekyll and Mr Hyde is a classic example of that."

"So, where does that leave me?" Karen said more to herself than to Bryant.

"If your man is a psychopath, then you are dealing with a very dangerous individual who won't give you much leeway and could appear normal if you passed him in the street. I have met many psychopaths who came from all walks of life. A doctor, scientist, a top five per cent engineering graduate from a prestigious French university, and a senior detective in Germany. They are all around us. I don't envy your task."

"Neither do I, Professor Bryant. Thank you so much for your time, it's been helpful," Karen replied, her mind darting back to Rutland-Pym, who now on reflection didn't fit the profile unless it was an elaborate ruse.

"My pleasure. Call me if you need anything else."

Karen hung up and spent a few more minutes padding around on the grass processing her conversation before heading back in.

47

SANDRA LESSING OFFERED Karen a weak smile as she answered her door dressed in casual grey joggers, white T-shirt, and flip-flops.

"Sandra, I'm Detective Chief Inspector Karen Heath from York police. Sorry about the lateness of my visit, but I wondered if you would have a free moment?"

"Of course, please, come in." Sandra led her through to the lounge at the front of the house and offered Karen a seat. "Can I get you a tea or coffee?" she asked in a shaky voice.

"Thanks, but I'm okay. I don't want to take up too much of your time but thank you for agreeing to see me. I'm the senior investigating officer dealing with the murders of Ruth Tate and Leah Hayes."

Sandra placed a hand on her chest and stifled a sob. Her eyes moistened. Karen noticed the distress as Sandra's body slumped into the sofa, her eyes drifting around the room.

"I know this must be difficult for you."

Sandra nodded and sniffed. "I'm so shocked. We all are. None of us can believe it. I've been doing the best I can to support the rest of the women in our group. But there's only so much I can say and do." Sandra shook her head in disbelief as she glanced at the floor. "Why would anyone do something like that?"

"That's what we're trying to find out. You run a business networking group for women, correct?"

"Yes. I've been running it for about five years. I own a recruitment company, twenty-three staff. Five are admin and the rest are recruitment consultants. I remember how hard it was to get business as a female when I first started in recruitment over fifteen years ago. The number of potential contracts I lost to my male counterparts made me realise how important it was for women to have a support network group."

"I see. And how long had Ruth and Leah been members?" Karen asked.

"Gosh. I could get you precise dates, but off the top of my head Ruth had been with my group for about three years. Leah was with us for just over a year. Both found it invaluable as a way of learning from others who were more experienced as female business owners. It was an opportunity to learn from each other what worked best in terms of marketing approaches, advertising, and managing finances. We also operated a referral network, so we could recommend each other to clients if they were looking for certain professionals. It was a way for us to all grow our businesses."

Sandra's focus softened as she gazed around her lounge while finger-combing her short blonde bobbed hair. She spoke affectionately about Ruth and Leah. They were both strong-minded, focused and dedicated to their careers, with Leah often being the joker among the group, which left many members in stitches as they listened to her jokes and stories.

"Sandra, did either Ruth or Leah ever mention any concerns they had for their safety?"

Sandra turned to Karen, a look of horror on her face as her eyes widened and her jaw dropped. "What do you mean?"

"Well, did they ever mention any unwelcome attention from strangers? Had they expressed concerns about being followed?"

"No. Not to me. We are a very close-knit group, and I'm sure if either of them had problems like that, then we would have known about it. We are very safety conscious. Our meetings always take place in coffee shops first thing in the morning when they are quiet, and we can hear ourselves talk. I don't organise any meetings in the evenings unless it's a celebratory dinner, or drinks, or attending any local commerce events."

Sandra gasped. "Oh my God, do you think someone has been following us? Are my ladies in danger?"

Karen raised a hand to reassure the woman. "I don't think it's linked to your group. Perhaps it was an unfortunate coincidence both Ruth and Leah were members. I think it would be wise for the moment to not arrange any more meetings, and I'll need a list of all your members and their contact details. We'd like to contact them to offer advice about personal safety."

"So... so my members are in danger? Why else would you contact them?" Sandra stuttered as her panic grew and her chest heaved. She dropped her head into her hands. "Oh God."

"There is no intelligence to suggest Ruth and Leah were specifically targeted due to their affiliation with your networking group. Until we can establish a firm motive, I need to make sure we remind your members to stay vigilant and not put themselves in situations which could endanger their safety."

Sandra inhaled and exhaled as she fought to calm herself. She rose from her chair and retrieved her case from the hallway before returning and providing Karen with all the contact details. Karen thanked her for her time and gave her a business card before leaving.

48

Melody Faulkner was proving harder to take than his earlier two victims. She led a busy and successful life which meant she was rarely at home, and if she was, it would entail her arriving closer to midnight, having six hours sleep and rising at six a.m. six days a week. Melody left at seven a.m. on those mornings as her first clients would be in after eight and she needed to prepare her team. On the second Tuesday of every month, she would visit one of her businesses in Leeds. On the third Tuesday of every month, she would visit Harrogate for the same reason. He knew her schedule very well.

Six weeks of following her had led to this moment. He couldn't wait any longer. He followed at a discreet distance, always keeping two cars in between his own and Melody's white BMW X3. She was a glamorous woman who paid meticulous detail to what she wore and how she looked. She always styled her hair perfectly, applied make-up precisely, and pressed her clothes immaculately. The only times he had seen her make-up free with messy hair was when she put out her rubbish and even that carried finesse. She washed the plastic containers, neatly folded the cardboard packaging, and pinched the metal tins at the top.

Melody slowed ahead, so he applied his brakes and dropped back to allow a few more cars to overtake him. He watched as the X3 stopped for a moment outside the King's convenience store before moving off again and taking the next left that led to a small open-air car park big enough for a dozen cars. He moved off, keeping his speed steady before he took the next left as well. Melody had pulled into a parking space and had already left her vehicle by the time he arrived. He glimpsed her in his rear-view mirror as she disappeared on to the main road.

He waited until she was out of sight before he left his vehicle and trotted over towards the main road. Peering around the corner, he spotted Melody at the cashpoint before she darted into the King's convenience store. He thought this might help him as he made his way back to his car and crouched in the dark waiting for her return.

It was a tense few minutes before he heard heels clipping on the ground and the jangling of car keys. He popped his head up to see Melody enter the small car park and make her way to her car. He crept between the cars, careful to keep the sound of his footsteps to a minimum as he closed the gap. Melody had popped the boot of her car and was sliding two bags of shopping into the boot. The rustling of the plastic was enough to mask his approach. With a second to go, Melody must have sensed something and glanced over her shoulder. But it was too late as he threw his arm around her neck and pulled her backwards.

A strained scream like a wounded fox tore through the silent night air. Melody clawed at his arm. Her falling body weight pushed him back as he struggled to keep his hold. Melody hit the ground with a heavy thud as another strained scream bubbled up from her throat. He needed to be fast. It would only be moments before a nosy neighbour pulled back a curtain to see what was going on. As Melody wrestled with him on the ground, tugging at his arm to take in air, he released his grip and punched her in the temple. Her head bounced off the ground, the sound like a cracking egg. It had an immediate effect. He had silenced her.

With his heart hammering in his chest, he glanced around, not sure if anyone was looking. There were too many windows to check and the longer he hung around, the greater the chance of being spotted. He rifled through her handbag and retrieved the phone, stuffing it in his back pocket before closing the boot lid on the X3. One last look around to check if the coast was still clear. He looped his hands under her armpits and dragged her towards his car.

It took all his effort to haul her limp body on to the back seat. There wasn't time to tie her hands and wrists or tape her mouth. He could do that in a few minutes when he was away from the scene.

49

THE ADDRESS for Joel Bartram led them to a council-owned ground-floor apartment in a house converted into two properties.

"Let's hope he doesn't see us and do a bunk out of the back door," Karen said as she was about to ring on the buzzer but noticed the front door to the building was already ajar. "That's a good start."

The communal hallway was functional and clean, though a stale odour hung in the air. Jade scrunched her nose and glared at Karen with contempt.

"Don't give me that look. You could have turned down my request for you to come with me. Besides, it's not like you're standing in a pool of dried piss, but then again, the yellow staining you're standing on could be…"

Jade almost tumbled over her feet as she shifted her position. "Ew. That's bloody gross. I'm going to have to spray the soles of my shoes with anti-bac."

Karen shook her head in consternation. Jade's OCD was always a constant source of light entertainment for her. Despite two visits from police officers yesterday, Joel Bartram was nowhere to be found, but a quick check with the neighbours confirmed they had been woken by Bartram coming in at four a.m. this morning, knocking over empty beer bottles. Karen banged on his door with a fist. She waited a few moments before banging harder and for a few seconds longer.

"Fuck's sake," came the muffled voice from beyond the door and the sound of approaching footsteps. The door finally opened a few inches and the tired face of Joel Bartram stared back at them. His eyes were narrow and bloodshot. Hair dishevelled.

Karen held up her warrant card. "Joel Bartram?"

Bartram cleared his throat and ran his tongue over his lips. "Now what? Whatever it is, I didn't do it." Bartram went to close the door, but Karen had already placed a foot in the doorway. He tutted as he glanced towards the floor and then back at her.

"Not so fast, Joel. We just want a quick word. Won't take long." Karen leaned into the door and pushed it open, ignoring Bartram's protests as she walked through the darkened hallway peering into the kitchen on her right, the lounge on her left, and a single bedroom towards the rear. Karen didn't cross into the bedroom, the overnight stale smell of sweat and farts providing an impenetrable barrier to her entry. Karen turned and walked back towards the lounge. "In here," she demanded.

Joel let out a deep sigh and followed her instructions, with Jade following behind to make sure he didn't do a runner.

Karen surveyed the messy lounge. The sofa had seen better days with deeply pitted cushions. A small coffee table with tea stain rings sat in the middle of the room. The orange floral curtains didn't match the magnolia woodchip walls, and a few prints on a wall looked as if they'd come from a second-hand charity shop. A small TV was perched on an upturned beer crate. "It looks like you've made yourself at home here." Karen wandered over to a chest of drawers piled high on top with an assortment of jumble, or so she thought. As she got closer, she noticed at least a dozen mobile phones thrown over a pile of clothes, a few gold chains, a car stereo, two laptops, and an iPad. "We have a real Aladdin's cave here, don't we?"

Bartram yawned and then dropped into the sofa. "It's all legit. Stuff my mates don't want."

Karen rolled her eyes before walking over to Bartram. "Of course, it is. Looks like you've turned your hand at a bit of breaking and entering?"

Bartram groaned and stood. "I swear, give me a break. It's all legit."

Karen shoved him in the chest and pushed him back down. "I didn't say you could go anywhere. You can stay put until I'm finished with you. It's your lucky day today because we're not here about your new career as a tea leaf. I'm the senior investigating officer handling the abduction and murder of two women in a week. Both of them live within two miles of your address."

Bartram shrugged as he rubbed his chest. "So?"

"The fact you were cautioned two years ago for stalking a woman suggests you may be of interest to us. Your MO is to rob women from behind, each robbery becoming more violent."

Bartram tried to stand in protest, but Karen shoved him with both hands. "Stay where you are. I won't tell you again." Karen glared at him as she clenched her jaw.

"This is bloody assault. I'm going to make a formal complaint."

"Assault? Really? If you don't shut up, I'll ram that bloody iPad down your throat," Karen said, throwing a thumb over her shoulder. "Then you might have grounds for a complaint," Karen added with a smile.

Jade stood in the doorway, arms folded across her chest, a slight smile the only sign of her amusement.

"The last victim said you tried to choke her to death, and you had a smile on your face while you did that. What kind of sicko does that?" Karen asked, leaning forward, hands on her hips. "Someone attacked our two victims from behind and strangled them to death. The attacker took their mobile phones in both cases. I'm wondering what the chances are we might find their mobile phones in the pile behind me. Hmm?"

"Whoa. That ain't me. You can check all those phones. But I don't know what you're talking about."

"I'm just wondering if you moved up from attacking and robbing women to attacking and killing them?"

Bartram shook his head in defiance. "I'm telling you, it's not me."

"Prison records state you were a bit of a fantasist. Obsessed with fantasising over strangling women and listening to their screams. That's what you told one of your cellmates. So it set off alarm bells for us. Where were you last Friday night?"

"I dunno," he huffed.

"Not good enough! This will be the last time I ask. Think carefully or I'll arrange for you to be strip-searched and inspected with the biggest anal probe we can find!"

Jade threw a hand over her mouth as a snigger escaped her lips.

"Where were you Friday night?" Karen shouted.

"Party. I was at a party. About thirty people there. I've got an alibi."

"That wasn't hard, was it?"

Karen asked him where he was on the night Ruth's body was dumped. This time he was vaguer and could only offer the usual "I was at home" reply.

"Jade, bag up those phones. Are there any other phones on the property?" Karen asked, snapping on a pair of latex gloves.

Bartram shook his head and sunk back into the sofa.

"Good, because we're going to look around your property, and if you're lying, you'll be sitting in a cell within the hour. Now keep your arse parked there. Jade, get a few officers to take over. I want this place turned over."

50

"WHERE DO you come up with this stuff?" Jade asked, still chuckling to herself.

Karen shrugged. "Well, people like Bartram get on my tits when they don't answer my questions, so a little bending of the truth seems to get them talking."

Jade shook her head and stared at Karen. "Well, you need balls. Does he go in our possible pile?" Jade asked as she tucked into a late breakfast of scrambled eggs on toast in a café close to town.

Karen spread a thin layer of marmalade on her toast and took a bite before nodding her approval at the taste. "I'm not sure to be honest. It's a big step up from attacking and robbing women to killing them. It's also a big leap to go from being a fantasist about strangling women to seeing it through."

"True. But it's possible. We've seen it in murderers before. A surge of adrenaline and red mist bridges the gap between hurting someone and taking their life."

"I know, Jade, but if he was our killer and based on what Professor Bryant has told me, he would have come across as a lot more confident, articulate, and methodical. His apartment looked like a council tip. His bed sheets were dirty, and he looked untidy. Based on what Professor Bryant has told me, I can't see Bartram as our killer."

They settled into eating their breakfast in silence, and for Karen she welcomed the caffeine hit from the strong coffee. There was something about having breakfast in a café which seemed to lift people's spirits. Karen noticed various conversations from different tables. And that's what she liked. Places like this generated conversation. No one hid behind text or WhatsApp messages which stripped the world of the art of face-to-face conversation. She felt sorry for the younger generation, those still in school and at university who spent much of their time forming and maintaining virtual friendships with people they rarely met face to face.

Karen placed her knife down and pointed a finger in Jade's direction. "Mind you, I remember Professor Bryant saying psychopaths are hiding in plain sight and we could walk past one and not notice them. It doesn't matter whether they are killers or business professionals. They leverage their ruthless personality for their own gains." Karen glanced at the ceiling as she recalled more of the conversation. "They can be good actors and appear very normal. Bartram came across like a pathetic wimp who shot his mouth off too much. What if that was the side of his personality he wanted to show everyone?"

"Even if that's the case, where did he take Ruth and Leah?" Jade asked. "I can't imagine him taking them back to his apartment. It's too public and his neighbours are vigilant."

"A lock-up, a garage, a derelict house, even an old crack den. He could take them anywhere," Karen remarked, as she fished her phone from her bag. "But it got me thinking," Karen added, scrolling through the list of contacts and calling Professor Bryant.

"Professor Bryant speaking."

"Professor, it's Detective Chief Inspector Karen Heath here," Karen said in a hushed tone, keen to make sure the nearest tables couldn't hear her.

"Detective chief inspector, it's good to hear from you. Is everything okay?" he asked, his voice firm and commanding.

"Yes, but I wanted to pick your brain again. I remember reviewing the notes on Carson's interview. There was no mention of where Carson was taking his victims in between abducting them and dumping their bodies. Did he mention anything to you?"

"He did. I recall he didn't cooperate with detectives during his interviews. However, on one of my prison visits he let slip he had a hiding place where he spent a lot of time and took his victims. I visited the location and found it fascinating. The police didn't take any further action even though I had informed them about the information."

Karen heard the rustling of paper at Bryant's end before she continued.

"Did he say why he spent a lot of time at this place?"

"Carson said it was his sanctuary. He had stumbled upon the location, but it suited his needs."

"So, if someone was copying Carson, would they also go as far as having some kind of hiding place? Somewhere he kept his abductees?" Karen asked.

"If they idolised Carson that much, they would seek to replicate *everything* he did down to a tee. So yes."

Could she imagine Bartram having a sanctuary? She doubted it, but she had to keep an open mind.

"May I suggest something, detective chief inspector?"

"Sure."

"I can take you to the place Carson called his sanctuary. It used to be a Priory, but now it's abandoned. All three victims were held there. It might not help you, but it's part of the jigsaw puzzle and it makes sense to step into the mind of your perpetrator. Think like them. See the world through their eyes. Shift your mind into a different plane of processing." Bryant drew in a breath and exhaled slowly down the line. "Anyway, the offer is there should you feel it's helpful."

Karen thought about it for a moment as she watched the quizzical look on Jade's face. "I think that would be useful. Are you available in the next hour as my sergeant and I are out and about on enquiries at the moment?"

"Let me check my diary." A brief pause followed. "I can. My next appointment is in three hours. That gives me plenty of time to meet you and get back to prepare for my client. I'll text you the address and I look forward to seeing you there."

"Thanks, professor, we'll see you soon."

51

KAREN FOLLOWED Jade's navigation as they headed south out of the city centre. The further they travelled, the narrower the roads became until Karen slowed her speed through single-track roads. She prayed no one would come the other way as there was nowhere to pull up. Tall hedges hemmed them in, shielding her view of the surrounding countryside, which featured in nearly every journey she took.

"Much further?" she asked.

"Um, one sec," Jade replied, pinching her phone screen to zoom out. "Not far. To the end of this road, right at the junction and maybe half a mile up on the right."

Karen continued down the lane and spotted signposts for nearby villages. Appleton Roebuck was to her right, Acaster Selby to her left, and Ryther straight ahead.

"The former RAF base, Acaster Malbis, is a quarter of a mile to our left." Jade looked out of the passenger window as the hedgerow thinned out and she glimpsed flat, open fields. A treeline in the distance marked the perimeter of the base where in an earlier homicide case, a prostitute called Sallyanne Faulkner had been murdered and her hand chopped off.

"The one thing I would say about York and the surrounding area is it's a small place. It's surprising how so many of our investigations have been within a short distance of each other," Jade remarked. "London is so vast we would never return to the same location in months or years."

Karen nodded as she tapped her fingers on the steering wheel in time with a song on the radio. She took a right and continued until she turned right again and down a dusty, single-track lane which had seen better days. A rusty gate leaned against a tree. The grass beyond had not been cut for years, and the hedges were growing in all directions. "I was thinking the same," Karen said as she spotted a large ornate abandoned building at the end of the lane. As Karen approached, she saw Professor Bryant standing beside a gleaming black Mercedes.

"Show off," Jade muttered under her breath as Karen pulled in behind Bryant's car, switched off the ignition and stepped out.

Karen threw Jade a wry grin.

"Good, you found it," Bryant said as he approached.

"Just about. Professor Bryant, this is Detective Sergeant Jade Whiting."

Bryant shook Jade's hand before turning to face the imposing mansion. "This was Norton Priory. As you can see it's had better days. Abandoned over twenty-five years ago and changed hands many times since then, but because of council red tape and its Grade II listing, many proposals haven't progressed, so it's been languishing in its sorrowful state for a long time."

It was an imposing building in Karen's opinion. Three stories high, built of reddish orange brick, with ashlar dressings and a Welsh slate roof. She noticed eight chimney stacks protruding from the roof. This building wasn't double-fronted, it was triple-fronted with an imposing doorway which drew her eyes to the centre of the building.

"This was Carson's sanctuary, a place where he wouldn't be disturbed or discovered," Bryant said. "But now, only urban explorers visit here," he added, pointing to the peeled-away metal door. "Come with me."

Karen and Jade looked at each other before following Bryant through the gap and into an imposing hallway with grand stairs snaking up through the central spine of the building.

A distinct chill in the air made the hairs on the back of Karen's neck stand on end. Light flooded in through the tall, slender windows. The smell of stale, rotting wood permeated the air. Blue wallpaper lined the walls, and though the central stair runner carpet had been removed, the ornate, dark brown, newel post and spindles added a touch of elegance to the abandoned structure.

"This way," Bryant instructed as he took the steps. Each tread creaked as they headed up to the first floor, the sound echoing around the cavernous space. He led them along the hallway.

Karen ran her finger along a white cast-iron radiator, one of many dotted at regular intervals along the hallway. *These things cost a fortune nowadays.*

The detectives followed Bryant into a room off the hallway which at one time Karen assumed was an office when she spotted a desk pushed to one corner and several filing cabinets, their drawers open, and paper scattered on the floor. Various charts hung off the walls, though Karen was unsure what they related to because a fine layer of grey dust coated them.

Bryant led them over to a radiator beneath the window. "This is where Carson held each of his victims. They were handcuffed to the radiator, and he kept a bucket close by. He sat at a desk," Bryant said, pointing towards the corner of the room, "and studied his victims, often engaging in one-sided conversations with them. Carson occasionally sat beside them having a cup of tea. Other than keeping them handcuffed to the radiator, he didn't harm them until the end. There were no violent or sexual assaults. No torture. Nothing physical. It was mind games."

Karen moved away from the radiator and walked around the room taking it in. It was a large space with tall ceilings and ornate woodwork. She imagined the room and the building itself had looked magnificent in its heyday. "Mind games?"

Bryant nodded. "He wanted to exert his authority and control. He did that through silence to begin with and then conversation. He felt powerful here." Bryant threw his hands up towards the ceiling. "Nothing could be more grandiose than this, which was how he liked it. It was his sanctuary, a place he felt safe and in control."

Karen took a few moments to absorb the atmosphere. Silent, chilling and strangely isolating, even though there were three of them in the room. She imagined how each victim might have felt. Lonely, scared, terrified, and help-less were words which sprang to mind.

"So, Carson was a real psycho then? Not just an inflated ego?" Karen asked as she returned to where Jade and Bryant were standing beside the window.

"Oh, he was a psychopath. Calm and collected under pres-sure with something we call in medical terms as a 'resilience to chaos', which meant he thrived in situations others would find stressful. He was a con artist who could be charming and charismatic. Carson was a thrill seeker because he lacked fear and lacked conscience, which blunted his emotions." Bryant turned to Karen. "You are looking for someone with the same traits I have discussed with you here. I did this when profiling for the South Wales Police on one of their cases, and then with Kent Police. If I can be of help, you only have to ask."

"Thank you, professor. It has been interesting. We need to get back now."

Bryant checked his phone. "I must too. I need to prepare for my next appointment," he said, leading them out of the building.

52

KAREN DROPPED her handbag by her desk and promptly headed back out of her office and made her way to Kelly's office. Another officer was leaving as Karen arrived, so she stepped to one side to let her colleague through. "Ma'am, do you have a minute?"

"Sure. Come in and grab a seat. How are things going? Are we making much progress?" Kelly asked as she shuffled papers into a plastic sleeve and placed it to one side. "That's budgets done for this month."

"We are hitting a few dead ends at the moment."

"Suspects?"

"Two, possibly three. Howard Rutland-Pym, who had spoken to Ruth before she left, was the exhibition organiser and the last person to see Ruth Tate alive. And Joel Bartram, an ex-con done for attacking women from behind and robbing them. He's a fantasist who fantasised about strangling women and hearing their screams. And I've just spoken to my contact at SCAS who informed me of their nationwide hunt for a serial killer strangler called Carl Munro."

Kelly chewed on her bottom lip and nodded. "Are either of the first two contenders?"

"Bartram I would say is a no. I don't think he's got it in him, and he doesn't fit the profile. Rutland-Pym, possible. We are running more checks on him now. I've already brought him in for an interview, but I didn't get much from him."

"And Munro?"

"Munro is the only one with confirmed form and linked to a series of murders across the country and a number of attempted abductions. SCAS are unable to confirm Munro's whereabouts as he moves around a lot."

"So he could be on our patch?" Kelly asked.

"It's a strong possibility. Gabby, my liaison at SCAS, said she'd update me with more results from her checks." Karen explained Munro's tendency to switch between his interest in different serial killers and the adoption of their MO.

"Right, that sounds like crap. We don't want to find ourselves in this position for much longer," Kelly stressed. "The press conferences should have thrown up new information?"

Karen shook her head. "A few interesting calls, but more speculation than anything else. We just haven't got anything concrete. And the only link between Ruth and Leah we've found so far is they were both part of a women in business networking group."

"Do you think he's targeting women in that group specifically?"

"I don't think so, ma'am. Sandra Lessing, who runs the group, is mortified. I've asked her to cancel any future meetings until we have this wrapped up. I've got my team contacting her members to offer them personal safety advice."

"That's a good call. Well done."

"Thanks, ma'am. We're reviewing all mobile phone traces near the victims' residences and where they were found. Using cell site triangulation, we can identify if any mobile numbers appear in all four locations during a twenty-four-hour period in the run-up to discovering each body."

"Long shot," Kelly remarked.

What else do you want me to do? Karen thought.

"On another note, I've been speaking to Professor Bryant, a criminal psychologist. He has studied psychopathic serial killers for many years now and is only one of two people to have visited Bruce Carson in prison as part of his lifetime of study into this subset of murderers. Having spoken to the professor at length, I believe we are dealing with a copycat who is enacting everything Bruce Carson did during his reign. Professor Bryant has got into the minds of psychopaths and has interviewed Carson at length. He knows him better than most people."

"So how does that help us?" Kelly asked with a shake of her head and a shrug of her shoulder. "We don't need a shrink telling us how to do our job."

"I appreciate that, ma'am. I think he could be of value to us. He could help us to get into the mindset of the killer and understand what kind of individual we are dealing with and what we should be looking for. From what I can gather, such an individual would be unique but act very normal. They carry certain traits, and it is those we need to focus on."

Kelly grimaced. "I'm not comfortable with that."

"Neither am I, ma'am. But we are running out of options. He's helped South Wales and Kent police forces in recent cases. His work helped both forces to firm up a suspect profile, which assisted officers in apprehending the killers in both cases. It might be worth offering his opinion to our team?"

Kelly pondered their predicament and rolled a pen around her fingers. "South Wales and Kent police forces?"

"Yes, ma'am. I've checked a few of the press articles online and both chief constables mentioned and thanked him. I was wondering if you could have a word with the CC and get his office to do the due diligence. Worth a shot if they rate him?"

"Okay, leave it with me, Karen. I'll put in a request with the CC. It would need to be signed off, but I would rather his office contact the chief constables of both forces because I want the decision to come from the top of the chain. If it backfires, both of us are protected."

Karen smiled and rose from her seat. "Thanks, ma'am."

53

HE UNLOCKED the door and pushed it open, taking his position in the doorway as he watched Melody Faulkner dig her heels into the floor and push herself back. Her breaths were fast and ragged as she pressed herself into the wall. He tightened his jaw. An overpowering smell of excrement, sweat, and urine punctured the air and filled his nostrils.

He remained silent, gazing at her, his lips twitching as he took notice of what he felt. Very little in fact. No anger, fear, or hammering of his heart in his chest. No throbbing veins in his neck and no sweaty palms. This was more like it. It had taken a while to get there, but he was satisfied with the progress he had made. The stillness of mind and body. But the inquisitiveness was still there and the subconscious calling to snuff out another life.

Stepping into the room and walking over to the desk, he placed his car keys on it along with a bag of food he had bought for her. He turned and faced Melody, her eyes following his every step. He faced a strange juxtaposition. Do away with her now or keep her for a while longer.

"Normally, you would have outstayed your welcome, but there's something about you I find fascinating." He picked up a chair and walked over to her, setting it down in front of her before taking a seat just inches away. She shrunk away from him, which made him smile. "A strong-minded businesswoman. I've seen the way you manage your staff. A strong, confident voice. Empathy mixed with a shrewd business mind. And of course, dazzling beauty. So, what would you like to talk about? How are you coping with your enforced stay?"

Melody trembled, her bottom lip quivering as tears broke from her eyes. "Please. Please let me go. If you want money, I've got lots of it. I can transfer it all to you right now and you could let me go."

He offered her a small smile and a shake of his head. "It's not about money. There are plenty of others who have amassed a bigger fortune than you who could sit here in front of me. You must have heard the phrase 'It's not you, it's me'. Well, it applies here. You are nothing more than a pawn in my experiment. There was something about you which drew me in. In fact, I can remember the exact place where I first noticed you." He laughed as the recollection surfaced in his mind. "Waitrose, Foss Islands Road. You were dithering over which bottle of red wine to choose. So consumed were you in your thoughts, you didn't notice me. I studied you for a few moments before walking away. From that point onwards I needed to know everything about you."

Melody's shoulders shook as fear gripped her body, her legs shaking uncontrollably. A timid and desperate squeal whistled from her throat.

He nodded as he leaned forward and stroked her dark locks. "A thing of beauty. Luckily for you, I'm not interested in your looks. If I were a sick, demented, twisted sexual predator, I would have broken your body and made you bleed in ways you would never have imagined."

The soft squeal grew louder before an ear-shattering scream bounced from wall to wall.

"That won't help you. No one knows you're here and no one will come and rescue you. The next time someone sees you, your body will be cold and lifeless. There'll be a few touching eulogies as your friends and family gather to say goodbye to you. Which is nice, isn't it? And I'll be sitting at the back listening. What would they think if they knew they were sitting shoulder to shoulder with the person who killed you? Wow! That's sick, right?" he asked.

Melody closed her eyes and sobbed into her hands. "Please. Stop. Let me go."

The man inhaled deeply and stood before picking up the chair and returning it to one side of the desk. He picked up his keys and removed a sandwich and a bottle of water from the bag, placing it down beside her before walking away. "You should eat. Oh, and try to use the bucket next time. We live in a civilised society, not a Kolkata back-street. Do you want me to bring you a change of clothes?"

Melody continued to sob into her hands.

He raised a brow as he stopped in the doorway, glancing back over his shoulder. "I'll take that as a no."

54

Bart Lynch, the CSI manager, had also been in touch, and at last there was progress on the forensic front. They had discovered a single hair fibre on Leah's clothing following a second sweep. The fibre had been tucked into a seam, and it would have been missed on a visual inspection. However, it was spotted under magnification. Karen's hopes were dashed when DNA checks confirmed no match at Leah's home address or on the DNA Database. It was progress and something Karen informed Kelly of.

Karen and the team had spent the next few hours chasing up a new lead called into the control room. A group of cyclists travelling along the single lane track by Brieryend Wood had spotted a man standing in the trees the day before the discovery of Leah's body. At the time, they didn't think much of it until they heard the announcement about the discovery of Leah's body. The team was working flat out to discover the identity of the individual.

An appeal to the public needed to go out as a priority, but Karen accepted there could be a reasonable explanation for him being there. He could have been a walker who'd stopped to take a break, but with the cyclists commenting about the lack of vehicles in either direction close to the scene, and how he'd turned his back on them as they'd ridden past, the news tingled Karen's spidey senses.

"Karen, have you got a moment?" Kelly asked, striding into Karen's office.

Karen sat up straight. "Of course, ma'am. Everything okay?"

"We've had the sign-off and clearance to talk to Professor Bryant in an official capacity. The CC spoke to his counterparts in South Wales and Kent. Both forces spoke highly of the professor and his valuable insights. So, I don't see any harm in us talking to him, either."

That was great news as far as Karen was concerned. Though she had spoken to him on several occasions, having his input in an official capacity could prove invaluable. "Excellent news. I'll call him."

Kelly stepped in closer to Karen's desk. "I want us to tread with caution. He may have helped two other forces, but we need to keep our own boundaries. Involve him, but he is not going to come to the SCU. There is far too much confidential information and I don't want him seeing that."

It was a strange and cautious request, but Karen understood the reasoning behind it.

"Discuss the case with him, show him the crime scene photographs, get his input, but that's as far as it goes, Karen. If he has anything of importance, then I would like you to relay it to the rest of the team."

"Understood, ma'am," Karen said, and was about to continue, when Ed hurried into Karen's room with a sheet of paper in his hand.

"Ma'am, sorry to interrupt, but we've received an email from someone claiming to be the killer."

Karen jumped up from her seat. "What?" she said, taking the note from Ed and reading it before passing it over to Kelly.

"Stop me before it's too late!" Kelly said, reading the one line. "Hoax?"

Karen shrugged. "I think we must take every piece of information seriously. Ed, can you get on to the high-tech unit and see if we can trace the IP?"

"Will do," Ed replied, before dashing back to his desk.

Karen pursed her lips as confusion spread across her face. She relayed some points Professor Bryant revealed about how a real copycat would follow most steps that Carson had carried out during his reign. "This isn't the MO of someone copying Carson. Carson made no contact with the police before his capture. But it could be Munro. He latches on to a serial killer and adopts most of their MO but adds his own twist. The email could be his twist? SCAS said Munro hid out in remote locations and woodlands. Brieryend Wood where Leah was discovered is a remote wooded location, Munro could have been hiding out there."

"Yes, but Ruth was murdered over a week ago too," Kelly said, "why now? Why contact us after two murders? Is there any significance in that?"

"I don't know, ma'am. From what I can gather during my conversations with the professor, we are looking for someone who is intelligent, confident, has a lot of bravado and is very calculated in *everything* they do. He could just be bored, but I doubt it. I think he's teasing us."

"Well, I'm not surprised. We've turned up nothing. Not a bloody sausage. A bunch of weak suspects, a hair fibre from forensics, no one caught on tape, and we are no nearer to catching him than we were a week ago. Of course, he's bloody teasing us. This isn't good enough. Can you imagine the grief I'm going to get from upstairs?" Kelly bristled, sucking in air through clenched teeth as her face reddened. "If it's Munro, then we're in for a rough ride. More than a dozen forces haven't tracked him down and neither have the NCA. What chance do we have?" Kelly ranted.

Karen swallowed. She hadn't seen Kelly this angry. But hints of the Terminator were bubbling to the surface.

Kelly headed to the open door before stopping and turning to face Karen. "Get a result, Karen, or both of us are going to look like a couple of incompetent morons and end up being shipped out of here. God help us if this has been sent to the press."

Kelly shook her head and left the room, leaving Karen stunned by her boss's outburst. Her head spun as a wave of heat flashed across her face. It felt like her silver necklace was choking off the air to her lungs. Having not felt like this since London when her panic attacks struck like hammer blows, Karen dropped into her seat and leaned forward as the first signs of panic swelled in her chest.

Breathe in 12345, breathe out 12345678. Shit. Get a grip. Breathe in 12345, breathe out 12345678. Slow it down. Slow it down.

55

KAREN HAD STEPPED out of her building and walked around the grounds of the base for thirty minutes waiting for the adrenaline spike to subside. Her body felt tired, her chest tight, and her limbs restless.

Kelly's reaction had taken her by surprise and dredged up awful flashbacks of her run-ins with DCI Skelton in London. The fresh air helped, the grass and trees calmed her. *Kelly's reaction was a natural response from any senior officer when a case is stalling*, Karen reasoned. *It's nothing personal*, she reminded herself.

Karen met Professor Bryant at the visitor reception an hour later and led him to a meeting room along the corridor.

"Thank you for coming in," Karen said as they both took a seat.

"It's my pleasure, though I sensed a frigidness in your tone," he replied, unbuttoning his jacket and retrieving a pad and pen from his case.

Karen took a sip of water to soothe her parched throat before continuing. "I put in a request for us to get your input on our case in a professional capacity. Our chief constable spoke to his counterparts in the South Wales and Kent forces who spoke of you highly. My request was approved, so I can now discuss aspects of the case with you and seek your opinion." Karen chose her words to avoid any suggestion Bryant would be ensconced into the investigation team.

Bryant broke out into a big smile and nodded. "Fantastic. I'm happy to help in whatever way I can."

"I was going to run through aspects of the case with you, but we've had a development." Karen retrieved a copy of the email from her folder and slid it across the table for Bryant to read.

He scanned the one line and narrowed his eyes.

"Genuine or a hoax?" Karen asked.

"I would say this is probably a hoax. If we are working on the assumption your copycat killer is enacting most details of Carson's movements during his reign, then he wouldn't be contacting the investigating team. Before the advent of the Internet and email, thrill seekers or malicious individuals would send handwritten letters and cassette recordings."

Bryant nodded as he glanced down at the email again.

He tilted his head to the side. "It was the issue which caused the delay in apprehending the Yorkshire Ripper. A hoax cassette recording and three handwritten letters sent to police taunting them for failing to catch him. John Humble, the individual concerned, threw a false accent, which led to

the investigation being moved away from the West Yorkshire area. It prolonged the Yorkshire Ripper's reign of
terror. Some twenty-five years later and advances in DNA
technology led to Humble finally being uncovered as the
hoaxer."

Karen nodded. "Okay. That's helpful."

THOUGH BRYANT HAD ALLAYED a few of her fears, she
wasn't about to disregard the email altogether. With Kelly's
outburst still ringing in Karen's mind, she needed to throw
resources into validating the email.

"You said probably a hoax, professor?"

"I did. Though he is attempting to copy Carson down to a
tee, if we look hard enough, there will be slight nuances
which become apparent. Few copycat crimes are exact
replicas of the event that inspired them. Instead, an imitator
lifts and copies certain elements such as motivation, tech-
nique, or setting, et cetera of the original crime. Our job is
to identify which of those elements will give us the greatest
chance of unlocking the identity of your killer."

Karen felt overwhelmed. The case was testing her in ways
she hadn't been tested for a long time. There was so much
information to take in, but sifting through it was giving her
a headache.

Karen went on to discuss Munro and the insights she'd
gathered so far on that suspect. "Considering Munro likes
to add his own twist to his killing spree, maybe he's
copying Carson to a degree, and the email is his twist?"
Karen said, thinking back to her conversation with Kelly.

"That's a distinct possibility. It's almost impossible to copy a serial killer's MO to a tee. There will be certain slight nuances. Munro may have both psychopathic and socio-pathic tendencies, which cause him to switch direction in how he operates with little effort. If Munro carries both traits, then he would indeed be highly dangerous and an unpredictable individual." Bryant shrugged. "Perhaps that's why forces up and down the country have been unable to locate and capture him."

It wasn't what Karen wanted to hear.

Bryant interlocked his fingers on the table and leaned forward. "With the aid of EEGs and brain scans, scientists have recently discovered that psychopaths have significant impairments which affect their ability to feel emotions, read other people's cues, and learn from their mistakes." He paused as he took a sip of water. "They are often untreat-able. I can't stress enough just how *distinctive* such a group of individuals are. Coming face to face with them can be electrifying, if also unsettling. They lie and manipulate yet feel no compunction or regret."

"How are we supposed to find him? If he's well organised, methodical, and forensically aware, we are looking for someone who walks around wearing a Harry Potter invisi-bility cloak!" Karen said, blowing out her cheeks and staring at the ceiling. "And to top it off, he would appear normal."

"If I had to build a profile of this individual on the little I know, I would say he's a white male, of above-average intelligence, thirty to forty-five years old, and lives alone. He probably has a small social circle, and his victims prob-ably resemble someone from his past. An ex-partner, or his mother. There will be similar physical characteristics that pull him in at a subconscious level. I think he's a very complex individual and probably one of the most dangerous men you will ever meet."

Karen jotted down a few observations before looking up. "Do you think he hates women?"

"Possibly, but at a subconscious level. Something he's not aware of but a key driver behind his behaviour."

They spent the next thirty minutes going through further details surrounding the case, including a review of photographs from the crime scenes. Bryant offered his opinion. Karen listened and challenged, not intending to disagree with him, but to aid her own deeper understanding.

As Karen led Bryant back to reception, he was at pains to stress how difficult the challenge was they faced. "DCI, I remember a convicted rapist I once interviewed in Germany. A complete psychopath. In the interview, he described how he had kidnapped a woman, tied her to a tree in a forest, raped her for two days, then slit her throat and left her for dead. He told the story, then concluded with an unforgettable non sequitur. "Do you have a lady in your life?" he asked. "Because it's important to practise the three Cs—caring, communication and compassion. That's the secret to a good relationship. I try to practise the three Cs in all my relationships." He then explained how he'd abducted another three women and put them through the same ordeal. He spoke without hesitation, clearly unaware how bizarre this self-help platitude sounded after his awful confession."

Karen pressed her lips together. "Sounds like catching this man is going to be harder than I thought."

Bryant shook Karen's hand. "I'm heading back to the office now, so will get to work picking through my case notes."

56

KAREN LEFT WORK a few hours later and headed straight to Zac's. The meeting with Professor Bryant had left her more confused than ever. They were skirting around the edges of the investigation but struggling to grip on to anything with substance. But something about the sighting from the cyclists niggled her. Call it a gut instinct, but first thing tomorrow morning she would arrange for her officers to take the cyclist who had called in the sighting to the exact spot. *How close is it to the spot where Leah's body was found? Is he scouting the area as a potential site for disposing of a body?* Then a horrible thought flashed through her mind. *Can there be another undiscovered body at that location?*

Karen rang the doorbell and leaned against the door frame, her body tired and exhausted. She had hardly eaten all day and her brain felt frazzled.

"Oh my God, you look dreadful," Zac said as he opened the door. "Are you okay?"

Karen didn't have the energy to string a coherent sentence together. She shook her head. "I've had it today. Done. In." She stumbled through the doorway and dropped her bag before slipping off her jacket and hanging it on the newel post.

Zac swept her up in his arms and hugged her tight.

Karen buried her head in his chest and closed her eyes, feeling his heartbeat against her cheek. If she could fall asleep standing up, she would. It felt as if Zac was holding her up as her body loosened and her shoulders sagged.

"I've got some leftover spag bol. How about if I heat it up for you, and you can have a glass of red with it?" Zac suggested.

All Karen could do was nod as her eyes remained clamped tight. Her stomach grumbled.

"Plonk yourself on the sofa and I'll bring the food to you in a few minutes," Zac said, peeling himself away from Karen's grip and heading off to the kitchen.

Karen flopped on to the sofa and flipped her head back. The cushions swallowed her as her body relaxed. Every part of her ached as she heard the ping of the microwave in the background. "I don't want to go to work tomorrow," she muttered. "Why can't I win the lottery?"

"Here, get this down you. You look shattered." Zac placed a large glass of red on the coffee table in front of them and handed Karen a bowl and fork.

"Can't you feed me? My arms won't work," she groaned.

Zac laughed. "Bad day? Or shouldn't I ask?"

Karen shook her head as she willed her upper eyelids to open. "This case is slipping through my fingers."

"Well if you want to talk about it, I'm all ears. But I think you need to get some food inside you, drink this gorgeous Shiraz, have a shower, and get a good night's sleep. In that order."

She reached out and grabbed Zac's hand and squeezed it tight. "What have I done to deserve you? You're so good to me."

"I could say the same about you." He leaned in and kissed Karen before cupping her chin in his hand. "You're not alone now. We share the good and bad times. We pick each other up when we are down, and we laugh when times are good. That's what we do as a couple. And if you've had a shit day at work then I'm here for you. I want to take care of you, and I want you to be happy. One of these days you'll realise how much of an impact you've had on my life and Summer's."

Karen kissed him before sitting up and cupping the bowl in one hand. It was empty minutes later when she placed it back on the table and scooped up her glass of wine. Both hit the spot but made her even more sleepy.

"Thank you. I really needed this." Her eyes moistened as she looked at him, a wave of deep emotion washing over her. It felt like a hand was pushing against her chest, but it wasn't the feeling she associated with a panic attack, it was something else. A softer sensation which overwhelmed her. She wanted to cry tears of happiness. Floods of the stuff, but she didn't know why. Maybe it was a need to release the stress, anguish, and frustration of the day. She wasn't sure. It was a strange experience, one she had never felt before, like her heart and mind had been elevated to a higher plane.

"Are you okay?" Zac asked, throwing his arm around her shoulder and pulling her into him.

"Yeah. Sorry. I think it's been one of those days. And having you here… Well. I can't explain…"

"Shssh. No explanation needed. How about you grab a long hot shower and get into bed. I'll wash and tidy up and be up not long after."

Twenty minutes later, Karen was fast asleep, her head resting against Zac's hairy chest and her naked body pressed against his skin.

57

"MORNING," Jade said as she appeared in Karen's doorway. "You look bright and breezy. Did you sleep well?"

"Like a log. I went back to Zac's last night and could barely keep my eyes open. Bless him. He heated leftovers for me and gave me a glass of wine. Both disappeared in a matter of seconds. But I was just brain-dead. I had a shower and crashed out."

Jade laughed. "Hardly a romantic evening."

Karen smirked. "If he was hoping for anything more then he went to bed disappointed."

Jade took the chair opposite Karen. "What are you up to?"

"Don't laugh, but after talking to Professor Bryant I did some research into the careers and work commonly associated with those carrying the psychopathic trait. No idea why I looked, out of curiosity, I guess. Any idea what the number-one profession is for a psychopath?"

Jade narrowed her eyes and stared at an empty spot on the wall beside her. She shrugged. "I don't know. A shop owner."

"Wrong. According to a top Oxford University psychologist, the number-one job for a psychopath is a business executive. Followed by a lawyer, media personality, salesperson, and a surgeon or healthcare professional."

"A business executive?" Jade questioned as she folded her arms across her chest.

Karen nodded. "Yep, and after them come journalists, coppers, a religious person, chef or someone in the military."

"Ha. I knew coppers would come somewhere on the list. I've come across a few unhinged ones in my time. So, we could be looking for someone similar? It doesn't narrow the field does it?"

Karen had to agree. They needed something more tangible, and they needed evidence. A car caught on camera, a witness, bodily fluids or hair fibres. But they had drawn a blank on most fronts so far.

"Have you seen the latest online press articles?" Jade asked.

"Not yet. Dare I?"

"The press is going into overdrive about the two murders. All it's going to do is whip up fear. There's already talk on Facebook about setting up vigilante patrols at night to offer a visible deterrent. A female empowerment group is offering free rape alarms to anyone who contacts them. And we had an increase in the number of calls to the incident line putting forward names."

Karen groaned. She needed the press working for them not against them. It surprised her she hadn't heard from her intrepid reporter, Henry Beavis. But a thought sprang to mind. "I'll give Henry a call. He's desperate to get something off us. If I can get him to write a piece supporting our work and downplaying the fear element, it might help us."

"It's worth a try. The team is still going through CCTV obtained from all premises in and around the restaurant where Leah was. The footage helped us to track her across the city centre, though we haven't seen anyone trailing her on foot or by car. There were plenty of people around, but no one acting in an odd manner."

"I think we can probably rule out Joel Bartram," Karen commented. "He's got an alibi for one night. He was in the pub, and they've confirmed it by checking their own CCTV. However, he can't vouch for his movements after eleven p.m. on both nights. We know Leah was killed after nine p.m. if the positioning of her arms is anything to go by. So that leaves Ruth who was killed about three a.m. He wouldn't kill one and not the other."

"True."

"Anything from Bartram's apartment?" Karen asked.

"Nothing to further our case. However, officers from the robbery unit have been able to identify the owners of four mobile phones and the iPad. All stolen from residential burglaries. They are checking against forensics recovered from the scenes to see if any match Bartram. Oh, and his bed sheets had semen stains linked to him as well as other bodily fluids. There were long dark hair fibres recovered from his sofa and a hairbrush in his bedroom. None of them link back to Leah or Ruth."

"Looks like we can rule him out for the time being," Karen said.

Jade rose from her seat and stretched her arms above her head before letting out a yawn. "There's a remembrance vigil tonight on the steps of York Minster for Ruth and Leah. Preet is going to go along for a few minutes on her way home."

"That's good of her. Can you remind her if Henry Beavis is there, which no doubt he will be, she needs to give him a wide berth? I'll call Henry now." Karen said, grabbing her phone.

58

KAREN WAS deep in conversation with Henry Beavis when Jade dashed back into her office waving a sheet of paper.

Karen furrowed her brow in confusion, her lips forming an O. "Henry, something's come up. I'll have to call you back." Karen fell silent as she listened to Henry at the other end. "Yes, I know. That's why I was calling you. But Jade has just popped into my office with an urgent issue, so I'll call you back when I get a chance." Karen hung up and rolled her eyes as she stared at the screen for a second. "What's that?"

"We've had another email," Jade said, thrusting the single sheet of paper in Karen's direction.

Karen jumped up from her seat and snatched it from Jade's hand, her brow furrowing as she read the one line aloud. "I told you to stop me. It's too late." Karen jabbed a thumb into her temple and closed her eyes. "I don't get it. I'm confused. Is he reminding us about his last email or has there been another abduction?"

"Let me check," Jade said, grabbing Karen's desk phone.

While Jade was on the phone, Karen reread the message. It could only mean one thing. He had killed again.

Jade put down the phone. "No reports of another body being discovered, but they are dealing with a misper who didn't show up for work at one of her salons and isn't answering her mobile or her landline at home. Last seen Monday night leaving work. And there was an attempted abduction north of the city. A woman out jogging was attacked. She was approached by a hooded man who grabbed her around the neck and pull her into some bushes."

"Have we got a name for the misper?"

"Melody Faulkner. They are sending the details through to your computer now."

"And the attempted abduction?" Karen asked.

"Judith Turness, aged thirty-four, an event organiser. Officers have interviewed her, but the description of her attacker is vague. White male, medium build. Black clothing. There's a small open-air car park beyond the bushes which dog owners use. My guess he was parked there. Unfortunately, there's no CCTV, but SOCO are taking impressions of fresh tyre marks."

"Get a police notice put up in the car park asking for any information," Karen said before dropping back in her seat and wiggling her mouse to wake up the screen. It was a few moments before an email popped up in her inbox, and as she opened the attachment, she sighed in desperation. Melody bore more than a striking resemblance to Leah and Ruth. The same dark hair, pronounced cheekbones, and full lips. It would have been easy to mistake all three women for sisters.

"Shit. Melody Faulkner, aged thirty-four, single, owner of three successful hair and beauty salons in York, Leeds, and Harrogate. The wives of several Leeds United football players are frequent clients of her Leeds salon," Karen said.

"Knowing how quickly our perp has disposed of his victims, if Melody is one of them, it's likely we'll be searching for Melody's body," Jade said.

"Get a ping trace on her phone as a priority. Let's find out where she was last picked up. Any digital breadcrumb trail from the first email?"

"Someone used a VPN, a Virtual Private Network, to hide the message and sent it from a Gmail account," Jade explained. "The high-tech team said they can't trace the computer IP address using the email header because the email was sent behind a VPN which masked the IP address. Normally a device's Internet connection is routed through their ISP, their Internet Service Provider, but when they use a VPN, their connection is routed through a private server."

"I thought as much. We've dealt with crap like this back in London. As good as VPNs are, they make our job so much harder. The problem is we don't know who the user is so we can't get a court order to get their ISP to release data on usage logs and connection logs."

"I know, Karen. Even if the high-tech team could trace the computer IP address, we wouldn't be able to see the Google server, and no matter how hard we tried to request it from Google, they wouldn't give it to us partly because they would only have the details of the VPN service used, but everything behind it would be encrypted."

"What else do we know about Melody's disappearance?" Karen asked, grabbing her phone and heading towards the main floor to liaise with her team.

Jade followed on Karen's shoulder. "She lives on her own, and uniformed officers visited there yesterday evening. They also checked with neighbours. No one has seen her. A successful businesswoman who's built her business up from scratch. According to the manager of one of her branches, Melody was on the lookout for a fourth location and looking to open up an online store selling hair and beauty products. She was due to open up the York branch on Tuesday morning as contractors were due in to service the air conditioning system. The guys were left waiting an hour until other members of staff arrived."

"And that's when they tried to contact her?" Karen said, pushing through the main door.

"Yep. She was never late. A stickler for punctuality and timekeeping. The manager of the York salon called it in when Melody didn't answer either phone on Tuesday morning. Officers have confirmed Melody's white BMW X3 isn't at her address."

As Karen added Melody's name to the board and rallied her team around her, she instructed Jade to set up an alert for Melody's car on the ANPR system and check York Hospital admissions in case she'd been involved in an accident.

"Will do. I'll check with her manager of the York salon. It might help if we know if her X3 has a tracker fitted."

"Good shout, Jade," Karen replied, turning towards her team ready to brief them.

59

HE COULD HEAR Melody's frustrated sobs before he unlocked the door. The sound of metal scraping on metal brought a smile to his face as he heard her squeal.

"Please help. Help!" Melody screamed.

Turning the key in the lock, he opened the door and stood in the doorway, hands on hips. Her desperate pleas petered out when she realised her rescuers hadn't found her. Her sobs turned into hysteria as she fought to yank her wrist from the handcuffs securing her to the radiator.

He could tell she had been trying for ages to free herself. Welts and cuts to her wrist seeped blood, forming a sticky and shiny improvised bracelet as it congealed.

"Melody, as I've told you, you can scream as much as you want, but save your energy because no one is coming to save you. However, I have good news for you. You'll soon be joined by another, so you won't feel alone."

"Please, please stop. Don't hurt me." Her voice was deep, guttural, and desperate.

"Of course, I'm going to hurt you. I haven't brought you to this place on a sightseeing tour. These are the last four walls you will ever see," he said, fanning his arms out by his sides and looking around the dusty room. "It could do with a lick of paint, but this room carries meaning. It's where others like you pleaded to stop the noise in their heads."

Turning around, he picked up the chair and placed it in front of her and opened his white carrier bag, presenting her with a bottle of water, plastic of course, and a cheese roll which he unwrapped. Tearing off a piece, he offered the morsel to her mouth. She pursed her lips and turned away from him.

"Melody. That's not very nice. I'm trying to take care of you. You need to keep up your strength."

He offered the morsel to her mouth for a second time, and again, Melody closed her eyes, tightened her lips, and looked away. Tutting, he rose from his chair and grabbed the back of her hair with one hand, snapping her head back while jamming the small piece of roll into her mouth. With the heel of his hand, he pushed her jaw up to clamp her mouth shut. "Eat," he whispered in a calm tone, his face just a few inches away from hers.

Tears tumbled from Melody's eyes as snot dripped from her nose. Unable to chew because he was still pressing on her chin, she swallowed the piece whole and choked, coughing and spluttering the piece back into her mouth. Her eyes were a wild mixture of fear and sadness.

He pulled away, her final cough bringing up the piece of food and watery bile.

"You are a stubborn bitch. The world will be a much better place without you." He took a deep breath, held it for a few seconds, before releasing slowly, enjoying a sense of calm washing over him as he recentred. "Right, let's start again. I'll leave the roll here for you. I expect it to be gone when I return. If it's not, I will tie you down and clamp your jaws open before forcing it bit by bit down your throat whether or not you like it. I suspect you'll suffocate and choke to death. It isn't a nice way to go, especially when it's self-inflicted. So do yourself a favour and… eat… the roll."

Melody trembled with fear as she bum-shuffled back towards the wall and tucked her knees into her chest, wrapping her free arm around her shins.

"Understand?"

Melody's shoulders shook violently as she nodded once.

"Good. I'm glad you understand. I really don't want to be disappointed again. In fact, I have an even better idea for when I return. Rather than putting you through the harrowing experience of choking on a roll and going through the same palaver *every single* time," he rolled his eyes as he smiled, "I'll pull out every single one of your teeth with a pair of pliers."

Melody whimpered as a scream snagged in her throat. She clenched her hands into tight fists as she rocked back and forth.

He stood from his chair and crouched down beside her. Running his fingers through her dark hair, he sniffed a few of the locks before cupping her face in his hand. "You really are a thing of beauty even though the last few days have taken their toll on you. You're safe here with me. No one will find you, but all good things end one day. And for you, time is running out. You will share your last few hours on this earth in the company of another woman who is taking your place… Or am I just suggesting it to give you false hope?"

He smiled before standing to retrieve his carrier bag and car keys. The bucket he had left her remained empty. He tutted as he glanced back at her.

Melody's screams tore down the corridors and sounded like a demented soul trapped within the fabric of the building, begging to be released.

60

WITH CONCERN MOUNTING around Melody Faulkner's disappearance, Karen, Jade, and Ed headed to Melody's hair and beauty salon in Fossgate where they met Angie, the manager, hovering in the doorway.

Karen presented her warrant card before Angie led them to the office at the back of the salon. Angie had decided to close the salon after Melody's disappearance. *This is a stylish place*, Karen thought as she walked through the ground-floor unit. A plush seating area just off reception gave their customers an opportunity to relax either before or after their appointment, with a large espresso machine, a fridge stocked full of soft drinks, and a bowl of fresh fruit. Mirrored walls on either side gave the visual illusion of the salon being much larger than it was, but it was bright and airy in Karen's opinion.

Angie opened the door to Melody's office and invited the officers in first before she stepped in and close the door.

"Thank you for taking the time to see us." Karen checked her notes. "We understand the last time you saw Melody was on Monday night when she helped you to cash up and lock up?"

Angie chewed on her bottom lip and nodded. "Yes. She moves around all three branches but is here most of the time. She likes to have a hands-on approach with this branch because this was the first one she set up. It's her baby."

"Did she say where she was going after you locked up?" Karen asked.

"Off to the gym. She tries to go three or four times a week on her way home."

"Can we have the details, please?" Karen asked.

"Yes, she goes to Swift Fitness in town. Not far from here," Angie replied.

Karen nodded at Ed, who excused himself and went outside to contact the gym. "Does she have a partner?"

Angie shook her head. "Think she would like to, but she's a busy woman. I honestly don't think she would have enough time to devote to a relationship, and she has told me it wouldn't be fair to any bloke."

"Has anything happened at the salon that has caused her concern? Any financial difficulties?" Karen asked.

"No. All three salons are debt-free and super-successful. Melody had paid off her bank loans and was looking to take out another loan to fund the purchase of a fourth salon." Angie folded her arms across her chest and placed one foot over the other as her eyes moved around the officers.

"Did she mention anything about anyone following her, or any uncomfortable situations which she found herself in?"

"No."

"Have you noticed anyone lurking around outside in recent days?"

"Not as far as I'm aware. I can check with the other members of staff for you?" Angie replied.

"Yes, please." Karen retrieved a card from her purse and handed it to Angie. "You can call me on this number. I think we have all we need for the moment. Thank you for your time, Angie." Karen and Jade filed out of the small office and met Ed before heading back towards the car.

FIFTEEN MINUTES later they were outside Melody's house in Badger Hill. It was a pleasant neighbourhood to the east of town and only two miles from their station, with the sprawling York University campus sandwiched between the two locations.

"I've got a bad feeling about this. Melody fits the victim profile both in looks and career," Karen said as she stepped out of the car and made her way down the path to Melody's front door in Sails Drive. It was a stylish and slick new development of detached dwellings with small grass-fronted drives bordered by hedges.

"Me too," Jade replied, looking up and down the street.

Karen had called control to ask for a locksmith to meet
them there. After knocking and checking the rear of the
property, she had given the locksmith the go-ahead to gain
entry through the front door. Within ten minutes, Karen and
her team stood in the hallway and announced their presence. There were none of the usual smells of a dead body
or signs of a disturbance. The house was silent, clean, and
empty.

"Jade, you and Ed check upstairs. I'll check the ground
floor."

Karen moved from the hallway into the through-lounge. It
was spotless. Cream walls and carpets, a grey sofa, and a
huge TV sat on a low-level chest of drawers. The kitchen
was equally impressive and spanned the entire width of the
house with floor-to-ceiling bifold doors which opened on to
the garden.

"Nothing upstairs," Jade said as she met Karen in the
kitchen. "I've bagged up a hairbrush and her toothbrush,
just in case."

Karen nodded as she looked around the kitchen, running
her fingers across the large black marble island positioned
in the middle.

"Do you think he has her?" Ed asked as he looked out over
the garden.

"I hope not. Let's head back. I need a word with the super,"
Karen said as a ball of anxiety tightened in her chest. After
her last conversation with Kelly, she dreaded breaking the
news that the killer may have struck again. But without a
body, Karen still held on to the hope Melody was alive.

61

Detective Superintendent Laura Kelly glared at Karen. "When I said we needed a result, I didn't mean the news of another suspected abduction!" Kelly fumed, slapping her hand on the desk. "Christ."

"It wasn't the news I wanted either, ma'am."

"Okay. What do we know so far?" Kelly asked, returning to her seat.

"Melody Faulkner, owner of three high-end hair and beauty salons. Last seen Monday evening, and no one has heard from her since. We are running a trace on her phone, and we've been to her house. There appears to be no sign of a disturbance or anything to suggest she has come to harm. Jade found Melody's bank statements upstairs in her study, so we are contacting her bank to find out if her card has been used since Monday."

"ANPR?"

"We've run her plates through the system. Nothing yet. Hopefully, she has been picked up somewhere which can help us in building a timeline of her last known movements."

Karen discussed the probability of the two emails received as being genuine, and for the time being agreed with Kelly they needed to assume they were even though it didn't mirror Carson's behaviour during his reign.

Kelly glanced around her room as she processed the situation. "The minute this gets out it's going to cause panic. We have a major threat on our hands. Women aren't safe walking the streets until we catch this shitbag. I'm going to put in a request to have all leave cancelled for the next forty-eight hours and arrange for a stronger and visible police presence in town to reassure the public."

"I think we need to put out a press appeal for sightings of Melody," Karen suggested. "We can keep it general and explain Melody's absence is out of character for her, and we urge her to come forward and get help. We can also throw in the line of asking members of the public to stay vigilant for her and contact us if they have any sightings."

Kelly sighed. "That will be like stirring up a hornet's nest but based on the current situation it's a good idea. I'll contact the press team so they can put out a bulletin."

With every hour being crucial, Karen made her excuses and dashed back to the team. A wall of noise greeted Karen as she pushed through the double doors on to the main floor. Many of her officers were on the phones chasing down every scrap of information they could find.

"Anything yet?" Karen asked, stopping by Belinda's desk.

"Nothing so far, Karen. She has over a ninety thousand followers on her Insta page, over four thousand friends on her Facebook personal profile, and just over eleven hundred followers on her business Facebook page."

"Those numbers are just too big for us," Karen said, scrunching her nose. She turned to Ed. "Anything from Swift Fitness?"

"Yes, they've sent over video footage from their reception area. Melody was seen entering at seven-nineteen p.m. and leaving at eight forty-three p.m."

"Did anyone follow her out?"

"No. The next person to leave the gym was another female, nine minutes later. They don't have any CCTV covering the gym car park."

"Karen," Jade shouted to get Karen's attention. "Melody's X3 didn't have a tracker as far as we can tell. We are still checking with other providers, but a GPS car tracker is accurate, often down to within one to three metres of its location, but we have a ping location on her phone which last placed her in and around the Hull Road area."

Karen stepped over towards a large map of the city centre and found Hull Road. "She was on her way home."

Jade agreed. "We've been in contact with city control, and they spotted her vehicle on several of their cameras. They are sending it through to us."

"Great, let's head to the video room and grab a coffee on the way."

62

KAREN WAS on her second cup of coffee as she waited for the footage to arrive from the council video control room.

"Anyone would think the recording was being sent over from the other side of the world," Karen said, draining the last bitter remnants of her coffee and throwing the empty paper cup into the recycling bin.

"They clearly have a different definition of urgent to us," Jade said as she swivelled around in circles on the computer chair.

"Please stop! You're making me dizzy looking at you," Karen said with a shake of her head.

"Oh, come on. Everyone enjoys doing this. Go on, try it. You'll realise what you've been missing."

"I don't think so, Jade. When you've finished playing in the playground, we can have a chat about you needing to grow up," Karen said, throwing Jade a wink.

Another two hours passed before the footage came through. By then, Karen had already returned to her office to carry on reviewing the case notes before dashing back down to the video room. Squeezed around the monitor with Jade and Bel, Karen crammed in alongside them. They began by watching the council footage of Melody's white BMW X3 being picked up as she left the city centre. The registration plate triggered ANPR alerts during her journey.

Karen jotted down a few points knowing this was the last journey and the last time Melody had been seen alive. The gravity of the situation wasn't lost on her. She only hoped Melody was being held captive, but with their killer having only kept Ruth and Leah for hours before disposing of their bodies, she was bracing herself for the prospect they were looking for a third body.

Melody's car travelled along Hull Road, stopping for a few moments before setting off again and taking a left and turning off on to a side road.

"Is that it? Have we lost her?" Karen asked.

Belinda shook her head. "Hold on a moment. She reappears. There!" Bel pointed out, poking her finger at the screen.

They watched as Melody appeared from a side turning and walked the short distance to a cashpoint outside a small convenience store, called King's. Karen checked the time. Three minutes past nine. From the placement of the camera, it was hard to tell if anyone was observing her from across the street and there didn't appear to be anyone else lurking. A few customers popped in and out of the store while Melody was at the cashpoint. Melody then headed into King's herself before reappearing nineteen minutes later carrying a plastic carrier bag. She glanced up and down the road before heading off in the direction of where she had left her car.

"Bel, we need any CCTV footage from inside the store in case anyone followed her around the aisles."

"I'll call them after this," Belinda replied.

Three other women and two men left King's minutes after Melody but appeared to head off in different directions, with no one heading in the same direction as her. Karen made a note to get their images blown up for reference in case they were needed as part of an ongoing press appeal.

"What's the name of that side street?" Karen asked.

"Siward Street," Bel replied.

"That's minutes from her house. We have to assume our perp lay in wait for her," Karen commented. She was about to continue when Ty burst into the room.

"Melody might still be alive!" he said out of breath, as he handed Karen a sheet of paper.

There were three words in the body of the email. Karen read them out aloud. "She's still breathing."

63

KAREN SCRAMBLED every available officer to the area within minutes of receiving the email. She needed to take it seriously even though the sender was still unknown. Efforts by the high-tech team to identify an IP address had failed so far. With the suspect hidden behind the VPN, their task was almost impossible.

A long line of marked and unmarked police cars came to a halt outside King's convenience store. Traffic slowed in both directions. Pedestrians stopped and stared out of curiosity. A few young lads on bikes whipped out their phones and began recording the commotion, which would no doubt appear on TikTok or Instagram within minutes.

Karen gathered her officers in a large group around her. "Break up into pairs and start searching the area. One team will knock on every single door between the convenience store and Siward Street, the other team will focus on Siward Street," Karen said. "I know it's late, and there'll be residents who are getting ready for bed, but keep trying them, and the ones who don't answer we can try again first thing in the morning. We want any sightings of Melody Faulkner or any suspicious activity. Okay?"

Her officers nodded.

"It could be a car that's been cruising up and down this road. It could be an unidentified male lurking in the shadows beneath trees, in gardens, or in between houses. Make a note of anyone who has CCTV or a Ring doorbell. Once we've conducted our first sweep, I want you to go back to all those houses and obtain a copy of the footage. I've got a box of spare memory sticks in my boot, so grab yourself one."

Jade handed out a picture of Melody to every officer.

"Get the image in front of as many eyes as possible," Karen barked as passing traffic drowned out her voice.

The officers dispersed in all directions, a sense of urgency in their steps as they hurried away.

Karen and Jade entered King's convenience store. A few late-night shoppers strolled up and down the aisles picking up last-minute items. Karen went to the till point and saw a middle-aged Asian man standing behind the Perspex screen, probably mid- to late-forties, balding on top, thick black-rimmed glasses, wearing a loose black baggy polo shirt which looked three sizes too big for him.

"York police," Karen said, pressing her warrant card up against the Perspex screen. The man narrowed his eyes as he flipped his glasses on to his forehead and leaned in to take a closer look. "Do you recognise this lady? She came into your store on Monday evening shortly after nine p.m."

The man grimaced. "We have lots of customers. Many regulars. But sorry, I don't recognise her," he replied in a thick Indian accent.

"Please look again. We are concerned for her safety."

He gave the image a cursory glance before shaking his head again.

Karen tutted. She glanced over the man's shoulder and spotted a CCTV camera looking down at the till point. "Is that working?"

"Of course. Me and my wife are here seven days a week. At this time of night, it's very dangerous. Boys come in and hold up a knife or try to steal things."

"How far does it go back?" Karen asked.

"Thirty-day rolling period," he replied in a dry and flat monotone voice.

"Right, we'll need a copy. I'll send an officer in a few minutes," she said, before turning and heading for the front door. Karen grabbed the first available officer she saw and told them to grab a copy of the CCTV footage from Monday night.

Karen spent the next thirty minutes checking in with officers as she walked up and down Hull Road. So far, their enquiries had been less than encouraging. Karen knew she was clutching at straws. Had Melody visited the cashpoint and King's in the middle of the day, the outcome would have been different with many more sightings.

Static on Karen's radio had her pulling it out of her jacket. Officers had located Melody's BMW X3 further down the road. Karen raced down the road with Jade in tow, out of breath by the time she turned into Siward Street. Another fifty yards down on the right was a small open-air car park. Several officers were walking around the BMW, shining the torch from their phones into the cabin.

"Anything?" Karen shouted as she approached them.

Dan shook his head before getting down on his hands and knees to shine the light from his phone underneath the car.

A uniformed officer with him pointed the beam from his torch into the front passenger seat. "Nothing appears to be disturbed inside the car, ma'am."

Karen came and stood beside him, leaning in to take a closer look. Though it was dark, it appeared spotless inside. "Can you arrange for this to be put on a low-loader and recovered for forensic examination? Has anyone touched it?"

The officer shook his head. "No ma'am. We didn't want to disturb any evidence."

Karen stepped away from the vehicle and rested her hands on her hips as she looked around the area. A row of houses overlooked the car park. Officers were on the doorsteps making enquiries. There had to be CCTV or a Ring door-bell from one of those properties in the area.

"Melody was abducted from this spot. She could have been taken anywhere after this," Jade remarked.

"I know. She's just disappeared. There's hope still. I pray the email is genuine," Karen replied.

64

THE SMELL of warm croissants and coffee filled the main floor. Karen had ordered a massive morning delivery to gee up the team.

Tiredness and a lack of sleep had left their mark on the team as they pulled their weary bodies from their chairs and gathered around the whiteboard. Constant yawning, unshaven faces, and bleary eyes told Karen everything she needed to know. The team had worked through the night, and from what Karen could see, some hadn't gone home for a change of clothes, choosing to stay for the team meeting before heading home to get a few hours' sleep.

A search of the local area had continued all night. There had been no further sightings and little in the way of witness statements. CCTV and Ring doorbell footage from eleven houses were being studied. Their efforts hadn't gone unrewarded when one of the search officers found an expensive cream silk scarf beneath a car close by. It appeared new other than a few torn threads at the end, which Karen put down to foxes or cats. It was with forensics and being fast-tracked to be compared against the hair-brush taken from Melody's bedroom.

Kelly had demanded an update first thing this morning, which Karen had only just returned from as she took her place at the front of the room.

"Thank you for your hard work last night. I know everyone is shattered, but we need to stay positive. The day shift will carry on with the video analysis and all our main enquiries, but everyone who was up last night and helping with the search needs to go home. But before you do, let's have a quick catch-up," Karen said, her request met with plenty of nods.

"We've been through the details of all sex offenders registered in the York area and visited those of interest, but we haven't found anyone with the right MO," Ty started.

Sitting beside Ty, Ed nodded in agreement. "I began by checking prisoner release records for the last twelve months. Again, nothing matched our profile. I expanded the search to the past five years. Zilch."

"Anything from our press conferences?" Karen asked.

"We had a few calls to the incident hotline from concerned partners who thought their husbands or boyfriends were behaving suspiciously," Claire said.

"In what way?"

"Suddenly hiding their phones, going out at unusual hours, coming home and being elusive about where they were. We followed up on all those enquiries and ran searches on those individuals to see if any had earlier convictions. Other than one having two convictions for speeding, one for possession of class B, and another charged with shoplifting seventeen months ago, they were clean and didn't fit the profile of our suspect."

That reminded Karen she needed to call the professor to get his input. Turning to Bart Lynch, the CSI manager, who had joined them and sat towards the back of the team she asked, "Any further developments on the hair fibre found on Leah's clothing? You said it's not on the system, but were you able to do anything else with it?"

"I'm afraid not, Karen. I've got the DNA profile. Give me suspects to match it against."

"We are trying, mate. Not even the slightest match to Joel Bartram or Howard Rutland-Pym? Or is that hoping for too much of a lucky break?"

Bart offered her a sympathetic smile. "We analysed the nail scrapings from both victims and found remnants of soil samples that matched the areas where their bodies were discovered. Leah's body had nothing else, but we found a tiny thread caught beneath the thumb and first two fingers on the right hand of Ruth Tate."

Karen's heart quickened as she clasped her hands together as if praying for divine intervention in the hope of a miracle. The room fell silent as they hung on Bart's every word.

"We sent it off for analysis as we don't have that capability in-house. The result came through yesterday evening. As far as we can tell, the fibre was SMS."

Karen pinched her nose and closed her eyes for a few seconds as a wave of tiredness washed over her like a heavy cloak, dragging her shoulders down. "What does that mean?"

"SMS stands for spunbond meltblown spunbond, a tri-laminate non-woven fabric. It's made of the top layer of spunbond polypropylene, a middle layer of meltblown polypropylene, and a bottom layer of spunbond polypropylene again," Bart replied.

Karen raised a brow and blinked hard, her focus waning by the minute. "You've lost me. Plain English please."

"It's a breathable fabric with great water-repellent capabilities. It's what you'd find in surgical gowns, sterilisation wraps, disposable patient sheets, nappies, incontinence products, and coveralls like the Tyvek suits we use."

The penny dropped as Karen clicked her fingers. She saw the same realisation dawn on the faces of her officers. "That's why he hasn't left any forensic trace evidence. He's been wearing a coverall, and probably gloves and booties as well. Shit. Carson didn't leave any evidence, and maybe that was down to luck, but our perp has evolved Carson's approach and taken advantage of modern-day technology, equipment, and clothing to stay one step ahead of us."

Bart agreed. "It's difficult to tear. My guess is she put up a fight and scraped her nails across the fabric picking up one solitary thread."

"Thanks, Bart. That's fantastic. Listen team, we stay focused and positive. While there is a chance Melody is alive, we don't stop until we find her!"

65

KAREN DIALLED the professor's number as she headed back to her office.

"Detective chief inspector, it's a pleasure to hear from you. How are you getting on?"

"So-so. One step forward, two steps back. We've had a report of another missing female. We believe she was abducted on Monday evening."

"Ah, not good news. I'm sorry to hear that. And her body?"

"We haven't found her. Melody Faulkner could still be alive." Karen updated the professor on the emails.

"Have you been able to confirm if the emails are authentic and sent by your perpetrator?" Bryant asked.

"We haven't. I'm assuming they are. Equally, they could be a wind-up. Whoever sent them has cloaked their IP address."

"And does Melody Faulkner fit the victim profile of his earlier two victims?" he asked.

"On paper, she does. Very similar facial features and a successful businesswoman. Melody is his type. What are your thoughts on it?" There was silence at the other end of the line, but Karen heard Bryant's breathing.

"My first is that it may not be your perpetrator. Let me explain why. Carson never kept his victims longer than a few hours. Based on the information we have, it seems Ruth and Leah were held captive for only a few hours before they were killed and disposed of. Following the same pattern, Melody Faulkner would have been dead for at least two days already. I'm afraid you might be looking for a body."

Karen stepped into her office and walked over to the window, staring out across the lush green grass and trees which appeared so inviting. She dragged her mind away from the thought of being able to walk barefoot across the grass while listening to the birds in the trees.

"I'm not prepared to entertain the idea at the moment, professor. Yes, it could be a wind-up merchant getting a kick out of sending these emails. The thought of Melody lying in the middle of dense woodland or in a grassy verge is something I'm keen to push to the back of my mind. We have to stay hopeful."

"That's understandable and wise."

"Ideally, I wanted to call you in to discuss this face to face, but time isn't on our side, hence the reason for my call."

"Sure. Sure. Yes, it would be better, but we can do this over the phone. What do you need from me?" he asked.

"If we work on the assumption she is alive, then she is being held somewhere. Where are the likely places our perpetrator might hold Melody?"

"DCI, you need to find somewhere personal to him. He is a solitary individual, so he needs to be somewhere where he feels safe. He needs to be somewhere he won't feel exposed, such as a family home. However, living in a family home could make him too vulnerable to his neighbours. Alternatively, he could choose a former workplace or an abandoned building where he won't be seen or disturbed."

"Out of those, what would be the most likely hiding place for him?" Karen asked.

"He has to find a safe place where he and his victims cannot be found, like an abandoned house or building in a remote area. It must be secure so Melody can't escape. It needs to be a place where he can leave her and head off to work and act normally. Because a psychopath can't see any wrong in their behaviour, he could be working at this very minute in a shop, factory, or office. The next person who brushes past you could be carrying deep, disturbed psychopathic tendencies. Normal on the outside, deadly on the inside."

"Remote, safe, secure. Got it. God, this is so frustrating. We have so little to go on."

"Your perpetrator is a copycat. If he idolises Carson's work. He wants to eat, live, sleep, and breathe Carson's world. Yes, some of his behaviour hasn't mirrored Carson's MO completely, and often most copycats can't achieve that. With that in mind, he will be familiar with the places which meant a lot to Bruce Carson. And where possible, he may incorporate those into his plans."

Karen stood tall and pulled her shoulders back as her mind went into overdrive. Images flashed through at a rate of knots of the original case files on the Tick-Tock Man. The statements, pictures, and facts. Random pieces of the jigsaw were being dragged from different corners of her mind. She just needed to make sense of them. "Bruce Carson was a site foreman at a construction company and moved around several of their locations during his career before being laid off as they suffered financial difficulties. The company closed, and the sites were left abandoned and still are to this day. His victims were murdered at those spots. Our man may take his victims to one of those sites."

"That's plausible," he replied. "Or any other large, remote, abandoned, buildings close by."

"That's perfect, professor. I need to go as I've a message I need to review. I'll be in touch," Karen said, before hanging up abruptly and dashing back to the main floor.

66

KAREN'S DECISION had paid off to place a police notice in the car park close to where the attempted abduction of Judith Turness occurred. Though embarrassed, a courting couple had called in to mention that they had seen a man acting suspiciously at the far end of the car park. At first, they thought he was a dogger because he came close to their car, then he walked off into the trees and bushes. Spooked, the couple left moments later.

He stood beside what they described as a tatty VW two-tone blue and white camper van. Though Gabby had mentioned a blue and grey camper van, in the dark, white may have come off as grey.

Buoyed by the news, Karen had informed Gabby and immediately ordered a tracker dog to the scene and requested the help of NPAS, the National Police Air Serivce, to conduct a sweep looking for a heat source in the woodland area beyond the car park.

The feedback so far from officers at the scene was less than encouraging. If it was Munro, he'd long gone. But it raised concern in Karen's mind. Munro might have landed on her patch, and he was more dangerous than most suspects she'd dealt with.

With some of the team holding back to continue with the review of CCTV footage from properties close to where Melody Faulkner's car was discovered, Karen set off with the rest of her officers to the former address for TJH Construction, where Carson was once a site foreman.

The location took them north out of town until they arrived at a remote spot at the end of a lane which, judging by the overgrown verges and broken tarmac, had seen little traffic over the years. Karen was in the lead car, followed by three pool cars carrying Belinda, Jade, Preet and Ty, along with a few uniformed officers for backup. As they all exited the vehicles, they gathered by the gated entrance. Karen glanced through the rusty, tall, black gates to a derelict building beyond, with nothing in between them other than overgrown grass and weeds that had buried any signs of a road. In the middle of a rich and diverse green landscape stood this eyesore.

"It looks like someone's been here before," Karen said, pointing towards the broken chain once used to secure the gates together, which now hung from their frame, the padlock discarded on the floor.

"It's exchanged hands several times over the years. Various developers have submitted plans, but nothing came of it each time because of council objections. Some wanted to turn the site into an exclusive residential development, while others wanted to build a business centre," Belinda offered.

"Could be urban explorers?" Belinda suggested. "They love breaking into places like this and putting pictures and videos on their Instagram pages."

"We'll soon find out," Karen said, removing the chain and pushing the gates open wide enough for her team to squeeze through. The gates squealed on their rusty hinges and brushed against the overgrown weeds and grass.

Someone had torn the main door from its hinges, and it now hung precariously with only a few screws left. Karen instructed a few officers to scour the grounds and emphasised the need to stay in pairs and maintain radio communication, while the rest entered the dark and dusty building with her. Graffiti lined the walls, and discarded beer cans littered the floor. Karen kicked one accidentally, its metallic clang echoing around them as it skimmed along the floor and made everyone jump.

A corridor branched off to both her left and right from the main hallway. Karen sent Belinda and Ty with two uniformed officers down the left-hand corridor, four uniformed officers up the stairs to search the first floor, while Jade and Preet joined her searching the rooms of the right-hand corridor. Despite the warmth outside, an icy chill tickled Karen's neck. With the windows boarded up on the ground floor, a darkened gloom enveloped them. Years of neglect and decay had left a damp, stale mustiness that wasn't revolting, but more unpleasant. Paper and boxes lay scattered across the floor in each room.

"Shit!" Karen screamed, when a scurrying, tapping sound and a high-pitched noise broke the silence in one room they had entered. Her scream only made Jade and Preet do the same as they all jumped backwards unprepared for what it might be.

A large rat appeared from behind a box and raced along the edge of one wall before disappearing in a heap of clothing further along.

"Jesus, that was the size of a cat!" Jade squealed as her body shivered.

"Bit of an exaggeration, Jade," Karen groaned, tucking her balled fists into her chest.

"Says the woman who bloody screamed and nearly gave me a heart attack," Jade replied.

"It's a large heap of clothing. Who's going to have a look?" Karen asked.

Jade and Preet had already taken a few steps back towards the doorway leaving the solitary figure of Karen standing in the middle of the room.

Karen glanced over her shoulder and groaned again. "Seriously?"

Jade shrugged. "You're the boss. You have a duty of care for your officers. And if we're too scared and fearing for our safety, you need to lead by example."

Karen narrowed her eyes in the dark gloom as she stared at Jade. "I don't recall reading that in any police manual."

"There could be a body under that," Jade said as Karen tentatively stepped towards the pile.

The thought stopped Karen dead in her tracks. She let out a deep sigh. "Thanks for that, Jade. I was trying to push the thought from my mind." Karen paused, mustering up the courage to step forward. It took a few moments before she was within touching distance. With the tip of her shoe, she pushed away a few items, bracing herself. Kicking away more clothes, the pile collapsed, spreading them across the floor. Karen jumped back in shock and anticipation. Nothing.

"Clear," Karen said.

"Where's the rat?" Jade asked, taking a few steps forward with Preet over her shoulder.

"There must be a hole somewhere. It's more scared of us than we are of it," Karen said.

Jade raised a brow. "Speak for yourself. They are just horrible, and the fat rat's tail, yuck!"

They continued searching the rest of their corridor before returning to the main entrance where they met up with the rest of the officers. The search had turned up nothing. There was no evidence of anyone being held captive, though there was plenty to suggest people had been here as magazines had been found upstairs dated from six weeks ago.

It wasn't the result Karen hoped for. But perhaps the primary site was too obvious in her mind. Their perpetrator was methodical in his approach, in much the same way Carson was. Their suspect would have assumed the police would look here first.

Karen pulled out a sheet of paper from her pocket as her team gathered around her.

"TJH Construction had three smaller sites. I suggest we split up. We'll be able to cover the sites quicker. Jade, call in extra resources to meet us at those sites. Make sure they are taser trained. It would be helpful if we can get a few

AFOs to assist us. I want you to all be extra vigilant. Stay in pairs, keep comms open. Remember, this is a very dangerous individual. Let's go." Though the help of authorised firearms officers may have appeared a bit of an overkill, Karen wasn't prepared to take any chances.

67

KAREN HAD CHOSEN the second of the three sites to visit. Less than three miles away, it was the largest of the three locations and, for that reason, she had put in a request for more officers.

"It would be good to eliminate all three sites," Jade said, sitting in the passenger seat of Karen's car as it travelled along the country lanes.

Karen agreed in part with Jade's thoughts. "Yes and no. If we find nothing, it rules out one thread of our enquiry, but it leaves us with more questions than answers. Where else would our perpetrator take them?" She slowed behind a tractor trundling along the narrow lane, whipping up a storm of dust in its wake.

Karen's phone rang on the speakerphone system. Professor Bryant's name popped up on the screen.

"Hello, professor," Karen said, raising her voice to be heard over the loud tractor in front of them.

"Oh, DCI. Am I disturbing you? It sounds very loud there."

"No, it's fine. We are out and about visiting the former sites of TJH Construction. I thought about what you said regarding Carson. There is a possibility our copycat could take his victims to one of those former sites. We've just left the main building and are heading to a few of their satellite sites."

"Did you find anything at the first location?" Bryant asked.

"Nothing," Karen said, throwing a look in Jade's direction, and using her fingers to imitate the running of little legs.

Jade rolled her eyes and stared out the passenger window.

"Something else came to mind as a potential location your copycat might be using. Bruce Carson stayed in a former psychiatric hospital during his twenties. It's now derelict, closed many years ago. That's another possibility for you based on our earlier discussion."

Jade and Karen glanced at each other, confusion etched on their faces.

"Really? There's nothing in his records or case files to suggest he was treated at the loony bin," Karen remarked.

"You're correct. There are no records of it. He self-referred. From the beginning, he calculated his moves very carefully. I believe he had chosen his path long before then, but at that age was struggling to cope with the psychotic and psychiatric disturbances he was experiencing. Rather than bring his troubles to the attention of his doctor or health authorities he self-referred and paid for treatment himself."

"I don't get it, professor. Why wouldn't he have revealed that during his interviews?" Karen asked.

"Simple really. It was all about power from the very beginning. He established a reign of terror, he chose to conduct himself in a certain way during police interviews, and he has been behaving in a certain way since he got incarcerated. He didn't want to show any sign of weakness. That would have been out of character for his personality. It was a condition he chose to self-manage. He first attended High Royds Hospital, a former psychiatric hospital south of the village of Menston in West Yorkshire, but when they began asking too many questions, he discharged himself."

Karen listened, dumbfounded. How had Carson kept this under the radar for so long? "Professor, how did you hear about this?"

"He opened up confidentially in one of my interviews. Said that he had faced a few challenges and had tried to seek help, unsuccessfully. He trusted me enough to tell me and by then his reign of terror was over and he couldn't harm anyone while in prison."

Karen thumped the heel of her hand on the steering wheel and sighed.

"Anyway, he was treated for a short while at Banstead Hall Hospital, a former mental asylum, which has again been closed for many years. Bruce Carson took his last victim there as he knew the grounds well. He said it was his special, safe place."

Jade checked the location on her phone while Karen was speaking. "It's about fifteen minutes away from here."

"Okay. Thanks, professor. We'll head there now." Karen hung up. "Jade, get on to control and tell them we're taking a detour there. Arrange for the extra officers to meet us on that site. And get the team to find out anything they can on

High Royds Hospital. Former patients, staff, layouts of the building, everything."

A short while later, Karen pulled up alongside an entrance to the former Banstead Hall Hospital which sat in extensive grounds. Ringed by wire fencing with red signs telling the public to keep out and the presence of twenty-four-hour patrols, it seemed better protected than the earlier site they had visited. With her officers gathered by the entrance, they used a set of bolt croppers to cut through the chain holding the two large wrought-iron carriage gates together before driving the short distance to the cluster of buildings further down the long drive.

"It's a big place," Jade remarked, craning her neck to look up towards a tall building in front of them.

Three stories high, with large windows, it looked more like an expensive public school in its heyday than a Victorian built asylum. A central main tower poked up above the building with its tiled belfry atop housing a single bell. It was both impressive and chilling.

Karen looked around the grounds. *No sign of a camper van, could Munro be around here?* she wondered. Other than the main building, which was substantial in size, three other large buildings sat shoulder to shoulder with it, connected by ground-floor walkways and the remnants of a canopy which would have protected people in inclement weather as they moved between the buildings. Several other outbuildings were dotted around the grounds.

With over twenty officers at her disposal, Karen set about dividing them into small groups to search the grounds and buildings, while she entered the one in front of them with

Ty, Jade, and several uniformed officers. Before they started, she made it very clear that if they came across Munro, he was to be approached with caution.

68

THE BUILDING'S interior was cavernous as Karen entered and stood in the large reception area. The tall ceiling added to the expansive feel. A large, ornate staircase snaked up the wall in front of them and the original geometric terra-cotta floor tiles reminded visitors of its Victorian elegance. It could have once passed for a high-end hotel which welcomed guests into its large and salubrious surroundings, but now it was a shadow of its former self. With the once grand structure left to the elements and legal wranglings, particles of dust floated in the air, discarded food wrappers and empty beer cans littered the floor, graffiti marked the walls, and the faint smell of bodily excrement, human or otherwise, assaulted the nostrils.

There was no other option but to split her team while remaining in pairs. She sent Ty with one uniformed officer and Jade with another. A further two uniformed officers were dispatched in search of the basement, while Karen and her officer, PC Darren Cane, headed to the second floor. The stairs creaked underfoot as Karen made her way on to the first-floor landing, watching officers disappear down the labyrinth of corridors, as she continued to the next floor.

It was dark and dusty as she stood contemplating which of the three corridors to tackle first. "Let's take this one on the right," Karen said, heading for the first doorway off it. She snapped on a pair of latex gloves before trying the door handle. The door opened, its rusty hinges squealing to announce her arrival. Empty. She continued down the corridor, with PC Cane across the hallway.

"Anything?" she asked.

Cane shook his head.

Karen's phone rang in her pocket which startled her. Pulling it out, she checked the screen. It was Claire back in the office.

"Hi, Claire."

"Hi, Karen. How are you getting on?"

"We've just arrived at Banstead Hall Hospital and are beginning our search. Any news on the aerial and ground search at the abduction site?"

"Lots to update you on. NPAS have picked up a few heat sources in the woods and are directing officers on the ground to those locations. It's not easy underfoot with lots of overgrown bushes, shrubs and exposed tree roots. It's pretty dense."

A rush of excitement still hit Karen hard, even though they didn't know the specific nature of the heat sources. But again, thinking back to what Gabby had said, Munro had taken to hiding in the woodlands to avoid detection.

If he was the suspect in the car park, he could be close by. "Right, keep me informed. We can drop everything here and make our way to you if there are possible sightings."

"Understood. Also, the dog picked up a human scent, and officers are tracking it at the moment. It's probably nothing because it's a popular area with dog walkers and the dogging community... I mean the human kind." Claire laughed.

"Yes, it might be a dead end. But if it is Munro, then he can't be far," Karen said.

She was about to hang up when Claire stopped her. "Oh, Karen. Hang on a sec."

Karen waited while Claire talked to someone back in the office.

"Sorry, Karen. City CCTV control called a moment ago. They picked up a camper van matching the description three hours ago. It was snapped on camera two miles north of your location doing fifty in a thirty."

"Travelling away or towards?"

"Towards your direction," Claire said.

Karen thanked Claire before informing everyone to be extra vigilant.

The further they continued down the corridor, the darker it became. It felt like something out of a horror movie as chills of coldness crept up her spine. Once white walls were now dusty and grey, fine particles tickling her nose. Karen stopped in her tracks when she heard a noise. She couldn't make it out to begin with but signalled to PC Cane to get his attention. He came alongside her and paused, tuning into the noise.

The noise stopped for a few seconds before she heard it again. Perhaps the faint sound of whimpering. She narrowed her eyes as she looked at Cane who looked perplexed. "Trapped animal?"

Cane offered nothing more than a shrug.

Karen continued down the hallway, her steps slower and more cautious as she searched for the source. The corridor felt as if it was narrowing, the doors on either side closing in on her. She stopped towards the far end and stood outside a large ornate door. The sound came again. Karen nodded at Cane who withdrew his extendable baton and flicked it open, placing it across his shoulder ready to strike. Karen's heart thundered in her chest. Her mouth was so dry and parched from both anticipation and the clouds of dust. Karen tried the handle but found it locked. With something on the other side, she needed to get in fast. She stepped back and told Cane to kick the door open.

Karen's phone rang in her bag, but she ignored it, her mind focused on what might wait for them on the other side of the door.

Cane took a few steps back and launched himself forward, landing the sole of his foot alongside the handle. The door rattled in its frame. He tried again; the frame splintered but held. The third attempt sent shards of wood in all directions as the door flew open.

Karen peered in and stood dumbfounded. Another corridor! It was like a never-ending maze. The only difference being this corridor was only twenty or thirty feet long with one solitary door at the end. Karen made her way forward and then stopped to place her head closer to the door, she furrowed her brow into deep lines of confusion. The whimpering sound came again. This time it didn't sound like an animal. Not at all. A human being was behind that door.

"You ready?" Karen whispered. Cane nodded, his baton held aloft ready to strike.

Karen tried the handle, expecting it to be locked, but to her surprise it opened. Pushing the door open a few inches, she saw nothing but blackness. Stepping to one side, she let Cane grab his torch from his utility belt and enter first. The beam lit up the room. Empty other than a chair in the middle and the terrified face of Melody Faulkner staring at them, tied to a chair with silver duct tape across her mouth. Her lanky and matted hair clung to her sweaty face as she shook her head like demons has possessed her body. Melody's muffled screams intensified as Karen dashed towards her.

A heavy thud, followed by what sounded like a plank of wood falling on the bare wooden floor, took Karen by surprise as she gasped and spun on her heels. The torch flew from Cane's hand as he collapsed to the floor with a dull thud, the beam of light bouncing wildly around the darkened space.

Karen didn't have time to react as a figure in the darkness raced towards her.

69

MELODY'S muffled screams turned into a chesty roar as she shook her head in Karen's direction. Karen took a step back in the darkness and raised her hands to defend herself, but the force of the figure crashing into her sent her sprawling backwards. She landed with a heavy thump, her head bouncing off the wooden floor. Waves of pain raced down her legs, leaving them numb for a few moments. She blinked hard as she stared up towards the darkened ceiling, her mind in turmoil, her senses muddled, pain spreading throughout her body.

The man raced around behind her and yanked her into a seating position. His arm tightening around her neck.

Karen, dazed and in pain, froze when she felt the icy blade of a knife press into her temple.

"That's it. You stay nice and calm. I wouldn't want you to hurt yourself."

A familiar voice hit her like a speeding express train as a heavy feeling of dread washed over her. A spike of adrenaline tensed her limbs. Her mind spun out of control. *No!*

"Professor, what are you doing?" she said, her voice strained as she fought for air.

"Having my moment of glory. Do not make any rash movements. I'm sure you've imagined what Ruth and Leah went through in their last moments as they gasped for air. Well, you'll find out."

Karen held her hands out in front of her, drawing on all her experience and training. She was in no position to fight back, nor did she want to antagonise Professor Bryant even further. She couldn't think straight. Everything she had been doing over the last few days lay in tatters around her. She had relied on Professor Bryant for his insights but had played right into his hands.

Karen's phone rang again. It buzzed against the wooden floor, the contents of her handbag scattered around her.

"If I don't answer, they'll know I'm in trouble," Karen said.

"That's irrelevant, DCI. Answer it and put it on loudspeaker. One wrong word from you, and I'll squeeze every drop of air from you right where you're sitting, and Melody can watch her saviour die."

Karen tapped around on the ground, her fingers grabbing the phone. She pressed the green button and put the call on loudspeaker.

"Karen, it's Claire. I thought you should know straight away I found some crucial evidence. I've been sitting here looking at the CCTV footage from a restaurant across the road from the one Leah Hayes was in. I spotted Professor

Bryant twice peering in through the window of Lucia in Grape Lane before going in himself. He left an hour after Leah left. Why didn't he tell us?"

Bryant squeezed harder. "Careful what you say," he whispered.

"I'm not sure," Karen replied.

Claire continued. "I think he's our man. We found doorbell footage close to the car park where Melody left her X3. It's grainy, but we believe it was Professor Bryant who followed her. It was him all along. He's played us. It took a bit of persuasion and digging around, but we gained access to former staff and patient records of High Royds Hospital. Professor Bryant was a junior doctor when Bruce Carson self-referred."

Karen didn't know what to say. Her mind was blank, confusion clouding her judgement.

"Karen, are you there? Is everything okay?"

"Um, yes. Everything is good. Thanks for the update. I'll be in touch. Toodle-pip."

Bryant grabbed her phone and cut off the call before throwing her phone to the other end of the room.

Karen saw an opportunity to take the upper hand as he loosened his grip. She swung around and threw a weak punch in Bryant's direction. She turned on to her hands and knees, attempting to get up, but Bryant had the upper hand as he stood over her. Karen wasn't sure what she felt first, the punch connecting with her cheekbone, or the pain as it spread across her face. The second one connected with the side of her head, sending her crashing to the floor, her head hitting the floorboards again as her vision darkened.

70

KAREN WOKE with a hammering headache and blinding pain that blurred her vision. Her body ached as she tried to pull herself up, but a stab of pain shot down her left arm. Her left wrist was cuffed to a long radiator using her own handcuffs. Tentatively, she reached and prodded her scalp, feeling for blood, but found none. As her vision returned the room stopped spinning. It was a different room than the one she had been in. Small and darker with no windows for natural daylight, and just a small bulb in the ceiling casting the faintest of yellow light. The walls had white cushioning attached to them and dirt covered the floor leaving a grittiness on the fingers of her right hand. There was no furniture and only one door.

The headache softened as she took a few deep breaths to reorientate herself. Her brow furrowed as she stared ahead and saw the figure of Melody Faulkner at the other end of the radiator, her right wrist secured by handcuffs too. Melody bowed her head, her bedraggled, sweaty, and matted hair clinging to her face as she groaned.

Karen needed to think fast. She figured the professor would be close by. She shuffled her feet across the space between herself and Melody, and nudged Melody's leg with her foot. "Melody, I'm a police officer. Can you hear me?" Karen whispered.

Melody slowly lifted her head, her eyes peering through the thick strands of hair which clung to her eyelids. She nodded once.

"Everything's going to be okay. There are other officers here and they'll find us." Thinking they might have been moved to a different location in the building, Karen asked, "Do you know where we are?"

Melody nodded once. She cleared her throat. "The isolation room. He told me this was the place where they locked up the most dangerous and insane people with no contact with the outside world. The room is hidden, and no one can hear or find us." Melody's breath was laboured as she coughed and winced.

Karen tugged at her restraint, the metal cuff pressing red scorelines into her skin. Sweat greased her palms as her head continued to pound. She stared at the door. "Hello! We are in here!" she called out. After a long moment of silence, she shouted again. "Help! We are in here!"

Being trapped without her bag or radio, she hoped her officers were converging on the second floor. The conversation with Claire would alert her team.

Melody sobbed.

"Melody, listen to me. Everything is going to be fine. I won't let him harm you."

Melody shook her head. "He's going to kill us, and no one can help. We aren't in that building any more."

Karen furrowed her brow. "I don't understand. What do you mean?"

Melody's sobs turned into ear-piercing screams. "I'm going to die!"

"Melody. I swear. You are going to be fine. What did you mean?"

The woman sniffed loudly. "He put us on a trolley and took us through an underground tunnel before bringing us to this building. They won't find us."

Karen's mind spun. "Shit."

The handle on the door turned, making Karen snap her head to her right, holding her breath for a moment. Professor Bryant appeared.

"Shit, indeed. I was listening outside. And I must agree with Melody, they won't find you." Bryant stepped into the room and came within a few feet of where Karen sat on the floor, her back up against the wall, her left arm hanging from the radiator. "I know this place like the back of my hand. As you know, I was a junior doctor here. These buildings have so many passageways and rooms it would blow your mind, all connected by underground tunnels which were used to move living and deceased patients and equipment between buildings. There was a time when the most challenging patients didn't see daylight for weeks. They were sedated to ensure compliance and moved around beneath the buildings as a way to bring them back in line by frequently changing their surroundings."

Karen bristled with anger as both hands curled into fists. Bryant had just been stringing them along. It was nothing more than a big ruse to gain their acceptance which allowed him to stay one step ahead of them. The more she thought about it, the more Bryant fitted the profile he had explained to her. "There's nowhere for you to go. I have more than a dozen officers scouring these buildings, with reinforcements on the way. It's only a matter of time before they rescue us."

Bryant laughed. "Well, they would need to find you first." He smiled as he looked around the cushioned walls. "We called this room the hole, but it was known as the isolation room. Solitary confinement for the untreatable. Of course, none of them knew they were untreatable when they were first admitted. But there was only so much we could do. These walls could tell a few stories that would make your toes curl."

"You've made your point. There is nothing left for you to do, and nowhere for you to go. Let's end this peacefully. No one else has to get hurt, and if there is something you want then we can come to an agreement," Karen said, hoping she could begin a dialogue with him that would buy her time.

Bryant shook his head in defiance. "A commendable effort, but we both know how this will end. This was nothing more than an experiment."

"Oh, I think it was more than that. You became so absorbed with Carson's notoriety and fame that it rubbed off on you and you wanted to experience it for yourself."

Bryant grimaced. "Very astute. A good assessment. Anyway, an urgent matter has arisen. I need to distract your officers and steer them away from here, so I have more time for you both. They are getting too close for my liking."

Karen watched as Bryant backed up towards the door then turned to close it behind him. His footsteps faded into the distance.

71

K~AREN~ ~STARED~ at the door and then at Melody before returning her gaze to the door. Her eyes narrowed. *He didn't lock it.* Karen weighed up her limited options. Either he had forgotten, or it was a deliberate ploy with Bryant waiting in the corridor for her to emerge.

She tugged at her wrist and winced. The cuff wasn't as tight as it should be, but it was tight enough. Karen narrowed her hand into a point and tucked her thumb into her palm. She tried to pull her hand through, but it jammed when the metal met her knuckles. She leaned back to give herself more leverage and pulled again, baring her teeth as a growl tore from her throat. *Shit.*

"It's no use," Melody muttered as she bowed her head in resignation.

"I'm not going to give up on us," Karen grunted as she tugged harder this time. The metal sliced into her skin, the first sign of red raw flesh appearing. It stung more than she had imagined as her fingers sprang out from their conical shape to fight the pain. She blew out an exasperated breath as the bloodied wound ached. *This can't be it?*

Karen glanced over her shoulder knowing time wasn't on her side. Acting on instinct more than anything else, Karen used her right index finger to collect blood before smearing it around her knuckles. The open wound stung like hell as she dipped her grubby finger in again. She added more blood at the point where the cuff was catching on her joints. It wasn't oil or Vaseline, but it would do. Taking a few deep breaths to prepare herself, Karen leaned back, closed her eyes, and gritted her teeth as she pulled with all her might. The searing heat and intense pain took her breath away as she twisted her left hand back and forth to free herself. Unwilling to give up, she wedged her feet against the wall, the skin tearing from her hand as she fell back, her hand free.

"Fuck!" Karen hissed through gritted teeth and shut eyes as she rolled on to her side and tucked her left hand into her chest, curling her body into a ball. Her hand throbbed and burned as if a thousand bees had stung it. She remained motionless for what felt like minutes, willing the pain to subside. Karen knew she had damaged her hand. Strips of ragged skin hung from her knuckles and blood bubbled to the surface from the open wounds.

Pulling herself on to her knees, Karen got to her feet and staggered to the door. Pressing her left hand across her chest, she turned the handle and opened the door just an inch to peer through. The corridor was empty. There was no sign of him. Pulling the door further, she poked her head out and glanced in both directions. There was only one other door at the far end. It was now or never.

"I'm going to get help, Melody. I won't be long."

Melody glanced up and pushed her hair away from her face, tears cascading from her eyes. Karen wanted to take her with, but there was no way she could free her from the cuffs. It was a horrible predicament to find herself in and she knew she didn't have any choice. The best chance of saving Melody would be to get help. Karen ran to the door at the far end and tried the handle. To her surprise it was open. It led out into another corridor which headed in two directions. Again, there were doors at both ends and nothing in between. It was hard for Karen to make out a specific location, but she noticed an exit sign above the door she was running towards. She pushed against it and found it locked. Throwing her shoulder into it for a second time didn't help as pain shot through her body. *Shit.*

Karen turned and raced in the opposite direction, trying the door, and expecting it to be locked again. This one opened as she found herself in a stairwell. She glanced over the handrail. The stairs led down to lower floors and up one floor. Gathering all her strength, Karen raced down the steps stopping at the next floor and trying the handle. Locked. Her heart pounded against her ribcage as adrenaline coursed through her veins. She raced down the steps to the ground floor and tried the handle. Locked. The door had a small glass panel at head height, only six inches square. Karen peered through it and saw nothing but another dark gloomy corridor with rooms heading off it. Then a flutter of movement caught her eye. A figure at the far end. One of her officers?

Please, God. Let it be one of my officers.

She hammered a balled fist on the door. "Hey! Over here. Help."

The figure turned and walked towards her, and as the silhouette came into focus, Karen gasped. The professor was heading in her direction, stalking her like prey.

Panic gripped her. Her eyes widened in fear as the air caught in her throat. She had nowhere else to run. With no choice, Karen turned and staggered up the stairs as a door opened behind her.

"There's no point in running, Karen," Bryant shouted as he climbed the steps. "There's nowhere for you to go. Your officers are looking in the wrong place. They are putting on quite a show out there."

Karen's legs couldn't take her any quicker as she tried to speed up. Her foot slipped, sending her crashing face first. The edge of the steps jabbed into her ribcage and shins. She screamed in agony as she clamoured to her feet again. Each step sent shooting bolts of pain through her body as she hobbled up the stairs, soon passing the floor where Melody was being held. She looked up. There was only one other escape route, the roof.

Glancing over her shoulder and back down the stairs, Karen noticed that Bryant wasn't far behind and gaining by the second. Breathless and running on adrenaline, she reached the exit sign for the roof and pushed the emergency door bar as hard as she could, praying it would be unlocked. The door flew open, taking her by surprise. Brilliant sunshine pierced her eyeballs and blinded her. She placed her right hand over her eyes to shield them from the worst of the glare. Unlike the other buildings, the roof was flat and located about fifty yards behind the main buildings Karen had seen upon her arrival. Her officers were searching those buildings, and no doubt would start on this one soon.

Karen raced towards the edge and leaned over the brick wall which skirted its perimeter. "Help! I'm up here!" Karen shouted when she spotted a few officers close to one of the other buildings. Karen waved to catch their attention. A sigh of relief escaped her lips when she saw an officer point towards the roof before running in her direction.

Bryant stepped through the open fire exit door.

"It's over," Karen screamed as Bryant walked towards her.

"It's over for both of us," he replied.

72

"IT'S OVER, BRYANT," Karen repeated, backing away from the edge of the roof. She needed to hold him off and defuse the tension until reinforcements arrived.

"Perhaps, but the last thing I want is to end up in a cell like Bruce Carson. Yes, I learned so much from him. He fascinated me. Intrigued me. Carson's words were cold and measured. Not a hint of fear or remorse to this very day. That… is power. It wasn't about abducting women and squeezing the life from them. It was about power and being able to take a life without feeling fear, sadness, remorse, or guilt. Carson felt none of those." Bryant stepped towards the brick wall and peered over the edge.

Karen repositioned herself to maintain a gap so she could react if he lunged at her. Her body ached, her shins burned, her hand throbbed, and every breath sent shooting pains through her ribs. Perhaps she had broken one when she had fallen on the stairs, she wasn't sure. The distant sound of approaching sirens and officers shouting on the ground brought hope, but she needed to keep him talking.

"So it was power?" she asked.

Bryant nodded. "I've spent all my life studying the criminally insane. Understanding what made them commit their crimes. How they felt. Why they did it. And the more I learned, the more I realised they weren't weak. Confidence was not something they lacked. They were true to themselves and acted out of the need to satisfy a thrill or a need. Psychopaths are powerful human beings."

Karen didn't agree with a word Bryant spewed from his mouth, but arguing with him would only inflame the situation further.

"So you wanted a taste of it? You wanted to step into their shoes and experience the same thrill-seeking ride?"

Bryant nodded. "I'm surprised how easy it is to take a life. Gloria Kenny was my first. Two years ago, on the outskirts of Cork."

Sirens wailed around them and the chopping sound of an NPAS helicopter closing in on the scene had Karen staring at the sky. "It is over. No one else needs to die. Please. There's nowhere to go." With her officers racing to her aid and the AFOs taking up strategic positions, she only hoped that someone would reach her in time.

Bryant smiled before charging at her. A deep growl tore from his throat.

Karen's heart jumped in her chest as Bryant attacked like a rabid dog with teeth bared. She pulled her elbows into her sides and tucked her wrists together in front of her face to form a protective shield as the psychotic man closed in on her. She deflected his body away from her by taking a step to the side, the blow of his arm glancing off her arms as his weight carried him forward, causing him to lose his balance as he stumbled.

He spun around and closed in on Karen as she hobbled backwards, the pain in her hand intensifying. "Enough!" she shouted as Bryant lunged at her. He grabbed her by her jacket and pushed forward towards the wall at the edge of the roof space. Karen's eyes widened in fear as she clawed at his face. She saw nothing but cold evilness in his glassy gaze. She screamed as he released one hand and wrapped it around her throat, tipping her head back. Her chest tightened as a sudden and overwhelming sensation of dread washed over her, the thought of a tragic and horrific death crossing her mind. She tried to focus, but a shot of adrenaline stabbed her in the back, forcing her body to stiffen. Pain raced through her as he jammed her body against the wall. Karen screamed again as she clawed at his face, desperate to jab her thumb into his eyeball. But the reach of his arm was longer than hers. Spittle erupted from her mouth as she fought for her life.

With one hand pinning her against the wall by the throat, Bryant reached down and scooped his other arm behind her legs as he tried to lift her body over the wall and throw her off the roof. Karen kicked out as she swung her hands in his direction.

"Enough of this, you stupid bitch! Die with dignity!" Bryant shouted as he renewed efforts, spinning Karen around.

Karen gasped in pain as the cold hardness of the bricks pressed into her already bruised ribs, pushing the air from her lungs. Her eyes were wet with tears as she stared at the ground and the look of horror on the faces of the officers who had gathered below. Her body tensed in readiness for the fall. "No!" Karen shouted, flailing her arms and legs as she fought for survival. The whooping blades of the police helicopter drowned her own thoughts out as it circled overhead. With her body battered and bruised, images flashed through her mind.

Is this how my life is going to end? Falling three floors to the ground?

Karen thrust an elbow hoping to strike Bryant, but from her position with her head and shoulders hanging over the edge of the wall, her effort was weak and missed its target. Her head spun as a wave of dizziness took hold.

The sound struck her lips like a slap. A sharp pop. Karen hadn't had time to fully register what had happened when another pop echoed around her a second later.

Bryant's grip loosened as his body slumped to the roof with a soft thud, a pool of blood forming a halo around his head. He lay face up, his eyes wide and fixed staring at the blue sky, his mouth open in an O as if registering the shock.

Karen slid down the wall and crumpled in a heap on the floor, tears rolling down her cheeks, her mind numb, her senses dulled.

73

KAREN COUGHED and sputtered as she sobbed. The body of Professor Bryant lay just a few feet from her. She tried to move, but her body wouldn't let her. Exhausted and in pain, her body had shut down. Each movement left her wincing.

The fire exit door burst open, startling her. Two advanced firearms officers stormed through, guns poised and trained on Bryant's lifeless body. Further uniformed officers ran through and surrounded his body, while others gathered around Karen.

"Karen!" Jade screamed as she ran through the doorway and pushed past her colleagues, before dropping to her knees, tears streaming from her bloodshot eyes. Seeing Karen's bloodied left hand, Jade reached to Karen's right hand and cupped it within hers. "Oh my God, I… I can't… I thought…" The words wouldn't come as Jade pulled her in for a hug.

The warmth of the embrace only weakened Karen further as she sobbed into Jade's shoulder. She tried to say something, but coughed and winced as spasms of pain crushed her breath.

"I'm so sorry we couldn't get to you sooner," Jade said. "We tried. Thank God you used the danger phrase 'toodle-pip' that you'd come up with for us as a team. The minute you said that we checked the tracker on your phone which told us you were in this building, but we couldn't get in. The main entrance was barricaded, and Bryant boarded up the ground-floor windows. Every door we attempted to open was locked, including the one to the fire exit stairwell. However, we managed to enter through a service door at the back. The main stairwell to the first floor was blocked with furniture so needed to be cleared first. Bryant had turned this place into a mini-fortress."

Karen nodded, exhaustion and shock leaving her numb. "Melody?"

"She's safe. We've got her," Jade said.

Even though she could barely move her head, Karen weakly nodded once.

"I need to get you off this roof as soon as possible, para-medics should be up in a second, but we needed to make the scene safe first and we weren't too sure what to expect when we got here," Jade said, throwing the look over her shoulder at Bryant's body. "What did he say?"

Karen stared at Bryant. "He killed Ruth and Leah as an experiment. He'd become obsessed with Carson and with the minds of psychopaths. I guess he had built a taste for it by listening to all their stories and had become so obsessed he wanted to experience it for himself. He enjoyed the thrill of power it gave him. The same thrill Carson spoke of during his prison visits." Karen gasped for breath as a shooting pain flashed across her chest. "There's another vic."

"What?" Jade replied.

Karen nodded weakly. "Gloria Kenny. Two years ago. Outskirts of Cork. We need to inform the Garda."

"Not right now. Let's get you sorted first."

Karen sunk into Jade's embrace as they looked at Bryant's body.

"Bastard," Jade spat. "And the families don't get to see justice for their loved ones."

"No," Karen whispered. "He played us. I feel like such a fucking idiot. If it wasn't for my hand and ribs, I would have thrown him off the roof myself," Karen said, gritting her teeth.

Jade squeezed Karen's arm softly before brushing sweaty hair away from her boss's face. "You're not an idiot. He fooled us all. He was clever, calculating, and conniving. It was all part of his game plan, and we weren't to know that. Don't forget South Wales and Kent forces fell for his game too. The CC authorised Bryant's offer of help after we had followed due diligence. So don't even entertain the idea that this is your fault."

Jade was right, but the outcome didn't sit comfortably with Karen.

Paramedics attended to Karen before strapping her into a chair and taking her from the building to a waiting ambulance. The last thing Karen saw before leaving the rooftop was a white sheet placed over Bryant's body while her team waited for forensic officers and Detective Superintendent Laura Kelly to arrive.

74

KAREN PULLED the white sheet over her and let her head sink into the pillows of the hospital bed. A few hours in A & E and the X-ray department had resulted in seventeen stitches to injuries to her left hand, lacerations to her shins, swathes of bandages, and the confirmation of one cracked rib. Her head was pounding because of fatigue and the comedown from her adrenaline spike. She stared at the ceiling, trying to make sense of the last few hours but finding it difficult to hang on to any thoughts. They swirled in her mind like a tornado, clamouring for attention, but out of reach.

Melody Faulkner lay in another bed somewhere within the hospital and Karen wanted to visit her, but she felt too tired to get up. PC Cane also underwent extensive X-rays and MRI scans after being admitted to the hospital. He had suffered a fractured shoulder blade and bruising to his cervical vertebrae. He would be off for a few months. She wanted to visit him too to thank him for his bravery.

There were so many people she wanted to thank it was hard to know where to start. When the time allowed, she wanted to meet up with the two police snipers who had taken the shots, bringing Bryant down. Their skill and courage were commendable because at distance the margin for error was small. Karen's head had been only inches away from Bryant's and a slight change in wind direction could have altered the trajectory of each bullet.

The whooshing sound of the door opening and Zac's face poking through the gap distracted her from her thoughts. Seeing his concerned expression set her off again as her bottom lip trembled and her eyes misted over.

"Hey, you," Zac whispered softly as he entered the room and made his way over to her bed, coming around to the right so he could hold her hand. He leaned in and kissed her. "How are you holding up?"

Karen sniffed loudly and cleared her throat. "I've been in worse scrapes... I think," Karen said as a flashback of Skelton being gunned down close to her crossed her mind.

"I nearly shit a brick when they told me what happened. I was so worried," Zac said, a small smile breaking on his face. "You know how to live dangerously."

"Yeah, I know. I do have a bit of a reputation for finding myself in scary situations."

Tears squeezed from Zac's eyes as he blinked hard. "To think I nearly lost you. I don't know how I would have coped? You don't know how much you mean to me. To me and Summer," Zac said, his voice bitty and strained as he fought to compose himself. He stared at the ceiling looking for a distraction.

Karen squeezed his hand. "You both mean the world to me too. But we have dangerous jobs, and sometimes things can go wrong. But it's over. I'm here now, living and just about breathing," Karen said, attempting to laugh. "Ouch, that hurts."

They stared at each other for a few moments, both unsure of what to say next. Their eyes connected, conveying unspoken words.

Karen pursed her lips, her mind in turmoil, her heart aching, her body battered and bruised. She intertwined her fingers with his and studied his features. He had a soft, kind and caring look, one she had seen many times before while lying naked beside him. The impact on each other's lives had happened so quickly and was nothing short of amazing. And the thought of life without him was something she never wanted to entertain.

"I love you, Zac."

Zac leaned in closer and kissed her again. "I love you, too."

With a smile, Karen confessed, "I've been wanting to tell you for the last few days, but I was nervous about how you would react. I've never told a man I love them because I've never felt this way."

"I'm honoured," Zac replied, with a wink. "You sure it's not because of my cooking?"

"Oi, you cheeky git. I'm being serious."

He stroked her face. "I know. I'm pulling your leg."

Karen rolled her eyes. "I've had enough leg-pulling in the last few hours to last me a lifetime."

They both laughed.

"When I looked at the drop, I…" Karen's voice was sombre and serious for a moment.

"Hey, listen. There will be plenty of time to talk about this. You need to focus on getting better. I want you to stay with us and we will look after you until you're ready to go back to your apartment."

Karen nodded and looked towards the door as it swished open again. Detective Superintendent Laura Kelly appeared with flowers.

"Ma'am," Karen said, looking both surprised and shocked at her unexpected visitor. She glanced up at Zac.

Zac cleared his throat. "I'll leave you in peace for a little bit and pop back later. Ma'am," Zac nodded as he left.

Kelly placed the flowers on the table beside Karen's bed. "Are you ok? You gave us a bit of a fright."

Karen blushed in embarrassment. "I'm doing okay. Not the outcome I wanted, but at least Bryant can't hurt anyone else now."

Kelly nodded.

"I am really sorry we asked Bryant for help, ma'am. I'm so angry I didn't see through him."

Kelly shook ahead. "No need to apologise. He screwed us all over. Three different forces duped by a very clever man. We'll have to refer ourselves for an independent investigation as will South Wales and Kent. And I suspect professional help outside of the police will come under heavy scrutiny, and stricter rules will be needed. They all want to speak to you. But you have my full support and that of the CC. We all have a lesson to learn."

"Of course, thank you, ma'am."

"Right, I need to head back to the station. Take time off to recuperate. Get yourself fighting fit before you come back."

"I will do, ma'am. But I want to pop in soon to say thank the team for all their hard work."

Kelly nodded as she made her way back towards the door. "Just to say thank you. Nothing more. You'll be in big trouble if I see you sitting behind your desk," Kelly said, looking over her shoulder, a smile on her face.

No sooner had Kelly left, than the door opened again with Jade peering around the corner. "Safe to come in?" she beamed.

"Blimey, it's like Piccadilly Circus."

"You should be so grateful people care about you that much," Jade replied, placing a chunky KitKat on Karen's lap.

"That's different. Beats having a tub of grapes," Karen said, eyeing up the chocolate. "Been ordered to take at least a week off by the super. Can you imagine me sitting at home with my feet up doing diddly-squat?"

"No, but I would make the most of it. Get Zac to wait on you hand and foot."

"He's already offered."

"Bless him. You've got a good one there."

Karen's face softened as she thought of Zac again. She had finally told him, and Jade was right. "Oh don't worry, I intend to. How are you? You were a tad emotional up there."

"Excuse me, so were you."

"What do you expect? I had a bloody lunatic trying to throw me off a three-storey building."

"Well, he didn't try hard enough," Jade teased.

"I'll remember that when I'm doing your appraisal." Karen reached out and held Jade's hand for a moment, her face turning serious. "Thank you for caring. I haven't told anyone yet, but it was the worst experience of my life. I honestly thought this was it."

Jade eyes moistened. "So did I. I can't afford to lose you. You're my best mate."

"Ditto. Now bugger off and go downstairs to get me a decent coffee so I can enjoy this KitKat properly."

Jade did a mock salute before heading off. "Back in five."

Karen let out a long sigh. Her eyes felt heavy. It wasn't long before she fell asleep. The KitKat would have to wait.

75

"Ready?" Jade asked, resting the laptop on the table over Karen's bed and angling the screen so Karen could see better.

Having slept soundly for two nights, Karen felt more human this morning as she finger-combed her hair in readiness. "Yep," she replied, glancing over to Belinda, Ty, and Ed who had just arrived to visit her.

Jade checked her watch and then pressed the icon for the Zoom app. It took a few moments for the call to connect.

"Hi, Karen!" came a chorus of voices through the speakers. Her officers had gathered around Dan's desk and were all smiles and waves as they tried to squeeze in on the screen.

Smiling, Karen waved back. "Hey, everyone. Hope you're all behaving yourselves."

"We always do," an officer replied from the assembled crowd at Dan's end.

"How are you feeling?" Dan asked, leaning into his monitor.

"Been better. Thankfully, the painkillers are doing a fantastic job of spacing me out. Hopefully they'll release me in the next few days because there is only so much hospital food I can stomach."

Roars of laughter created an echo of static through the tinny speakers.

"Listen, everyone. I just wanted to say thank you to all of you. You did a tremendous job on a very challenging case, and many of you put yourselves in very dangerous situations," Karen said, before glancing up at her team members in the room with her. "I'm very proud of each and every one of you. And when I get back, I expect loads of flowers and chocolates to be sitting on my desk or you're all fired." Karen winced as she laughed, clutching her side.

More laughter from her officers.

"Right, that's enough touchy-feely stuff. Get back to work and see you soon."

A chorus of best wishes and smiles and waves filled the screen before Jade disconnected the call.

Karen wiped a small tear from her eye. "It must be smoky in here," she laughed.

Belinda, Ty, and Ed said their goodbyes before dashing out the door.

After they'd gone, Jade grabbed a wheelchair from the corner and helped Karen as she moved gingerly into it. Once she was settled and pain-free, Jade wheeled Karen down the corridor towards Melody's room.

"The chair suits you, not long 'til you can have your own," Jade said.

"You are so lucky I can't get up and punch you in the face."

Jade stopped by a door and pushed it open before reversing in and pulling Karen's chair through the doorway. As Jade spun her around, Karen saw Melody propped up in her bed. She looked better than the last time Karen had seen her. With her dark hair pulled back in a ponytail, showcasing her clean face, and wearing a blue hospital gown, it would be hard for anyone to know the ordeal Melody had been through.

"Hi, Melody. How are you doing?" Karen asked.

Melody nodded and smiled. "I'm okay, but things are tough."

"They will be. I hear they're releasing you later today."

"Yes. I'm going to take a bit of time off. The hospital has put me in touch with a counsellor, as they feel I need to talk through my ordeal."

Karen nodded and felt sympathy for her. Karen's boss had suggested that Karen would need to do the same. And it was something she wasn't looking forward to.

"Anyway, I just wanted to pop in and say hello and make sure you're okay."

"Thank you. Thank you for everything. You saved my life."

Karen smiled. "It wasn't just me. All my officers had a part to play in saving both of us." Karen squeezed Melody's leg before saying goodbye.

Jade wheeled her out of the room and down the corridor before turning into another room. PC Darren Cane was sat up in bed with his eyes closed and a pair of headphones on.

He must have sensed the door opening as he opened his eyes and whipped off his headphones. "Ma'am."

Jade wheeled Karen alongside his bed. "I wanted to come along and see you yesterday, but I was a bit out of it."

"That's okay, ma'am. How are you?" Cane asked.

"I've still got a few days here and then it's bed rest at home. How's your shoulder blade?"

Cane rolled his eyes. "It hurts a bit if I move too quickly. And if I try to laugh it feels like I'm being stabbed in the back. The doctor's coming round later and I'm hoping to be discharged tomorrow morning."

Karen's tone was grittier than usual. "Excellent. I wanted to say thank you for your bravery."

"I didn't get a chance to do much. But I appreciate your kind words."

"You did more than you realise. I hope you get some rest and let me know if there's anything you need."

"Thank you, ma'am."

After some quick goodbyes, Jade wheeled Karen back to her room and helped her into bed. Each step of movement was as painful as ever as the painkillers wore off.

"Is there anything I can get you?"

"No. I think I need some sleep," Karen replied.

"Okay, I'll leave you to it. Drop me a text if there's anything you need and I'll pop in tomorrow."

As Jade was about to leave, Karen grabbed her arm and swallowed hard, fighting back the emotion. "Thank you. Thank you for everything."

Jade squeezed Karen's hand, her eyes shimmering with unshed tears. "Just doing my job. Now rest up. We've got a celebration to look forward to when you're up and about."

With a final glance at her friend, Jade stepped into the quiet corridor, the hospital door closing with a soft click that echoed a job well done.

CURRENT BOOK LIST

Hop over to my website for a current list of books:

http://jaynadal.com/current-books/